Advance praise for

A HISTORY OF HANDS

"In a world not so far or long away, but every bit as distant as if it were another universe, *A History of Hands* imagines Depression-era California as it has never been imagined before. Here, Rod Val Moore takes up the grotesque tradition of Nathaniel West to turn his eye toward California's sparsely populated Central Coast, where drifters, charlatans, and earnest naïfs cross paths to transform forever the life of one isolated boy with troublesome hands. But what really sets this book apart is the knock-dead gorgeous writing which, like the characters and landscape it depicts, seems almost to come from another world—one that shares uncanny parallels with our own and that refracts them back at us with something between the microscopic precision of science and the skewed eloquence of translation. *A History of Hands* is a miracle tonic all its own, and you will not want to miss it."

—Katharine Haake, author of
The Time of Quarantine

"Rod Val Moore's *A History of Hands* is a paralytically funny run through the labyrinths of ontology, consciousness, imagination, illness, family, plight; like Omensetter's *Luck* meets *The Simpsons,* only Bart is paralyzed. *A History of Hands* quirks and hurts, successfully rising precariously above pathos through humor and philosophy, where the protagonist/victim Virge, alluding to Virgil, lies on the verge with his family, on the cusps of cruelty, affection, antagonism, and love. On top of that, the language is thick and layered and fabulous, it sucks you in and blows you out like prana, like breath. This is a novel of subtlety, complexity, humor, and wonder."

—Chuck Rosenthal, author of
Loop's Progress and *West of Eden*

b

A HISTORY OF HANDS

A HISTORY OF HANDS

a novel

Rod Val Moore

UNIVERSITY OF MASSACHUSETTS PRESS
Amherst and Boston

Printed in the United States of America

ISBN 978-1-62534-096-2
Set in Adobe Caslon Pro
Printed and bound by Maple Press, Inc.

Library of Congress Cataloging-in-Publication Data

Moore, Rod, 1952–
A history of hands : a novel / by Rod Val Moore.
pages cm
ISBN 978-1-62534-096-2 (pbk. : alk. paper)
I. Title.
PS3563.O645H57 2014
813'.54—dc23

2013051128

British Library Cataloguing-in-Publication Data
A catalogue record for this book is available from the British Library.

For Lisa and Aaron

A HISTORY OF HANDS

1

Here's the idea of them, a faint picture of three figures, emerging from a door in single file. Their bodies slant forward a bit, so perfectly parallel to one another that they must form a family. The one in the lead, maybe inspiring the slant, is a young man, skinny, cartoonish, his head like a pink bead at the end of a wire. Who follows? It must be his wiry mother, followed by the one who must, by nature, be his wiry dad.

And they appear as if in a kind of real life, larger than real life perhaps, and all of this in a blighted year, a blighted era.

Still, they emerge like vertical sparks from the darkness of a clapboard farmhouse, until this inner light of theirs fades in the coastal sunshine, and their three right feet, shoes dull as dust, extend at the same time, and poise there, hesitant at the edge of the front porch.

Until the walk begins.

It's after supper, always the time for the afternoon constitutional, a stroll that, according to their own rules, must be undertaken when the clock says it's time, and performed in solemnity, so that any complaints regarding hunger, or poverty in general, are to be discounted, in fact to be deemed, for the duration of the outing, inadmissible.

There is no way to guess that something untoward will happen in the course of the day, in this penurious but breezy February, a season when the verdant and sugary colors of spring have already arrived, a day of picture-perfect glimpses of the sea, while golden poppies along the wayside, goblet size, fit for a king, sway to a silly melody.

But there is no king, because California forbids any such personage. The only monarchy is in the royal bees that buzz the mustard flowers shooting up among the grasses, each petal painted with fairy brushes, as in a fairy dream. All around, both the pretty and the sickly shades of green sweep out and away from them like direction arrows, as if this family, delicate trio, were the center, or the source, of an exuberance.

My mouth can already taste the summer flavors, one of the three calls out, and by this he means hurrah, and may this good green world go on forever.

La primavera! another says out loud, tentatively, and by this she means more or less the same.

Oh my Lord, says a third, not in prayer, just pleasure and surprise.

And still, years later, nothing about that day will be remembered besides the one untoward thing—the moment that one of them, Virgil himself, young man, face mild as pine, takes a step that never ends. Down he'll go, tipping and toppling, till his mild face meets the ground. Maybe pulled down by a demon? That's one of many explanations. It's true that at first he'll feel like he's collapsing inward, but then, in falling, move flaccidly forward. And then down.

But before that moment comes, every way is clear, every possibility arrayed before him. The dark dirt path under his soles is artfully strewn with wet eucalyptus leaves, slippery but finely tinted, fiery, and it's a pleasure to note every variation of flame. A breeze whips up from offshore, and brings with it the seltzer scent of anemones, the tide pool kind. Virgil and his parents are inching westward, toward the edge of things, toward the cliffs that mark the limits of their farm, cliffs that carry the farm and the continent's whole weight behind them.

All this at the very fringe of the solid half of the world.

No hurry at all, one of them says, thick and barely audible.

Why quicken the pace? asks another.

Then comes silence, pondering.

They are in no hurry to decide. The clock tells them exactly when to leave the house. After that things can get a little unorganized. Moving along at first at a pace that is measured, step after step, as in some practiced ceremony, then losing their measure and drawing apart, the three figures advance like chess pieces toward the edge of the board, where, if they get that far, they'll gape down and wonder, for the millionth time, if there is an easier way to get down to the white sand beach than the frightening little trail along the cliff.

But they're not there yet. If they knew that one of them was likely to fall down, or fall ill, they might reverse themselves right away, rush home, take their seats around the kitchen table, rethink their circumstances in the glow of thin electricity, stay up late in the kitchen with watery coffee that, properly sipped, softens the time, the time it takes to watch the fire fade to black inside the stove.

Oh, but all this branching and fuzziness! remarks young Virgil, usually known as Virge.

He means not fuzziness, but furiousness, and not the foliage all around but the foliage inside him. A cedar or juniper, narrow and sometimes on fire, is one image that Virge keeps coming back to, investigating, wondering if it could be a metaphor for soul. For furiousness. His left shoe, lacking metaphor, is more down at the heel than the other, and he walks a little lopsided, a little on fire, and his red fanned-out ears are translucent.

The farm fields on either side of the path, dark in coastal light, show pale stubs, and stubs of stubs, but nothing more. One field runs along the side of a once fine barn, their own, painted grandly on the side with an ad. It's a man in a turban, a sultan, face too narrow, holding up a Sultan-brand cigarette, showing yellow teeth, and yellower gums and tongue.

This is the one that smokes smoothest by far, reads his speech balloon, barely, since the ad has faded in the always slanting-at-it sun, and the cigarette and the hand holding it have turned all beige, so that the cigarette has become the sultan's sixth finger.

For many, the year has set a bad example, as years and properties go. A good year for a stumble and a fall.

Virge's own lackings are the same as that of his parents, and theirs almost but not quite the same as his, but some celebration, some lust for things, must ever rise to the surface.

Today, smiles Dad, sliding a finger along the brim of his hat, snapping his teeth.

But goes no further with the thought. He melts, silent, leaving the one word as prologue.

How hard it is for him, for anyone, to articulate truth after truth in sequence, without resorting to stretches of reconsideration.

Then, a minute later, he starts over.

Today, he says, still fingering the brim of his hat, is a day meant to enjoy . . . enjoy . . . whatchamacallem? The *exilirs,* and Lamont mangles the word with energy, like someone who could say it a thousand times but never get it right.

Elixirs, corrects his wife, generously, as if she had coined the word herself.

Yes, yes, he goes on, a little less shakily. Welcome all you, you all, what did you say?—all you exhilarations of life.

Well, says the mother, a little less generous. I guess we'll leave it at that.

So Lamont, the dad, the husband, pauses on the path, taking her seriously, gathers his jacket fabric closer against colder air. Later he produces a pipe, knuckles it, stems it, and then, smiling down at the rounded and nearly spherical ends of his shoes, in full concentration, as if such shoes are yet more objects of joy, sucks in whatever medicine the smoke contains, bowl up close against his nose, cheeks rosy with reflected flame.

Welcome as always, he beams, glancing up, and his wife, Almy, stops too, turns to him to consider, while Virge, gangly, though grown and full of grown opinions, lopes a ways up ahead.

Oh, she mutters, as if to herself. Oh, they are welcome, bienvenido, those elixirs and whatever else you've got.

And out here on the path every Sunday such speeches surely are expected, along with oceanic oxygen and iodine and the other invisible but life-giving gasses of the out-of-doors, more salubrious by far than the air they must breathe indoors, which, according to Almy, is forever stale, because the house sits in a slight depression, behind a slight western rise, and they can't feel the great ocean give off any of its vitalizers or bromines.

Don't forget, continues Almy, snug and superior in a camel-brown coat thrown on over the apron she wore when baking two morning pies. Don't forget, she repeats, lest we omit them, each and every vitamin. They're free of charge, you know. Courtesy of the sun. But what do we do for the sun as a mark of gratitude?

Bow to the sun god, says Virge, barely in earshot. That's one suggestion. And subtly, Almy does so, lifting her arms like an actress, while Virge, walking backward, rolls his eyeballs in sarcasm, some surprise. Then she looks out over the ocean, and the other two can't help but follow suit, and so all three of them see where the sun is halfway hidden behind a low bank of clouds, displaying only its lower half, its baby's bottom, golden and a little sticky.

Then back to walking. After a while, Mont speaks his mind a second time.

The dad, he cries, is father to the child, and he cups one hand to his mouth to amplify the sound, because Virge is a swift walker, and is already several steps ahead, shifting uphill and downhill along the leafy path, proceeding in a mincing and squirrelly way, always approaching that point on the path where he is predestined to fall.

Did you hear me, Son? I meant, I mean, for you to put on a show for us.

Mont says this twice, louder each time, and Virge can hear him, even as he gets farther ahead, and why not, because his hearing is outstanding. So he slows his pace and thinks about what Mont is really saying, and how odd to be invited, as it appears to him, to remain a child, when it's a fact that at times he feels like one who is, or ought to be, father to the dad.

Why, he yells back over his shoulder, a show? And with his ear turned in that direction, now he hears everything.

Watch what he does, says Mont to Almy. Watch what he's apt to be up to next.

Oh don't, she sighs.

Watch to see what a loon your boy is whenever he thinks he's alone.

But, as far as Virge is concerned, though he takes in these comments, he chooses to understand, partly, that he has heard them wrong. It would make more sense to comment on how alone the boy is when he thinks he's a loon.

But it's no place for such considerations, here in this corner of Arcadia, though it's true the wolf is at the door, and it turns out to be impossible for a farmer to grow a thing or raise a thing, true that cats and plow horses can both fall dead overnight, that a house can turn shaky and shabby, can have a rat or two living underneath it somewhere, though there is some pride to be taken, to be insisted on, in that it was once a reasonable house, that it was built in better times, that there are curlicues carved by craftsmen into the front porch pillars, and gilly flowers acid-etched forever in the four corners of the entry glass.

Put on one of your shows for us, Virge, Mont repeats, louder this time. He and Almy float along side by side, like ice skaters, though earlier it was less congenial than this, as there was, at the very onset of the promenade, a degree of marital friction. It is a fact that Mont is the type who can suddenly grow bristly, derisive. Almy, for her part, can get very narrow and athletic. But now things are nicer, it's almost blissful, and the wife's hand slips into the husband's jacket pocket, and for long minutes just stays there, and Mont, slipping his own hand in the same pocket, plays with her fingers there with purpose, as if handling an important set of keys.

It's always best, says Almy, casting her eyes heavenward. It's always better, she warmly observes, to listen, than to be listened to.

But this marriage is slightly tainted, and the taint creeps back a little, now and then. Sometimes the awkwardness arises when they walk, as they walk now, past the little rubber hut, so-called because its roof is nothing more than a big sheet of rubber that got stretched and nailed over the top when a strong Pacific storm blew off the regular shingled roof.

More importantly, more unpleasantly, one day the rubber hut was open and inviting, and Virge, nine or ten at the time, got in there and somehow the rose dust, poison to vermin, got stuffed, or stuffed itself, into his mouth. The details are blurred except it's not hard to picture how the fine powder ran through his fingers and even steamed upward, yellowish clouds rising and falling as he tossed handfuls in the air, and at some point there must have also followed a time of chewing, a time of swallowing. A day later the boy fell ill, and later missed a year of school, because, or often because, of rose dust. Cause and effect don't ride on either fact or opinion. True it was an unknown fever that kept him out for the year, but it was the opinion of one doctor, a young man named Noster who clicked his heels at intervals as if to highlight his precision, and what he said, snickering at farmers, was that fevers are aggravated by the effects of lots of farm products that enter the bloodstream and carry toxins throughout the circulatory shapes, resulting in plasmalysis, hemospasm, gears loose, what have you.

Once, gratefully, past the hut, Mont stops holding his breath and releases his pipe smoke out into the world, but it returns to wreathe his head in ghostly laurels. He's satisfied, and the tobacco smell is sweet and oaken in his nose and hair, and still sweet and oaken when a stray wisp floats its way to Virge, who has a sense of smell to match a sense of hearing.

No, no, he hears Mont say, mockingly.

No, no, Mont repeats. Listen to you. You're going backwards again, aren't you? And his mother replies, but Virge doesn't catch it.

Oh yeah? comes the voice of the father. Well, if not a goon, then a loon. And I don't mind one bit if I do say so.

And Virge, who may be, according to some reckonings, too old to be living with his parents, isn't confused this time. He weighs the words, the rhyme. There's the sound of a hard click inside, near his liver, or kidney, but that's just his organs rearranging themselves into optimal positions for both a walk outdoors, and resistance to fatherly needling.

Better, after all, to think of happier times. To think of childhood games! Hide and Go Seek Them, Hare Go Down the Foxhole, Which

One Is the Witch, Beau-Regarde, Horse Won't You Come in the House Now?

Youth is often carefree, and given to larks, but all that Virge can admit is that he knows of these games because once, years before, he read a game book. He was seldom free to play, most often too stork-like and fragile, never fully participant in his own youth, perhaps to his discredit, and here it is a few years into manhood, and the rules of the games, which he does know, will sometimes morbidly absorb him, especially when he makes an attempt to play, always coming up short against the fact that no one else is there. Hide from whom? Which witch? The horse, in his own experience, is dead.

Here and there, wherever sunlight hits the ground, all in fractured focus under trees, Virge moves in twirly motions, but subtly, without absolutely reverting to childhood, without playing any formal and famous game. Just modestly launching himself, holding down his tie, he jumps in order to come down feet first in a puddle, and maybe it's enough of a show to satisfy his dad, but in truth for him it's a puddle of light, fiery light of afternoon, not water, and it's a surprise when he comes down that drops of light sting him in his heels and shins.

There, he says, speaking one word at a time, letting silence stand in for soliloquy. He knows he has to have a plan to break out of the patterns of morbidity, his well-known re-absorptions, and one word is fewer than two words, and so on. But it's also advisable to keep a sharp lookout, look further and more keenly than the others, even accept light for water, water for light.

Mother, Dad, he says out loud, straightening, not looking back, not much caring if they hear, using them more as points in his mind, and in this case it looks like they're finally, for now, only that, only points.

A little further down the path, closer to the railroad embankment and tracks that mark the property line, Virge at last starts to get some good ocean smells, like the oiliness of fish scales, the tang of seaweed ropes and driftwood, a hint of pure salt, even seafood, and it's true there are hobos on the beach sometimes, living, as his dad explains, in driftwood tepees and lean-tos, who, steps from the ocean, drink clam chowder, cold, out of tin cans.

This one view of ocean, he observes for their benefit, has the wedge shape, doesn't it, of a glass of water.

But they're too far back to hear.

THIS PIECE OF OCEAN, he cries, throwing his voice over his shoulder. Virge turns and sees they've stopped dead in their tracks, each one wagging a finger under the other's nose.

Part of the routine.

Here he is, Virge, one who has a quality of fitfulness, a wide mind that can only be applied to narrowness, or vice versa, and when applied, only applied for years at a time on one thing at a time. On any Sunday walk lately, he'll determine a distant point and run toward it, as if that were the point of the walk. But even that's a challenge. As he runs, he'll stutter in his step, as in a state of mild disruption. Fits and starts is how he describes this motion to himself. At the same time, as he fits, and starts, his features take on an expression of studied kindness, or if not that, random amazement. Amazed at what? Lately he's grown a mustache, then trimmed it down to look like two sharp punctuation marks that indicate, he'd like to think, a verbal skill, a frankness, the sense that what he says is worthy of quotation. All is well because all is trim and square.

Clothing also dresses the soul. Of course he's too warm today, he admits, but it's what holidays demand, and his wool coat marks the fellow who knows what the other fellows know is high class.

Then Virge slides accidentally, momentarily, on the moist scum of fallen leaves. Big shoes act sometimes like skis! It's so slippery he loses some balance but, this time, does not fall.

There could be a problem with the young man. People react negatively to him at times. When they look at him they appear not to care too much for his hands, or his mouth. Or there could be no problem at all, just an effect he gives, an impression. It's how he holds his left arm out an inch or so away from the body, keeping the right arm curved across the ribs, as if he were rubbing or about to rub his belly in hunger, and it's true that not long ago the whole family had gone hungry for days, and he picked up the habit of massaging the emptiness, and even slept face down in those days, the arm frozen in that spot. Now, now that they've eaten all right again for a while, he can't seem to break the habit, knowing that it brands him as pitiful. Also, as he walks, he will sometimes make more dips with his shoulders than others otherwise like him, young men of the same age and social class, and this time, when he discovers after a certain number of steps that again he's been swooping or dipping, he stops doing it of course. Still it's another occasion for absorption. The morbid sort. This is not to be allowed, he commands, determining that he will have to picture himself more often as something else, as not a cedar or a juniper but a marble pillar on fire, classic and Greek, but healthy as California.

Put on, put on a show for us. Somebody's father did say that. Put on a costume, put on a wig. Act the clown, the loon, the goon, the hound. In uncoiling himself away from his bad posture, bad habits, to light his pillar on fire, it becomes possible to become somebody new, or at least become oneself, plus at least one part that's new.

But then he's just steps away from falling down.

Later that evening, looking back on the bad stumble, it will seem as if there was no very good reason for it, no earthly reason for him to trip and fall down, certainly not to go down so hard. Not God nor a demon knocking you down, but God or a demon picking you up and using your head as a hammer. Try to explain that. That the leaves got slippery again and he just went down? But not quite like that. Funny that just before he falls he felt like someone else was walking the path, coming up from the ocean, toward him, planning to tackle and attack.

Well, ghosts have been known to trip up the living. Ghosts have been known to lie flat on the ground flat and make themselves a half-inch thick, and slippery.

But the accident isn't yet. Virge keeps on moving forward toward his stumbling block. The day lengthens, turns toward evening. He might see his shadow stretched behind him, but can't bring himself to look. Reverts to his slightly dipping shoulders, his slightly curving arm.

The trees along the way are not cedars, but shaggy old men, old eucalyptus. Gum trees, but where is the gum? Propped against one trunk is a downed branch that can be selected for use as a stick. Walking three-legged is easier than two in some ways, harder in others.

Oh, he says, comforting himself. I like it, and what I like is music. Boogie and woogie or something.

Sticks play percussion, a noise to crack back together the apartness. He is too old to live with his parents, but there's humor in it, a strain of narcissism and mockery about it for him almost all the time. The music in his head, a jumpy jazz, suggests a different and improved walk. He cautiously picks up the pace a bit and waves one elbow in the air, keeping another hand on a thigh bone. Syncopated, almost. It's hard to get right without getting low to the ground. Squirrelly flexible. He's never been this loose, this less of a galumph.

I shall pull you or tip you down, he thinks someone says, in as real a voice as any, slobbery in his ear, likely imaginary. Or maybe it's a sly hobo from the beach, or a fairy who's been hunkering in wait. A dreamy trick to make you take a dive. During the fall, on his way down, Virge wrenches his head back in time to see that the mother and the dad are far behind, not even walking, just standing still on the path, not looking at each other, not speaking.

What keeps us upright most of the time? Why not fall constantly?

If it comes to a fall, then fall all the way, per the saying. Something soft cushions his elbows, but next the face lurches forward, chest hinges down hard, no time to outstretch palms to break the impact.

And even then he keeps smiling, stays hearty, since there is no immediate pain. Maybe no fall! If no one sees you go down, you didn't go down. Or are we all already fallen, since Adam and Eve? Nobody knows anything new. They'll come along eventually, the frozen parents. One problem is that as his face presses against the dirt mass, he has the nasty sense of how he doesn't bounce, but sinks.

Later, Virge speaks through scraped lips, mumbling senselessly during the long interval between falling and the arrival of help.

Dust am I, the dust of the day, he says, or it comes out nearly that, but so slowly, one word at a time. But as he says it he sees that there's no dust, just mud, or moistness, many sickle-shaped leaves providing a pillow effect, spots of mold visible everywhere, and even down here you can sense the fading daylight, though finally the shadow is reduced, and there comes to his ears more clearly than before the distant cries of crows, as if they are far below ground.

Finally, no remorse. No shame in it after all, and no smells at the moment, so he sticks his tongue out to taste, and judge things that way. Musty and sour-sweet is the taste of earth, he learns, from his sampling of dirt's many spices.

A leaf, the shape of his tongue, adheres to his tongue perfectly, glued on. Everything sticky in this dirt pot. What he'd like to do is reach up and flick the thing away. But how? It's agonizing that the arms and hands are dead, have died, been buried where they fell, without eulogy.

Dead is too strong a term. Better to say his arms and hands are asleep, so, don't shout, don't wake them.

Didn't this all happen once before? All of this, and several times? Yes, but to a boy it doesn't matter, you're expected to fall. That's what's meant, when you're little, when the dad says something like, put on a show. You fall on purpose to entertain, you lick at the dirt to get a laugh.

What that makes him now? The neck muscles are perfectly alive, the lungs heaving because at least the air didn't get knocked out. At eye level there is a tiny world to explore: ants, half red and half black, bright as oil, but smaller still are orange mites that, if we squint with greater eye control, come into focus, no larger than poppy seeds, as small to the ants as the ants are to us. What this teaches is to keep an eye to the ground, to fall down with enthusiasm.

But then there's his loss of all feeling in his hands, half of his arms. Limbs do fall asleep but do they turn as plain and distant as his feel now, like the blood has been replaced with someone else's?

Spongiform arms. Mushrooms, lichens, and molds are all, after all, living things.

Along the length of him, though, there are trickles of warmth. There's a quality in the earth that doesn't heal but reassures, and this quality, this gift, makes for a slow, physical melting. There are crevices in this dirt that his body might eventually pour into. The underground realm of the crows.

Far behind, Almy and Mont are coming, at least Virge believes they are because he can feel their syncopated footsteps echoing like hooves. Someone, half-horse, half-dog, barks.

Our clown is down, is what his dad is shouting, with a terrible note of fear.

Still it's a lousy thing to say, and Virge is twisting his legs in such a way that his whole body turns upright.

It's the wrong word for me, he says to his folks, though they're not in earshot yet. In his opinion, the ground is more clownish.

But now here they are, parents looming like scarecrows overhead, with opposite expressions, one looking down at him in studied innocence, the other biting her lip like she's the one who tripped him up. But Almy pants raggedly, making gagging sounds at the back of her throat, as if unable to call for aid, but no, that's the sound of mothering clucking. He'd forgotten it, hasn't heard the sound in years, but it's welcome enough, a contrast to his dad's Germanic silence, the expression on his face changing from distaste to heroic weakness, his jowls sagging down slowly to hang like tea bags. It's Almy who at last falls to her knees, not to touch her boy, since she has always been averse to touch, at least with the tips of the fingers or the full hands. But then Mont uses his hand to stroke Virge's crown in a circular way, as if he wants to dry his hair, or arrange the victim to look a little more groomed.

Get up, Virge, he whispers, and then, in an attack of irritability, or awkward love, says the same thing louder, more impatiently, as if speaking to a foreigner.

It's me who's crazy, Mont continues, sounding desperate. It's your Dad who's the loon. I fell down. Not you, not you.

Meanwhile Almy clasps her hands in prayer, fervent and full of her vague acting ability.

Dear Lord, she prays, won't you please make everything come out as sunshine in the end?

Por favor, she adds, though not as one who speaks Spanish, just one who sometimes likes to add easy snips of it to her prayers in order to turn them, as she explains it, a few degrees more holy.

She shoulders Mont out of the way and touches his head painfully, maybe to make up for lack of previous contact, squeezing his skull so that he wants to yell at her to stop.

Still there's always room for humor, and the phrase he wants, but can't get the mouth to mouthe, is, Blessed Indeed Art Thou, as well as How They Soothe, Thy Blessed Hands. But he'll have to set them aside for later, treasures in their box, because there's in fact no room for making fun of her, given that her fingers do start to come alive, do start to carry what feels like an electric charge. And what if it is curative, what if these hands are hands of power, current passing through her that originates in heaven and grounds itself just under his body? Virge feels happy at the touch of her hand, already cured, and there is still a lot of pain, but it must be her pain he's feeling, not his. Almy has always had a rocky quality, with her cascade of coppery blond curls, her moss-green frocks, her skin scent of egg shells, the pebbles she carries in her apron pocket to fish out for sorting and sucking. Any impulse he might have had to make fun of her evaporates, and instead he wants to say, very sincerely, but can't get his mouth to move on the sincere version either, things like, You are some kind of a blessing, and Your hands make me feel a little better.

Earlier, there were ways to be separated from Mont and Almy while all the time living in their midst, and that seemed like the right way, and the only way. Be there, but be elsewhere, by entering a structure of apprehension and absorption. This new crisis makes everything more difficult and much from the discarded past is reactivated. Recently, it hasn't been so difficult to build a layer within a layer, a flame within a fort, as he likes to picture it—and by applying layers to himself he can feel airier. On arctic expeditions, all conversation stops when the oxygen gets low. The result is eerie silence, but the empty minutes are crucial to understanding the route, the road through the years, your seat at the banquet of life, the crumbs, or the feast, at will. Accidents and ailments marked his childhood, but those weren't enough to reach the lost soul stage. There may be no problem with the young man, other than one important one: that Mont and Almy always act as if there is a problem.

He knows for certain, lying there, that whatever is wrong with him is not his most feared disease, and a bird chirping from a branch says more or less the same thing. No polio no polio.

Almy, all business now, takes her hands off his head with a jerk. Later, as if controlled by strings, the comforting hands find their way back to his scalp, to his relief.

I can tell, she continues, mouth twisted with concentration. I can tell just by touching his head here, and here, by rubbing his poor scalp a little, and paying attention to the shape of his skull, that this won't be a case of the polio. *Gracias a dios.*

His nose comes up higher into the air for a moment, sniffing, canine, but her hands stay on him to keep him down. What an afternoon of ugly usages, he thinks. Goon, polio. Two words in the language. Golio and poon. Maybe he is or has one or the other, but not both, oh no, no one comes down with both.

If you're right, you're right as rain, snaps Mont, sitting some distance away now, forehead near his knees.

Just continue the treatment anyway, whispers Virge, enjoying his mother's motherly touch, but his lips have sunk back some into the dirt, and so he raises the volume, addressing himself more to Mont this time, though it's still only a whisper.

Say, Dad, he wheezes. Rearrange me, will you?

But Mont can make no move at all at first, and his face denotes nothing other than tremendous concentration. It's perhaps easier to not move than to move, but in the end he succeeds in grabbing his son's dead hands and positioning them more aesthetically, more funeral-style.

There, that's done, and now what, he mutters in his deepest tones, like one who has dug a grave and waits to hear who to place in it. Virge feels no better. Then Mont reaches out one finger to flick debris out of his son's mustache hairs, and that actually does feel better, for both of them, and for a while they all stare at one another in slackness, Mont still angling forward, so that his face stays fairly close, a couple of inches from Virge's, his mouth working its way toward a question.

Did you say that it is or that it's not the bad disease, I mean, you know, the lung taint, I mean the polio?

Mont gets this out rapidly, glancing back at Almy to maybe get her to restate her opinion, but she has turned her eyes heavenward again, squinting at a speck or two, as if looking for the miracle, or flock of miracles, which could be about to appear there. But no, he sees now that she's just acting a little herself, and has her own way, just as he's seen before, of moving her shoulders and loosening her spine at the same time, letting it sway this way and that, stretching vertebrae, extending the neck and looking straight up in such a way that she could be Almy the bird watching heaven for a chance to dart her beak at God.

If our tongues look diseased in our mouths when we merely speak the names of diseases, then why utter them at all? Better to speak at great length on the flattering beauty of good health. Still, he can't help but recall that there definitely was a girl, Virge's own age, who fell down to the ground years before, and it was because she indeed had caught the infamous ailment, but the family was poorer than poor after all, farmers growing more dirt than crops, going barefoot and that kind of thing, the girl wearing hand-me-down prescription spectacles that unfortunately were dark glasses, so she always had to come up close to schoolmates to talk, and maybe how she caught the disease was by standing too close to others, walking barefoot where others walked in shoes. At any rate, he'd known this girl before she got sick, known her in grammar school, spoke with her at intervals, let her befriend him, or vice versa, played those games with her back in that time when he knew games. Maybe they had played a game of Beau-Regarde, though he remembers being sick around that time too, some other malady he probably caught from her standing so close. One day she disappeared from school and ended up, it was said, in the full embrace of the polio bug, failing and then failing further, to the point where she was provided by charity with a lung so she could come home from the hospital, and, although he never saw this, someone said that she got all set up in the middle of the living room, near the front window, as if for public viewing, and while her name, Alice, and her lung, supposedly made of iron, would be mentioned at times in the community there was no one who could claim to have actually visited her, only those who said they had stopped for a moment on the road to try to peer through the glass, trying to catch a glimpse into the interior, as if it were okay for her now to be made public, a kind of theater showing here's what happens to you when you are unlucky, and you are poor, and you invite disease into your life.

As for Alameda, aproned and camel-haired and tattered at the edges, probably more poor by now than grammar-school Alice, it's true, hens have recently been dying, inedibly so, and from this she exhibits a dreadful exhaustion, as if there are good gallinaceous reasons for her pessimism. But, in the meantime, in the here and now, she does also show off a youth and freshness in the face, a way of not often combing her blonde locks that gives the effect of a raw and rural giddiness. But no, she doesn't, it has to be admitted, possess any special powers in her hands, healing or even diagnostic. So maybe part of the arm and hand problem could be, for all Virge knows, to some small degree at least, polio, or semi-polio, if there is a semi-polio. But is the very worrying about and wondering about polio a symptom? Do they all have it, and all will end up in the living room window in iron lungs in the end? Virge would like to ask all this of a third or fourth party, but there are only parents nearby, parents he shouldn't even still be living with, and there's the awful notion that even when it's definitely not disease this or disease that, then it's this endless lying around in the twilight, the damp of the whole planet seeping up into you, turning you into just another part of the planet, damp and earthy, that probably causes polio in the first place.

Say, Dad, he says, politely.

Yes, son.

Guess what?

What?

I can't say it, Virge replies, but the surprise is that he's got his voice back to where it can be heard. Yet Mont's face, only an inch away now, goes blank.

Say what?

Dad, Virge repeats, having something further to say, but not saying it, because the old man, right there, is big-nosed, bug-eyed, face as sunset-orange as the moon. Mont is chewing on his own upper lip, his own mustache, also about to speak, but not speaking. His eyes are brighter since the uttering of the word Dad.

There is no feeling in either of the arms or hands is what Virge wants to say, but doesn't say it. Nor does he say that he might be a cripple now, and might not be able to make it all the way back home, though there does seem to be feeling, even a good feeling, all throughout the rest of him, and it's interesting that there is something especially vivacious in the legs.

But Mont starts taking action. He gets his hands into the act, digging them under and under, and sure enough, while he's a wiry man, with a chin set more concave than convex, he shows a sudden strength, and manages to hoist Virge up to rest face down like a log in his arms, and Virge, the basket case, can relax there like a bag of something, head drooping down at one end, feet at the other, while the father wobbles, and curses under his breath, then curses over his breath, but ultimately and pluckily stands and carries the boy's body forward in the dark, Virge's arms hanging straight down toward the ground, and his lax fingers inadvertently drawing a funny pattern in the damp earth as Mont weaves back up the path, then down the slight slope that leads to the beckoning homestead, though there are no lights on to help show the way.

Almy tails close behind, full of brooding and clucking, an instinct for vocalizing, but it's just Almy being Almy, and so Virge smiles, glancing backward at her, only to find her pointing tragically at the spectacle of his droopy arms.

Oh Virge, oh Virge, she bursts out at last, fist drawn in tight at her heart, but then, abruptly sobering, she stands straight, smirking, as if to revel in some discard she has made of all cares and strife. There's enough moonlight now for him to see her front teeth glittering a bit as she dons a cheery smile.

You just pick those hands up off the ground, she laughs, flipping her head, shaking a finger at him, maybe satirizing the kind of mom who would tell a grown son what to do, but a second later the glittering teeth have disappeared.

Virge wants to lift his arms, comfort her with fond gestures, but he just can't, and doesn't want to say that he can't, and finally she takes care of the problem herself by running ahead and getting Mont to kneel down in the dirt and do the picking up all over again, but this time with Virge face up and his arms crossed on his chest. But as soon as Mont moves forward again, oh well, Virge's arms fall away just the same, bouncing around like the loose ends of a garden hose.

Pick them up, Virge, she barks, angry now, but it's Mont, the one who's proving something with all this carrying, who stops in his tracks and turns, wheeling the poor young man around with him.

Don't you yell at anyone, he scowls. Not unless you don't want me to carry him anymore.

Virge, in other circumstances, could step into this exchange and put a stop to it, but he keeps his counsel and doesn't yell what he wants to yell: that the reason he can't move his arms is that they have passed away.

In the game of Beau-Regarde, or Beautiful Gaze, children run in mad circles on the lawn. Then, on a given signal, all must stand stock still, but with eyes fixed on whatever they happen to be looking at that moment of paralysis. The winner is the one who can stay frozen and sing the cleverest song about the things he or she can see. This is what Virge, carried like a baby, sings, though only to himself:

My father's face is full of woe,
My mother's dress is long and cotton.
Every time I put on a show
The end of the piece is pretty rotten.

Once inside the house, there's the surprise that Mont veers left to the kitchen, not right to Virge's bedroom, explaining as he turns on a dime that there, in the kitchen, specifically in the breakfast nook, all the delights of a happy convalescence are to be found: food, warmth, light, company. Here, laid out on the daisies-and-suzies fabric of the banquette, he'll be comfy as a bear cub in a winter cave, not to mention the fact, Mont winks, that those cherry pies will be very near to hand, and who's to say that the sickest member of the family shouldn't get the largest slice, or a whole pie, or, for that matter, both pies? But Virge needs no convincing. He has always loved the breakfast nook, but, once he's ensconced there, can consider nothing at all except how to lollygag, rolling his eyes in his head until he's dizzy, testing to see precisely which body parts can move and which can't. Inches away are the old folks, fussing all around, lifting his legs, putting a hot water bottle under the ankles and wrapping everything together with a blanket, straightening out his arms to rest at his side, so that he's more mummy than corpse, head propped at a sharp angle with a cushion from the living room. Almy creeps in with a vial of something, some tin of farmer's salve or other, udder cream maybe, but here Mont shakes his head, no no no, and Almy backs off, abashed, giggling, slamming the screen door on the way out.

Everything's going to be all right, someone says, and Virge realizes he's the one who said it, so it's not at all comforting. But he keeps thinking.

If this is polio, he asks, can we afford iron lungs? If I have to have one, what about the iron and does it go inside the body or go outside?

Eh, what a waste of thinking and talking, exclaims Mont. You're going to be fine and dandy, that's what. We'll get you an outside lung if you want, but check the inside ones carefully first.

Meanwhile Almy comes back from outside with a small dark early strawberry, every boy's favorite, and there it sits on the palm of her hand next to his nose like a ruby for a crown, though a little green around the edges, so that he goes cross-eyed trying to take it in. Very well, with an ease born of long practice, he drops his jaw for the treat, and when she pops it in—oh oh oh—it's one of the sourest he's had in ages, but of course it's February, and how could he have thought it might taste good, how could she have thought such a thing for that matter, but what else to do here and now but smile, and chew, and swallow and smile some more?

Sourness, it is said, can be health-giving, and sour strawberries are recommended for the weak at heart.

So he tells himself.

Not for long. Men must, it is said by a host of experts, die. A minute later Almy turns on the little electrical chandelier that hangs over the table, and it bursts on this time like a photographer's flash, blinding him, and of course he makes a move to cover his eyes with his hands, and of course the hands are still granite, still morbid, and still don't want to go anywhere. All right, here's how it begins, he thinks, here's how they start to put the armless monster on display, here's how they warm up the lizard, no the snake, because I'm a snake, in the terrarium. I could die not knowing how it feels to clasp a woman to my breast. But do snakes have breasts? To her breast, then.

Turn off the goddamned light, hisses Mont, the fussy and cross authority figure.

All right, Almy answers, switching it off again, feigning, or perhaps not feigning, a pretty perkiness, but in all this she doesn't look at her husband, but at her son, taking on the wide-eyed and mystified look of an innocent, a wronged party.

Just please don't, she goes on, use your farm language around the two of us, as I've pleaded ten thousand times.

Maybe it's because I'm a farmer, as I've said back to you ten thousand times.

Virge stares up into the yellow glare of the chandelier. Will he see a tiny angel emerge from the very center of the light wearing a sort of grin? Snickering at paralysis and death?

It's at this point that he decides to teach everyone, human and angel, a lesson in civility, and to do this by dying, but in this case he only falls asleep.

Upon awakening, an odd mix of things: one slice of cherry pie in front of him, runny as well as notably runty on the plate. No fork, so how's he supposed to eat it? What's surprising is that, lying next to the pie, there's what looks like a hank of black wire, which turns out, when he leans in for a closer look, to be a thick strand of human hair. A wig? Also, next to the plate, there's a shot glass filled to the brim, ready to overflow, with milk. How's he supposed to drink that? And even if he could pick it up, how not to spill it? On the floor nearby there's the walking stick, the eucalyptus branch he'd had at the time of the fall, miraculously restored to its owner, the leaves smelling stronger inside than they do outside. All this is evidence of hours having passed, but it's still inky night outside. The chandelier is still on, still blinding, thought not as much as before, and while there's no one else in the kitchen at that moment, it's almost as if these items have been left out for him as a test, or an incentive, temptations for the hands, as it were, that might trick appendages back to life just because of wanting something so bad?

But as the blind learn to make sharper use of the fingertips, it occurs to him that the paralyzed can and will make sharper use of the eyes, and what's welcome immediately about the collection on the table is how expertly he can look at it, how he can see everything better than in the unparalyzed past. Cherry red is the pie, for instance, but also cherry scarlet, which is different, and then there's the silvery glint of the pectin, the tree-bark browns and mottles of the buttery crust, the diamonds of sugar sprinkled across the top. Mont had to steal the cherries from a neighbor's tree, and see how the cherries themselves are whole but pinched, as if grabbed in a hurry. As for the walking stick, it has much the same odor as the syrup for coughs that Mont used to brew by gathering eucalyptus leaves and nuts that fell by the bushel and crushing them with a pestle to get the oil. It's not until his mother peeks in that Virge comes to life and the first thing he does is crane his neck and raise his head as far in one painful direction as it will go.

What's this hair for? he inquires, nervously far-sighted, nervously near.

Are you a little better, young man?

Probably not. I still can't move them.

Move what?

Oh, you know. My parents to tears.

I see.

I can't move my arms and hands, of course.

Can't or won't, sweetie?

Well, my hands, you know, are crazy hands. Goon hands. Curled up. They belong in a sideshow. Maybe in prison. Mother, would you come here and cut them off for me please?

Almy sometimes likes to hang her mouth open, as if forming a reply.

I thought, he goes on, petulantly, that that's what made you think there was some little touch of something involved. You know. The taint that ain't.

Maybe, maybe, she snaps finally, stepping forward into the middle of the kitchen, as if approaching the podium. His lips are near the trumpet, she heard a preacher say once, meaning the end of the world was nigh, and she repeats this now, as she likes to do from time to time.

No no no, he chimes in, enjoying, as always, her fondness for the apocalyptic.

No? she asks, eyes widening in surprise.

No trace of a taint, or a fever. Just sleeping. Part of me. Maybe forever, though.

Then the feeling in your arms, she prognoses, gesturing with her own arms, must be on its way back.

You sure? he laughs.

You'd better believe it. On its way back right now.

Do you know what Dad's doing?

What?

What's Dad doing?

Oh him, she sighs. Looking through his papers, I guess, looking for the phone numbers of some doctors. You'd like to see a doctor, wouldn't you, just to show him how well your arms and hands are doing?

I guess. Maybe he'll know how to wake them up, or how to remove them.

Such language has its effect. She storms out, one eye turned on him like the evil eye, and when she's gone he feels bad, wants her back, wants to snap his fingers to call her in, and the impulse is there, but where are the fingers, it's difficult to find hands when they're not part of the nervous system. He can see them, gentle and friendly in his lap, but they may as well be someone else's hands, or a stray pair of gloves thrown there by mistake.

Nearly morning, and Almy returns, comes up to him within an inch. There's illumination and wetness in the air, and her nose, in middle-age, he notes with his new vision, is turning cherry red with a network of tiny veins, fine threads transporting a little blood to the surface.

But they stay silent, and then Mont comes in, and the two of them, mother and dad, resort to pacing from corner to corner, sometimes comically bumping into one another, sometimes simultaneously stopping to stare at the invalid, and Virge stares back like a puppet with its wide eyes painted on, able to speak, just choosing not to.

Mont the father lets his fingers dangle in the slots of the stove, which isn't lit, expressing himself to no one but himself.

Hair swept up, a little gaunt and tall, vaguely Norwegian, vaguely arctic in appearance, with his over-sized ears, just like Virge's, and his gauntness.

Can't we talk? Mont asks after a time, as if fighting to keep from being interrupted. He steps forward, bobs and weaves.

Virge moves his head at all this, uncommitted.

My guess is that he's got a spider bite on him somewhere, Mont states at last, sitting down as near to Virge as is comfortable, making things cozy.

Oh, he doesn't know, Almy snaps, sidling over near them. Virge doesn't look at the spiders.

But it is true that she has had, indeed they all have had, a fear at one time or another of spiders, particularly after hearing the story of the distant cousin who was bitten by a spider and whose brain turned to liquid, then dripped drop by drop out both ears, but wouldn't die, and didn't die, for two long years after that.

No, no, says Virge, sharply, thoughtfully, unsure how comical to get in a situation like this.

Sometimes they're all one funny family together, sometimes not.

Oh well, he continues, maybe it was spiders. Some neighbor's dog was barking one night. Maybe at a very large spider? Frying pan spider the size of a frying pan? Wolf spider the size of a wolf?

No one seems to know how to laugh.

Well, what difference does it make? he goes on. I'm taking paralysis very well this time, aren't I?

Or get into any more poisons? asks Mont, rubbing his chin, looking sidelong though there's nothing to the side.

No one has been poisoned in an awfully long time, says Almy, swallowing darkly.

Yes, I grant you that, answers Mont. But you see, you always have to wonder how long the effects of a given poisoning can last.

And Virge is pleased to see that this question softens rather than hardens the air, as his mother advances to where the two of them are seated and lets her hand hover near the top of his head, just where his hairline sits, receded, at the very crown of his skull.

Just call some doctor, pleads Mont, shivering under the presence of her hand, then brushing it off as if it were a brain-drip spider. Call that handsome friend of yours, the one you fell in love with, what's his name, Dr. Noster, wasn't it? Speaking of spiders. That one reminded me of a black widow, Virge. A black widower. Like all the doctors. Half of them are dutchified or something, the other half quacks.

Oh, well, you've forgotten something, despite being the famous genius that you are, cracks Almy, cocking her head, putting her hands in her own hair now, her particular way of showing displeasure.

You've forgotten that he's not our doctor anymore.

Call him anyway, mutters Virge, a little weary after a certain number of years watching the two of them spin in circles of littleness and penury. A little tired of the unswerving attention to detail of it all.

You're forgetting, continues Almy, that your Noster got pretty sick of us last time. No, Virge, not sick of you. Sick of us having a sick son. Sick of us. Just us.

You know I'm sick too, claims Mont, coughing on the intake of breath, entertainingly. He gets up and goes to the stove again, slumps hard against it, still coughing, eyes hard, then soft.

Silence follows, and more silence comes after that. Virge, at length, falls asleep again to the sound of his mother listing things: one, a doctor, two, one doctor for both of you, three, one nurse, and on and on.

But some minutes later he jerks awake when Mont approaches him and whispers at him, with his unlit pipe between his teeth.

One doctor for both of us, Son, and he's already on his way. While you were having your forty winks, he was getting in his car in San Grande and heading down Highway Number One just to see us. Your mother got through on the phone. And what do you know, not a quack, no, but he is in fact dutchified, if that's okay.

Mont's got his hand out all this time, waiting for a handshake, and smirks a little when Virge keeps looking pointedly around the room, pretending he doesn't see the hand.

What kind of dutchified? he asks at last.

What do you mean? How many kinds are there? Your mother just told me he's an in-commonist, the type who emphasize what they have in common with everybody, and maybe that's a good thing, since you'd have to guess that he can't charge us much on those terms.

Well, but you always talk, Dad, about the ones who don't work.

Because I like some of them. Depends how desperate they are. Anyway, that's one reason for me to get out of here before he comes, don't you think?

The youngest men, especially after sitting for long periods, or in some athletic sensations, get a tingling in one leg or one arm, and this is not a disease, but still a type of paralysis. Some critical point is passed, sensation lost. A certain pamphlet Virge knows goes on about something that is really just loss of blood, and gives no reason why. Where does it go? Overall, to prevent episodes, dress should be kept comfortable. Flannels of a light heft or linens are to be worn next to the skin. No heavy underpants or undershirts, no damp fabric, or boiled wool. The ankles generate electricity, so bottle that with firmly gripping stockings or garters. Don't choose styles of headwear that bind or reshape the skull. "Sleeping limbs" are, to some, a thrill, while for others a source of shame. My leg is asleep! the patient will shout out loud, almost triumphant, while another will quietly groan that his leg just isn't there anymore, as if it were his eyes that had gone to sleep. For Virge there was an instance long ago where the ends of his fingers went numb, and as they revived there was such an itching, and then a noise, crackling like tiny logs on fire. Also his legs were once incapacitated too, not exactly paralyzed, just too weak to budge, and it's a fact that he spent several days in childhood in a wheelchair, a leather and bamboo contraption, and there it still sits, in one corner of his room, rubber wheels shedding a black powder on the floor, the thing a reminder of those long ago more sickly times, only now it's used as storage, the seat a place to pile storage boxes that perhaps hold jumbled puzzle pieces, or some of his or Mont's boyhood clothes, or bundles of bandages from the days when, every time he fell ill with the headache, Almy would wrap up his head Egyptian mummy-style, and what really cured the headache was the pleasure he took in her wrapping, how neatly and loosely she proceeded, exclaiming over the ease of bringing ancient history to life.

But this episode is different, in that both arms, from the shoulder sockets down, have lost all feeling. Curved and quiet, they lie next to him, apart from him, and that's all. Virge fell down, or was yanked down. So many mysteries. There has to be something in the story, he supposes, that would intrigue a true genius of the medical field, if there's such a one to be had.

There's that other mystery, the one that must be re-explained to each new doctor, the story of the rose dust and the rubber hut. And it's always hard for Almy not to claim, in moments of the coldest extremity, that everything was, to be blunt, the clear-cut fault of the father. Mont, according to her, left the hut unlocked, and so of course Virge would stumble in there and consume the dust, just as any all-American boy would do. God put the apple in the garden after all, so you can only blame God for the fall. The innocence of Eve reminds us of the innocence of Virge.

The progress of any disease is that it gets worse before getting better.

There are waves of sharp-as-nails aches and pricks everywhere, everywhere but the arms, the vexation of it so unpleasant that he requests this time, speaking to the light fixture, that everything but the arms be amputated and then taken away and burned, so that he live his life as merely a pair of arms, paralyzed but free of pain.

Later the pricks subside, but now the arms themselves look ghastly. They are shrunken and yellow, dusty to the touch, sulfuric. More pointedly, it feels sometimes like the process going on is that the mind, the thinking process, is deteriorating. His mind's unhinged, they might say of him, and while he can't imagine hinges, he does feel that his brain has opened, more like the sprung-up lid of a tin can.

His parents come back to the kitchen to check, and the nearer they get the sicker he feels. One of them, he's not sure which, it's hard to tell through the fog, asks if he wouldn't rather get up now and go to bed. Come on Virge, it's as if someone keeps saying, but no, no, he refuses to go, to his room or anywhere, the idea is it's morning already, and he won't get up. He could weep to look at himself, but won't. Nothing could be worse than to look like that and then to be picked up and carried like a sack.

To be treated like a baby, he says out loud, not making much sense, enunciating, though his voice is pitched so low there is no baby effect possible.

Here we go, baby, says Mont, and, on cue, they simply lunge and grab, but it's only to angle him up, build the pillow pile thicker underneath him.

There, there, Mont continues. That ought to have been of some comfort to you.

But oh, his poor arms, says Almy, picking one up in a clinical way and letting it drop, like she has been assigned the job of testing arms, checking them all for absence of vitality.

Keep the extremities out of it, retorts Mont, and Virge tries to make sense of that. He won't do any more chores without arms than he did with them, is what he imagines Mont will say next, but Mont says nothing of the kind.

In times gone by, Mont was young, hard-hitting, fond of grinning and tousling, like children's hair, his own hair. He had then an air of self-confidence composed via muscle and wealth, though blessed with neither. But success and self-absorption always bite each others' tails. It happened that the young couple, newly wedded, having inherited house and land, moved out to own it and farm it, and Mont, nervous and buttery, went at it mostly with boasts. Proud of gentrified improvements, both in mind and acreage. His body turning harder and thinner with every month of labor. It's economies that sink, not economizers, so he plunged into it with clammy hands, cunningly but too thriftily. We're raising cash like cows, he coached his family to say. Part of it was bad luck, the crop he finally settled on, on the suggestion of an almanac ad. Napoleon beets, according to the speech balloon of a liveried servant in the ad, were famed for flavor and health-tingling properties, but what wasn't said was that they do not flourish in every clime. The great moment came when he pulled the first one from the ground and held it up victoriously to the sky, but in the end Napoleon beets had the flavor of something non-beet, a quality more flinty in flavor and gummy in texture than was marketable. So Mont's work went mostly for nothing, and self bites on to the tail of nothing. Then came the eucalyptus oil, and that showed initial success, but never bringing in more than a few dollars. Mont dreamed of advertising his health-oil company on the side of the barn, and started to paint it himself, depicting a spray of sickle-shaped leaves, dripping golden oil from their tips, but then the tobacco people paid him to put up the cigarettes instead.

A year later he claimed to have shrunk an inch, but it was more that he had developed a cowering. Though taller than a lot of men, he undertook to hunch himself down in a way that would let him look up to those he came in contact with, like a servant, and the way he reinforced that, nodding too earnestly as they took him aside to speak of highly effective ways of salvaging a family and a life, grew more and more difficult for Virge to look at, the older he got.

Later, Mont took up pipe smoking, and showed a talent for it.

By late afternoon, Virge is worse than before. He finds himself breathing slowly and at the same time quite precisely, as with those who freeze to death, men on arctic expeditions he's read of, each breath coming in so thin and inadequate that those who recover report how they believed their lungs to have shrunk to the size of acorns, while all the time their hands claw at the air as if to scratch any remaining oxygen out of it.

Would Virge have had the strength to file such reports? You could only claw the air in desperation if you could move your hands.

Long minutes go by, ticked away by the copper kettle clock on the wall. He pictures himself, if he should live, reduced to a purely mental shape, perhaps only eyes left to stare, alternately, at the clock in horror, and at the vanishing body in horror.

Still, at least he would have the eyes, the mentality. How would it be if he were an idiot? Have they already or have they yet to invent the iron brain?

Almy comes in close at one point, breathing heavily herself, proving there's plenty of air to be had, and perhaps the warmth of her breath, rich with carbon dioxide, is enough to help him wise to the fact that his own lungs are just fine.

By supper time he's hungry, and after some spoon feeding he looks better and better, a little bit of new sensation coming in his arms even, like some substance is hardening and shrinking inside there, or starting to glow. Bioluminescent arms would be good. Death-o-meter readings seem to be going down. Yet maybe his thinking isn't as usual, because he utters a few things that don't make sense to the others, and causes some extraneous noise in the kitchen when he asks at one point if it isn't almost time for school.

You don't go to school anymore, comes the reply, though he can't tell who it is who speaks.

You already graduated, chum, the other points out, in a less anxious tone, so this must be Mont. You already got your diploma. You want me to bring you your diploma?

By now, whoever it is, is shouting a little.

No, that's all right, Virge softly answers, satisfied with what he hears, embarrassed by mistakes but entitled to his body, however whittled down. He smiles, laughs out loud at floating images of hands, many hands, all whittling, forever cutting downward.

He's going to be all right, whispers some golden father after a while, and to Virge the comment is balm.

You're going to be all right is a sentence that would wake the dead, and Virge opens his eyes, and feels nearly ready to lift his arms up like a sleepwalker would.

I should stretch them, he says to his dad, but they're paralyzed.

I know, answers Mont, clearly not listening, barely moving his lips, half responding to the sound of the voice, and half to the message.

I don't know squarely that he's going to be all right, says Almy.

But he's more alert. The pain of hearing her talk that way pricks him awake.

I beg your pardon, he puts in, but doesn't know that his voice is hardly a whisper, and besides, they've walked away from him now, and he sees that Almy as well has her back to him because the telephone has been ringing an awfully long time, and now she's answering it, shouting shrill questions into the horn.

It's the doctor, smiles Mont, winking at him. I'll bet you anything it's the Dutchman.

But doctor of what? Virge isn't able to recall how this has all come about, but the next thing that occurs to him is that one of the parents is ill, that something really terrible has happened, most likely to Mont, who has seemed so down lately, so ready to leave.

Here it is, eight in the evening now, and when she gets off the phone Almy explains that the physician in question, a Doctor E. L. Flanig, is still on his way, just car trouble down the coast, also that he's bringing an assistant, and now here's the best part, that Doctor Flanig has conveyed by telephone the fact that he most certainly and even easily and routinely recognizes the symptoms that Almy describes, knows already exactly what is broken and what is at stake, and is ready to effect a cure, or begin a cure, the moment he steps into the sick room. And not just cure in the traditional sense, because his treatment involves a fundamental transformation of the patient as a whole, and the results are guaranteed for many years.

That's a lot of years, says Mont, leering.

Oh, it's something, Almy muses, not sarcastic, her eyes opening toward her husband, a thin and unsophisticated expression on her face, like that of a very humble person unwrapping a gift.

Do you suppose, mutters Virge, disgusted with them, but not immune to either reaction, that we take what everyone says with a grain of salt?

Years back, Almy was equally not the same. Back then she was Alameda. Smarter than I am now, but less knowledgeable, is how she likes to put it. At her parents' home, a house in town, as she has explained many times, she played the piano without much talent but with an unusual grace, cupping her fingers with exaggeration, easily reaching the pedals with the reediest and readiest legs imaginable, bursting out at intervals with lyrics that were more improvised than read out of any song book, expressing in them an interest in the farm, especially, the runtier creatures of the barnyard among the newborns. She had no idea that she would end up one day really working a farm, so it was funny to think now how she had sung so much about piglets and lambs, great spider webs inside the barns, imagining an alternate life for herself, picturing herself freed from the bland suburban avenues of her youth and transported instead to the rural landscape, where she, according to the lyrics she made up on the spot, would hold and love great armfuls of farm babies. Of course in time she grew up, gave up the piano, wedded, and when the chance came to move to the coast, to take ownership of and then gingerly live and hope to thrive in her grandparents' house, she snatched at the opportunity, a little less interested than she used to be in the runts and such, and more interested now, as the more self-inspected adult she had become, in her husband's view of her and of the world, observing his way with the beets and the oil, eager to judge him but silent, not truly expecting failure but not surprised by it, taking up a more religious attitude toward the ups and downs than he could. In the end, she could lament their ruin, then shrug it off completely, not weeping, but whining, hardening in those areas subject to unanswered prayer, and softening with the acceptance of huge changes. What Almy needs, Virge judges now, twenty years of experience later, is exposure. Stardom. More makeup. They could all use a change, a little world travel. Different countries to look at might fix everything, but Almy needs it more than others. Virge needs it second of all. Let us out of here! they used to shout at one another, rattling imaginary bars, only half joking. And now, it's all backwards, all inside out, because Mont, the most homebound of all, is the one likely to go off to compare himself, themselves, to the rest of the world, or at least the rest of California.

For now, Mont just whistles and digs his hands deeper in his pockets.

I'll send you a postcard from the big city, he sniggers.

To leave us with the doctor? asks Virge.

As long as he don't or doesn't cost anything, nothing, he re-sniggers, mocking someone or other. Herr Flanig can work on me even, he adds, for all I care. I will submit at those rates to anyone.

He emphasized, says Almy, icily, misunderstanding the joke, that there will be no charge.

Does that make him an in-commonist? asks Virge, getting his voice back.

That's right, says Mont, stepping forward. They're the ones who won't work for a salary. That's how it works. They labor but they get paid in something else.

But Dad, that makes you one too in a way, when you don't have a job.

You don't have one either, he mutters, shrinking himself, retreating to the stove, opening the door of it a crack, maybe thinking of inserting his hand inside.

That's right, says Almy, taking Mont's side, as she is apt to do when Virge is talking. Nobody has a job, and nobody has the right to compare jobs.

So Virge bites his lip and determines then and there to get up. Turn on the spotlight, and he will swing his arms around, grab a biscuit from the breadbox and walk away, go on his own trip. So he concentrates every effort on getting the nerves underway. After a moment he is stretching his whole body out with the effort, bugging out his eyeballs.

Oh, Virge, says his mom, recognizing from far across the room what he's trying to do. Virge, don't.

He's sweating, trembling, back arched in such a way that only his head and his heels touch the banquette. A bad sight made sorrier by some dust that now drifts down from somewhere.

Virge, stop. Let the doctor fix it. You don't even know how.

He lets go, sinks back down, but then, sort of on its own, one of his rag-doll hands lifts itself half an inch, like a dying bird, and one finger, like a dying bird's eye, wanders here and there.

Astoundingly.

But then the hand immediately falls, dropping back into his lap, happy to be dead there again, but there is no doubt that his hand did move, and that this can be called a breakthrough. So much so that he feels ready to walk out the door. No one has seen his little triumph, his willowy motion, and Virge decides, after thinking it over for a long time, chin in the air because a tilted brain always clarifies the thinking, not to say anything, but just smile and smile, in what he believes to be a fairly sultanic fashion, at the two of them, no more desiring to speak of his happiness than to speak of his unhappiness.

Here, Virge, says his mom, bringing over a towel, I wish I'd done this when you had your fanny in the air.

It's the greatest possible embarrassment to a young man as, with Mont's help, she lifts his behind an inch from the banquette, and slips the towel underneath him, explaining that he should feel free to pee his pants if he wants, the towel will catch it, and they can worry about changing his pants later.

He holds it in, slightly humiliated. What do they expect, he wonders. After a moment he notices that they both have been staring at him all the while, as if watching for a sign, in his face, or somewhere, of recent urination.

Well, says Almy, turning away, looking out the window, they ought to be here any time.

Let him come, and come quickly, that's fine, says Mont, taking a pair of scissors out of a drawer with one hand and a tea towel in the other, and proceeding to idly snip the fabric into pieces, following the lines of the pattern.

Let him come, just not this minute though, repeats Mont, piling up the scraps with care as if to sew them back together later. Let him come after awhile because I don't want to be here to greet the son of a bitch.

Virge glances at Almy to catch her reaction to the bad language. But Almy is unmoved, her head thrown back in an exalted fashion.

Mont is certainly going to go.

The die is cast, he says, once Almy has left the kitchen.

So no more shows for me to put on, smiles Virge.

No more shows.

With his fingers back in the stove slots, Mont has a way of pursing his lips when trying out eloquence, and a way of slightly inflating in his suit when he wants to, all of which makes him look like an illustrious person, a judge of men.

But he is Mont and it can't last. At last he deflates, goes back to his cowering, comes over to sit down near Virge's head, and goes on, in a more bland tone of voice, to explain how down there in the city he'll be all right, not that anyone necessarily cares, but how he'll make money for those in need of money, not for those with looming doctor's bills, because after all there aren't going to be any such bills, so Virge mustn't feel guilty about that. No, after all, because the family's been broke for a while, he'll go door to door, selling bottles of eucalyptus cough syrup, because think how many folks will be bound to have a bad cough. Or for that matter he'll sell anything, it hardly matters, he just knows there's a million doors to knock on in a city that size, and it will take a year at least to get to them all.

So just think, he concludes. If one in ten of my knocks results in a sale of something, no matter what it is you're selling, that's a better deal than sitting around in farmland watching your son fall down.

Yes I guess so, is Virge's frosty rejoinder.

I didn't mean it that way, blurts Mont, rubbing his eyes as if to snap himself back to loving his son. But I guess you're old enough to think for yourself. Judge me on my merits.

But Virge has gone back to tensing muscles, back to the effort to wake up things. It's not so bad, they do move a hair, just not on his command. The arms are still not his, but not dead, just hibernating creatures. To look at them you'd think of two leathery bats maybe, wings folded and pink, shuddering at times in their sleep.

You listening to me? You give a damn about your dad? asks Mont, some degree of alarm showing on his glazed face.

I was only thinking of the shows. Of no more shows.

Virge's plastered-on smile might end everything, but he's unable to keep his head, when he does grin like that, from yanking to the side, from letting his eyes go anywhere but toward his old dad's drawn and even slightly heroic features.

You are going to get cured, says Mont, nodding vigorously, and his son murmurs some note of thanks and gently closes his eyes. When he opens them later Mont is still there, still both affirmational and confrontational in his gaze.

To put on a game of Hare Go Down the Foxhole, teams of four children each are formed. Team A assigns three of its members to clasp hands and stretch arms in such a way as to form a circle, or "hole," with the fourth member, the fox, standing a short way off. Team B picks one of its members to play the hare, who must jump through the hole head first. However, the fox is ready to pounce on the hare as soon as he or she is trying to stand up again. If the fox can knock down the dizzy hare, Team A scores a point. If the hare can regain its feet and remain steady there, despite the efforts of the fox to upset him, Team B scores a point. And so on.

Virge nods off and wakes up again. Arms almost alive! Sometimes moving. Perhaps everyone will creep away while he's asleep, and not come back, leaving him to work out his own recovery. It's the middle of the night again, he's slept through the entire day, and then there is the surprise of, and then the reassurance of, finding himself undisturbed in his kitchen kingdom. But no, he's wrong, Almy is there busying herself at the stove, and then she turns triumphantly with a bowl of soup and a little dark bottle of cod liver oil, which she pours on top of the soup as a glistening garnish.

You aren't a cripple, she says. All you've got is, something to be gotten, and gotten over. All you've got's an interruption.

That's what I tell myself, Mother. That's the word I used. Is Dad still around?

For now.

Doctor?

Not yet.

Well, your diagnosis is wrong. The cod stuff isn't designated in my case, due to its overly powerful flavor.

Oh, don't be such an egg, says Almy. Stir it in the soup and you won't taste it. But I guess your pa knows better how to treat the sad sacks of this world.

As if introducing someone on stage, she swings an arm out to the side and there comes Mont stepping into the circle of breakfast nook light with a certain style, the jauntiness of those who think they know exactly what they're doing, the optimism of one about to jump off the edge into some darkness.

My boy, he says, swinging his own arms wide. Off we go. Or, off go I, that is.

Then there's a surprise. Mont, without further prologue, stoops down and wriggles his arms underneath Virge's waist, smooth and efficient this time, and lifts his son up to his chest, holding him too tightly there, like a Ming vase that he fears to drop, but at last the father moves forward, a stiff and cautious bearer of the ill, inching through the darkness and narrowness of the long hallway, and it's Virge who somehow manages to keep the arms, this time, from falling.

Okay? asks Mont.

Oh this is bad, this is bad, Virge replies. Father, I'm sure you can appreciate humiliation. Can you?

No answer.

The hallway's so narrow that a long lock of Virge's hair, which has loosened itself from the rest and flopped out, brushes one wall, while the toes of his stockinged feet slide along the other wall. But after a minute Virge can also almost enjoy the warmth and containment of the hard muscular arms under his knees and spine, skin and bone arranged somehow like a properly laid out set of cushions. It's nice to relax, to pay melting attention for once to the garden of wallpaper flowers that covers the walls above the wainscoting, believing for a moment they are real.

Why don't you just set me down now, says the convalescent, half-heartedly. I could probably walk, you know.

But it's as if he doesn't exist, or can't be heard from down there at chest level, because Mont says nothing, just carries and marches, seemingly a man who knows what he's about in this moment and nothing else. As they advance, one sock on one dangling foot gets snagged on a nail head sticking out of the wall, gets pulled off completely, and falls to the floor. This house is undressing me, Virge concludes, but doesn't say it aloud.

In the bedroom, firm hands lower him onto the mattress.

Can you get my sock, he whispers as he gets tucked in.

In a minute, says Mont. There's something first.

Okay, but don't forget the sock.

Just listen. You know how you've spent so much time in your room over the years?

Not so much.

Don't whine. You know, when you were sickly.

That was fourth grade, mostly.

Yes, but didn't you spend that whole year in your room, pretty much?

Mont's voice, it's impossible not to notice, is especially musical and sonorous when low. Compared to it, all other voices in Virge's recollection are squeaky, ratlike.

For no reason, it seems like a good idea to look at the time on the clock. What time was it? He forgot the instant he knew.

I don't know. Are you going to get me the sock?

Wait a minute, Son. Just tell me. What have you been doing in here over the years? Reading, mostly?

I still do that.

I guess you do. We haven't been to the library in a long time.

Right. So why are we talking about things?

It's your favorite room in the house, isn't it?

Huh?

This one here I mean, Mont emphasizes, gesturing around the room.

Would you prefer I spend less time in here? I didn't mean to be ailing so often, and maybe we should go back to the breakfast nook, because I'm fine anywhere in the house.

No, no.

Look at me, Pop, and you might notice that I'm nearly middle-aged.

Don't you say that, whispers Mont fiercely. don't you say that to me.

Well, I mean because I can walk. Walking toward decrepitude.

Your mother and I, says Mont, ignoring him, we got this house when someone died. Remember that. We stumbled into it and it seems right that you should get things too even if nobody dies. I'm saying this room is yours now. Do with it what you want. Turn it into a library. I even wrote up a deed. You want me to get it now?

Get what?

Get you the deed to your room.

Oh. The deed? No.

You understand what I'm telling you?

I understand it, but I don't particularly care for it.

That's because you've been in this room so much you don't know how things work. Sons often inherit their rooms in this way.

Mont's voice cracks a little, but he's not crying. He seems determined that some little thing ought to be said here, but will not nor never be said, or as though he's bewildered by how to say it, and there he lingers, shifting his eyes back and forth, though as usual there is nothing to see on either side. Then, making a noise in his throat, and maybe it's the word goodbye, he steps back into a shadow and melts away into the pit of the long hallway, and Virge waits for a long time for him to come back in with the sock but waits in vain.

Then there's the darkness and silence, a strange contrast after many hours basking for so long under the light of the electrical chandelier. In contrast, the bedroom is arctic, sepulchral. More apropos. This is where he'd better be while failing to be healthy and failing, as a consequence, to knit people together, keep people home where, all faults aside, they truly do belong.

Then some hallway door closes, doesn't slam, but in the surrounding quiet he hears a door creak open and creak close, and there's a distinct sense of departure, and the realization that there has never been a departure quite like that in his lifetime. A blankness settles in, but with a clean and formal structure to it. It's not my home anymore, he thinks. It's my institution.

But Mont appears just then at Virge's window, his face sagging, sad beyond years, and he puts his lips to the glass, the old distortion trick, monster face but more horrible because of the sadness, then slides his lips all the way down to the sill where the window is open a crack.

I'll be back in two shakes, says Mont.

Huh?

Two shakes of a leg.

You must mean a thousand shakes of a leg.

No.

Well, you were the one talking about a million doors to knock on.

Mont straightens up, and raises his voice to be heard through the glass.

You're saying that I should write you a letter, right?

About what?

Well, I'll pick up a pen even when there's nothing to write about.

Mont steps away from the window then, his face looking more noble now, and twisted, as if by some tremendous ambition. He fades backwards from view, and this time it seems to be for good.

Consider the number one thousand, Virge reflects. Even one thousand shakes, if one counted the vibrations of a nervously trembling leg, would take only a few minutes.

Later he tries to remember what doctors in the past have prescribed. Not just for him, but for all the sickly in the world. The iron lung for sure, and, if he recalls aright something he read once, the iron loom. If a loom, then picture it in terms of warp and weft, strings stretched taut across the chest, knitting and patching the damage. If a lung, then there's always been one lung that tends to loom in his imagination, and it's enormous, the size of their house, with all three of them inside it like men in a submarine, a thousand dials to scrutinize and coordinate at all times, making sure no needle ever drifts into the red zone, but you have to knock on each dial, one at a time, to make sure the needle isn't stuck.

For hours, Virge can't sleep at all, convincing himself that he never specifically wished for anyone, least of all Mont, to go out alone into the world. It occurs to him that if he were to get up and go to the telephone and recite random phone number sequences to the operator, there would be a mathematical chance of reaching someone who had seen Mont passing by.

Then, for a long while, each subsequent thought is incompatible with the last.

The bed seems to him the size and approximate shape of a boat, one that could be rowed around the room with the right set of oars, right set of arms, then rowed out into the world. He gets up, awkwardly, and paces back and forth, his hands sagging ape style, lower than usual, near his knees. What a spectacle, he thinks, he's made of himself. Later he finally has to pee so urgently that he gathers the strength to walk on two steady feet to the bathroom, where he somehow shakes his pants down by twisting his torso a number of times, and proceeds to business as quietly as he can in all the tremendous silence of the house, getting a few drops on the floor. They'll dry. Then how to get the trousers back up? Well, wouldn't you know it, it's a question of lying prostrate on the cold hard tiles, wiggling himself approximately back into them, then getting up off the floor, not at all easy to do, arms decorations, then proceeding back to bed, struggling to use his brain there, losing his train of thought. I'll just bide my time on this particular boat or this particular mattress, he says to himself, locating himself. By the time he sees gray traces of morning through the window, his mind takes a different turn, and he can picture Mont far down the road already in that semi-marine light, at least some miles down the highway, thumb set out at an angle if and when a car should zoom by, the cuffs of his trousers wet from cutting through the roadside weeds, worried about other vagabonds on the road, or farmers with hunting rifles, or federal men with machine guns who might appear suddenly out of the morning gloom and mow any vagabonds down.

It's Mont's paranoia, he's the one who's often spoken of his fear of getting shot, so why should Virge be picturing such a thing? Banish the thought, and Virge begins the day, at dawn, in a state of vigilance and image-free concentration.

In the distant past, it appears that people were much less sure of themselves. No one had ambitions then, so no one left the homestead. It was as if nothing was fully formed, but existed in a doughlike state of general grayness and flexibility. What mild surprises or repercussions there were seemed to be absorbed or deadened by this early softness, when nothing truly bad was possible, though nothing truly good was ever on its way.

One evening, in that same doughy past, Mont and Almy had some noisy neighbors over, and Virge, small child, lay in bed, listening to the voices drifting down the long hallway, and oh so clearly he heard someone speak out loud the word Virge, and refer to the aforementioned as that sickly child. So in that way he had an early clue as to who he was, or what. This was back in the years when Mont and Almy might sometimes give a little party, inviting people they'd never met, who knows who, it didn't matter then. On this occasion, Virge was sent to bed before they came and lay awake late into the night, moody and sniffy with a bad cold, cautiously chewing off slivers of fingernails, as he often did in those days, for no other reason than to build tiny forts and cabins out of the slivers, piling them like logs on the very corner of the night stand then languidly sweeping them off with one hand, letting the hand play the part of a tidal wave or scourge of war. At the same time he was mentally hopped up, all ears, focused on the adult voices down the hall, hoping for useful words, maxims, topics. Even at that age, nine or ten maybe, he was anxious to have an older soul than the one he had.

And again this one perturbed voice that he would always recall, nasal and raw, the voice of a hayseed, the one that had already called him sickly, piped up, and rose in volume.

Don't the boy help you? Don't the boy do his share in the fields?

There was a silence, finally broken by someone saying, You said it yourself. The boy's more on this side of funny than the other.

Oh no, chimed in a female, presumably Almy, with evident contempt for modern society in her voice. Sickly? No, but maybe just a little lazy or something.

The boy's a twig, continued the one who had to be Mont, but I'm not going to be the one to snap him.

Sometimes you've got to face facts, came another, more darkly amused voice.

Finally another dead silence, this one so perfect and embarrassed that Virge could hear, or thought he could hear, the lighting of and inhaling of a pipe, and then the exhaling, and sure enough here came a cloud of tobacco smoke drifting up the dark hallway with the result that Virge, who was all during this childhood of his very sensitive to smoke of any kind, ended up with a coughing fit, and finally here were the heavy footfalls and here was his dad to poke his head in.

I thought you were asleep, he says.

In fact it was a routine they had on such sociable evenings in that distant past. Cigar, coughing, poke the head in.

This time Mont came in all the way and switched on the desk lamp, whipped a checkered handkerchief out of somewhere and draped it over the bulb to light up the walls like chess boards, and then stood close to Virge, looking down on him, burrowing his arms deep in the bottoms of his suit pockets in the way he always had, rocking back on his heels, forward on toes. Finally he withdrew a hand out from a pocket, and it turned out, as always in this routine, to hold a spoon already somehow brimming with the newly invented eucalyptus syrup. It was a heavy dose, quivering and black in the spoon like a dome of petroleum, and he slipped it straight into Virge's mouth as if on afterthought, but so pointedly that Virge couldn't resist it, had to go along, as always, with the treatment. This is how Mont was back then, this is the kind of dad he was: boyish and playful looking for his years, as if he could be a friend to the boy, but, like the boy, unathletic, easily spooked, easily irritated, fond of establishing harsh rules then forgetting them, not likely to say a lot, not known to talk to his son, trying hard, around the clock, to just be a farmer, trying to become the type who could stand on a rise, if there were a rise, and overlook with triumph, and rage at the naysayers, a field of something that grew, a fruited plain, something that would wave in the breeze.

As for Virge, he may have been mentally weak at that time, or, conversely, mentally gigantic, but he was, then as now, at least to some degree, good at measuring degrees of pain and dismissing the lowest degrees and highest degrees to better comprehend the median. Cough medicine had little value, then as now. What does it do after all but lay down a coating, a blanket to hide but not cure the soreness. Further, it doesn't make a boy drowsy, and if that isn't the main purpose of a drug, what is? After Mont retired from the bedroom, little Virge kicked off the counterpane, sat bolt up in bed with his hair all scrambled, not gentlemanly, only a kid with a cold. Nevertheless he was ready to get up and get to work, ready to march in the kitchen, grab a bite, and head out to a day of work in the fields, while all the party guests sat dumbfounded at this display. But when he got to the kitchen it was too late. His folks were already at the back door, Mont laughing, Almy scowling, both bidding adieu to guests already swallowed up in darkness.

What fate do I have to face? he asked, coming right up behind them, meaning what facts, not what fate. A wonder that he would ever say the word fate, because at the time he hardly knew the meaning of it.

In any event, Mont and Almy wheeled around to find him standing there in his footed pajamas, a picture of golden childhood, and were pleased but stumped to the last degree by his question, which he couldn't amend and say the way he meant, so they tried to explain all about his fate, but not so much with praise as with vague promises of pluck and boyish success, and he walked back to bed with the idea that fate was probably a word to be preferred over fact. What fate to face? At the time of that party, that evening, it had only been one year since the rose dust, and no, since then, he hadn't been so very well. True, he was a twig that could either snap or bend. The rose dust helps the roses, he kept telling himself, so eventually it will help me.

And now, years later, with Mont gone, time to reconsider fate. Everything is either above one or beneath one and there's no way of knowing up from down these days. Go soak your head, is one expression. Our father who art in heaven, another.

Anyway, there never was any real anchor to the family, never a hold-forever glue, and though things could get less cohesive now, it's not as if Mont's presence or absence would be so much to blame. Everything could be altered for the better or for the worse. Mont is definitely among the lost, the departed, though the reasons given didn't come across as convincing. The family needs income, true, and certain doctors or doctor are scheduled to pull into the driveway any minute. There is a logic to that, given the awful listlessness and lifelessness. He imagines there do occur miracles that preclude events, such as any physician's arrival, and wonders if his hands have come back to life for a moment, and yes, believes that maybe they have, but then takes this on faith, since it might be better not to know.

He'll check in with the hands later though. With room for optimism. To be successful is to pursue microscopic successes every minute. Virge, who has been sitting at his desk staring out the window for these little minutes, not succeeding at not dreading the doctor, stands up. He's always getting better at it, and this time pushes away the chair subtly with the backs of his knees. There's also an interior flexing motion he has adopted since the fall. Brain to spinal cord to shoulder zone. Just to check. With nothing as a result. Not this time. Both hands, he realizes, are pulsing inside because of illness or recovery. There's a regular blinking, a code, but that gives way to a gong sound, meaningless in itself, but when he lies down on the bed he floats in rhythm to the ringing for a long time.

And so there's nothing left to decide, no choice but assistance, waiting for the arrival of the German, or, as he imagines, angel who stands many leagues tall. At least one thing is different now for Virge, and that is that he's the owner now, and it's no small thing, of a piece of deeded property, so why not, he reasons, expect the doctor to come in and properly play the subordinate, acknowledge his position as one who takes orders rather than gives them. Or does it go without saying that Flanig will perform the surgery immediately upon entering the room?

Waiting and ringing lay waste to the will.

Virge gets up, lies down again and begins slowly breaking down, his ooze seeping into the sheets.

He's in bed but he's back on the dirt path, no one coming to his aid, the sheets having turned to soil. Soft with infinite depths, they are spongy, half alive, growing around him like gums around a broken tooth. Imagine a length of pipe left out of doors to rust during the wet years, dark metal crust flaking off into the soil, slowly staining the surroundings red as it's swallowed.

The doctor is here for you, announces Almy melodically, poking her head in.

The doctor is here for you, dumbly echoes Virge, hardly knowing what he's saying.

No, sir, not for me, she snorts. The doctor is here for you.

And she snorts again, getting up a head of steam, her neck angled against the door jamb like the neck of a delicate horse.

You're angry, he sulks.

No, she smiles. But getting there.

You want me, don't you, to be polite to the doctor, who has driven out here to see me.

But Almy only brings a hand to her mouth, as if to cough, but it's her way of switching to her other language. Aqui esta el señor, she explains, pronouncing it old-Spain style, like she has a mouth full of postage stamps. A second later Virge hears a voice in the kitchen, and supposes for a bright but hopeless moment that it's his old dad—gone for years, it feels like—that has come back. But no, it's only one voice, and no, it couldn't possibly be anybody's dad. It's the doctor, and the unwelcome fact—unwelcome in a doctor, anyway—is that his voice his high-pitched, and pointed.

2

What's his name? Is he in the kitchen? Is he?

Yes, that's where he is.

But I don't want him coming all the way in yet.

You look fine. Try to sit up a little. Shall we just march out to the kitchen to meet him, and if not, could I prop you up?

Virge nods no, meaning only that he feels distracted by a presence, something, two presences, advancing approximately in his direction from the far end of the hallway, both moving forward with a light stealthy tread, like housebreakers. Tiptoeing, even? The bedroom door stands open, too late to shut it, and the part of the hallway wall he can see from his angle becomes a shadow puppet theater, filled with stick-figures.

Who's out there? barks Virge, rudely imagining gypsies, foreign soldiers. He knows he'd be good, given the chance, at guarding the farm from intruders.

Did you hear me? asks Virge, more gently, humanly, Almy trying to shush him, but the stick figures keep coming. Next one of them appears in the doorway, shadow turned to flesh.

What Virge and Almy behold is an elderly man. Skin drawn tight as mummy skin across the skull.

You're not the doctor, says Virge, taking into account the advanced age, and thinking this must be someone more like a funeral director, or an ancestor.

But, in the end, this is the doctor, just superannuated and frail for the job, thin as a marionette but juiced up or drugged, not artificially, just using his mind, maybe, to achieve a level of energy beyond his years.

It's only me, the gentleman smiles. It's only your dear Dr. Flanig, he continues, sliding in and coming to a halt at the foot of the bed.

In a way, he's the picture of wisdom through the ages.

My dear doctor, Almy announces. Your dear doctor.

He's insubstantial to look at, at first sight, but all aglow, with lovely white teeth and white eyes glowing brightest within the general aura, giving the impression of having hoarded and preserved some elements of himself from some earlier time, some past period of precious and salvageable youth. At the same time there's something wrong, some sort of droop or sag below the neck, as if every ounce of his strength were being directed into his face. He may well have a way of winning one over, Virge imagines, but it's likely a false and or corrupt way, and must be resisted.

Is he, as Mont predicted, dutchified? An in-commonist? No way to know. Germany, Holland, Austria, Switzerland: these are all little blank cameos on the globe of Virge's brain.

No matter. The doctor takes a bow, two bows, very gracefully, one directed to each of them, as if having been born in a century even earlier than the last one.

Which of you is the patient? he laughs, spreading his palms.

But wait, Virge wants to say, where is the person who was walking with you in the hallway?

Mrs. B, we have rushed down to be with you, the doctor goes on, addressing himself to Virge, but speaking with great care out of one side of his mouth, as if unsure which one is a woman.

Thank you, says Almy, looking pleased with herself.

We came straight to the house, Madame, he repeats, snorting a bit, though the laugh is harsh. And we were anxious to arrive when we heard of the patient's condition, and drove at top speed. You see it's always a policy to come rushing to the distant sickbed when it can be done.

It was wonderful, I hope, offers Almy, awkwardly, but straightening her spine, warming up. You didn't drive too speedily, I hope.

It was too fast for some, he confides to her, finally now taking her by the hand and holding it firmly, like the knob of some door he's about to open.

I let Stuart drive the auto, he explains, and yes, my young man is hastier than I would be in such a journey, but this so-called break-the-neck speed of his, as he calls it, though I screamed at him the whole way to slow down, didn't break my neck as you can see. Just bent it back a little I suppose, to the point that I had to take my collar off, and for that I apologize.

It seems meant as an amusing anecdote, and Almy is maybe about to come up with something gay in return, when there's a disturbance in the doorway, and in comes the second figure, the so-called Stuart.

There's no big mystery to him, after all. By this time he's expected, and even already admired a little, at least for his reputed driving skills. On first impression he's too young to be a doctor, but then the other one is too old, so perhaps they represent two ends of the profession? There are other conjectures possible. Based merely on the blond hair, Stuart comes off as an athlete, a golf amateur, perhaps, or judging from the pair of small unframed glasses, a college student?

Now, shoulder to shoulder, the two newcomers stand, bearing a family resemblance to one another in one sense, in that both seem to lean when standing, both in the same direction, though they are differentiated too, not just by age but by facial expression: one superior, the other smirking. Also, one is dressed in a dark musty suit and, as mentioned, a shirt with no collar, while the other, Stuart, who looks to be near Virge's age, perhaps a year or two older, wears an aristocratic white pullover and similarly colorless pants. The two men are the same height, both thin as acrobats, tightrope walkers perhaps, though Stuart has a smaller, more angular and nervous skull, while Flanig's head is calm, neutral, round.

They are both holding hats, straw boaters, like flimsy shields in front of their groins.

But who will speak? It begins to seem that not another word will be said or needs to be said, that they can just observe Virge, if that's what they're doing, or kill time, if it's that, but at least they are glancing at him sometimes, with what might pass for diagnosis and concern, yet their eyes tend to dart toward one another, or outward, toward the walls. Perhaps they diagnose, Virge hopes, by studying the patient's room just as much as the patient.

Look at him as long as you want, Almy volunteers, as if she were running a freak show, though she says it innocently, gaily. In general she seems to take everything so far as a good sign, and good way to get her son back to normal.

I'll make us all some poorcakes, she announces, but doesn't stir, as if she's only determined to introduce into the silence a note, spread cheer among the ruins.

Served with that famous apple butter of yours? asks Flanig.

I'm sure I don't know what you mean, replies Almy, flushing.

Then no, no, but thank you.

Well, you've come in an open car, I see, Virge observes, realizing this could be the wrong way to greet people he doesn't know well, but it's hard to avoid the observation, due to the fact that the shoulders of Flanig's suit coat are covered in white stuff, like talcum, or years of dandruff, while Stuart's pullover is flecked with a black powder, but in both cases it's clear that it's two-tone dust from their long drive.

You came in the same automobile, repeats Virge, tentatively. What I'm trying to say is that we only see the particles that the color of your clothing bring to light. Oh forget it.

Still no answer or even a prolonged stare. The eyes of Virge's visitors roam and roam, never looking at anything in the room for more than two or three seconds at a time. Introductions are easier, he supposes, when there aren't two new acquaintances at once, when there is only one item to a category, since creating new categories for new items that come along is less of a labor than having to take every new thing and put it in the proper preexisting category. Better, if strangers are to brought into his room, to be brought in one at a time, and for each to have his or her own definition. As for what can be gleaned about his medical history, let that be explained to one doctor at a time, because it is too rough to take in all at once and too tiresome to put two and two together.

Did you bring the bags in? asks Flanig airily, looking at Virge so intently as he says this that Virge almost gets up to go look for them.

No, he stammers, at last.

Not you, my boy. I'm talking to my assistant.

I'll get it, Almy says, jumping up from her chair. And she and the doctor dart out of the room.

Stuart stays behind a second, polishing his glasses with a cloth. Hello, he says, putting them back on.

Hello, says Virge. I'd shake hands with you, but for the paraplegia.

The what?

Paralysis.

Paralysis? asks Stuart, his eyes widening. I have a good joke for you later about that. But Stuart is also a darter, and now he too flashes out of sight.

Two hours later, they all come back, all three of them, and resume their previous positions.

Flanig and Stuart are like me, and both of them will like me, Virge has assured himself repeatedly during their absence, with some small sense of victory, though all the while he's of a good mind to resist them, if he can, to somehow overturn their best efforts and send them home hanging their heads.

There's only one more thing for me to say to you, today, announces Dr. Flanig, nasal and, despite his rest, appearing more aged than earlier in the day. This is my philosophy in a nutshell, young Virgil, and I know you're listening too, Mother. He clears his throat, steps forward, raises his eyes to the ceiling, as if reciting from memory. I am aware, he says, of the unspeakable loss to physicians and patients, both, that results when they are inattentive to the laws of the mind, as well as to the laws of the body, especially the bones. I like to think of it as a kind of psycho-osteology, the mind to bone correspondences that I will endeavor to explain. The spirit, the soul, comes necessarily after. If at all!

He steps back, looks around.

Do you have any questions so far? he asks, with a look that dares them to ask.

But it seems Almy isn't listening closely, as she ignores everything he's said so far and goes on immediately, blandly, to tell the story of the falling-in-the-path incident, with an attention to detail that is torture to Virge. First there's the meal, then the baking of the holiday pies, the argument with Mr. Bingham her husband, the beautiful weather just after the rain. There's the stroll, the setting sun, the dusk, and only then the falling down, the picking up, and Virge's limp hands, forever dragging and dragging in the dirt. Then there's the family diagnoses, the theory of the spider bite, the certainty that it's not polio. She doesn't mention the rubber hut and the rose dust but she does bring up her prayers, and would they like her to say another prayer now, do they believe there is any healing power to prayer, and is that all right, do in-commonists say prayers?

Of course they do, replies Flanig, discounting her inquiry with a stern shrug, though it's not at all clear whether he is sworn to such practices, either prayer or in-commonism, himself.

You will undertake all your duties, then? he continues, turning toward Stuart, who nods his agreement and simultaneously holds up to his chest a worn leather doctor's bag. Stuart freezes, grinning, in that position, and again, there follows a long silence.

Boring. So Virge puts on a show. For them? For his dad? Letting his head roll and loll around on the pillow, he twists his lips and mumbles some incoherences, all in a parody, perhaps not a very good parody, of dementia praecox.

After a minute of this he stops and checks in with them to see what effect his performance has had, and while all three are carefully watching, it doesn't seem to have caused any particular concern.

Maybe from her own sense of boredom, Almy leaves the room, only to come dashing back a moment later with an instrument he's never seen before but once, a pump with a reservoir at one end.

Could this be of any help? she asks. It's for killing spiders and, as I mentioned, we began to wonder if he might have been bitten by a spider, and I would hate to see the two of you get bitten as well, though you may already have been.

The two men look at her, back toward Virge, as if to see if he might wish to confirm this claim.

Well? Almy snaps at the visitors, not spraying the poison but pointing it right at them. Flanig tries to speak, but can't, as if he's forgotten part of a story he wants to tell.

Is it the money? asks Almy, putting down the spray gun, nearly sobbing. If that's what you're worried about, we can pay you. Just not today, that's all.

Oh no.

Because you'll have to send a bill. I know you said no, but you are welcome to send a bill.

Mrs. Bingham, there's been a misunderstanding, coos Flanig. There's not only no charge, it is we who are to pay. We who are to pay you.

Well, well, she answers testily, as if the issue still hasn't been settled. Well, that's very good of course. Virge thanks you. Don't you, Virge? Do you mean today?

Today what?

That you pay us today?

Flanig bows.

Madame, he says, you flatter me. But no. Not quite today. Perhaps later today.

Then I'll tell you what he ate, continues Almy. When was that, Virge? Ten years ago, I guess. Ten years, Doctor Flanig, Doctor Stuart. Ten years nearly to the day.

Flanig and Stuart exchange looks, and laugh.

Oh dear no, the boy's not a doctor, says Flanig, blowing his nose now into a black handkerchief. You see, Stuart is to be the young man's chum. Do you understand? I've brought him along as a hired companion for your son.

Hired, did you say?

Oh, we pay you for that too, Flanig laughs, his tongue, tiny and dry, fluttering around whenever he speaks like a scrap of paper. What I meant to say is that Virge is to be the hired companion for Stuart. And what do you say to that, young man?

Which young man? asks Virge.

You, Virgil, my patient. Let me introduce you. Virgil Bingham, this is Stuart Sturdy.

Is that your real name? inquires Virge, politely, but somehow he manages to make it sound nosy.

Not at all, says Stuart, coming forward with his hand out for a shake. No. It's only what the doctor calls me. I'm a prop to him, and a crutch, or so he says. Therefore "Sturdy." My real name is Duquesne and very pleased to meet you.

It's gotten warm. Stuart sheepishly retracts his hand. Virge has the impression that everyone is uncomfortably close to one another in his already cramped little bedroom. Do they know that he is the owner of this room? By now he probably should have framed and hung the deed of property.

Then something welcome: somehow the four of them manage to drift apart, subtly, but in just the right ratio, so at last the cramped feeling lets up a bit, leaving room for the rest of the world to come in toward Virge more readily, spaciously. The doctor, who has inched forward, is the biggest obstacle to spaciousness right now, but it's all right, because there's nothing too terribly uninteresting about the description he launches into, an account of the growth of bone tissue, and other matters. Marrow is the key, one learns, because it's a powerful substance that manufactures red blood cells, without which all life would fail. As these cells are absorbed, the bones can begin to grow, in order to manufacture yet more marrow. A perfect loop is what this represents, if it weren't for the brain. Nearly everyone who falls ill, you could say, is suffering from a mental breakdown in this loop, suffering from a tendency to neurotically withhold permission to release the red blood cells and thus slowly underfeed the blood, a psychic stinginess that cheats the whole body, and makes enemies of those who once were friends.

And how, asks Virge, does this result in paralysis?

It doesn't. Your paralysis is not part of that story. Not yet. Well, wait, yes it is, in a way it is. Very probably it is.

The arrangement of bodies in the room shifts again while everyone appears to ponder this last pronouncement. Stuart moves behind Flanig, and, raising his hands above the doctor's shoulders, makes a few mysterious silent signals to Virge, film-actor's gestures which seem designed to warn, maybe to suggest that the doctor's words are not to be taken literally, or alternately, taken more literally than one might be inclined to take them. The blood cells, which Virge had never considered properly before, could be, deep inside him, a source of extraordinary vitality. Or not.

Later that evening the new arrivals appear in his room, shoulder to shoulder this time, with no surreptitious gestures from Stuart. It is the bones inside the arms, says Flanig, that present the gravest obstacles to health. Sad to say, it appears now to be the case that the patient's ossa are denser and heavier than normal, and will be more difficult to treat. And yes, this treatment would be expensive, but no, it is such a privilege to work on a case like this, why any doctor in the world would rush to this bedside if he knew the facts in the case.

Go on, urges Almy, sitting herself down at Virge's desk, unscrewing the fountain pen she keeps on a chain around her neck these days, and poising nib over paper, fingers instantly staining with black ink.

There is, this time, a brief silence.

Maybe there is no treatment, mumbles Virge, and he must admit that this would come as a relief.

But there's more to examine here, the doctor says, moving back and forth, but no, he doesn't say much about how to treat, just goes on and on about the history of paralysis in humans, how it appears in ancient representations, how to identify it in papyrus portraits of Egyptians, Peruvian ceramics, et cetera. Virge is lucky, he explains, because his lack of life is only in the arms and clearly isn't spreading out or multiplying in any way.

It's a lazy paralysis, Flanig concludes, and therefore vulnerable, not indestructible at all. So I say that things can and must improve, that my patient will get back the use of his bones, and, as a consequence, will get back the use of the flesh and blood and skin that mask those bones from view. This type of condition has been observed only twice before, and in both cases the patient (it was the same man each time) got up, and when I snapped my fingers in his face, resumed the regular routines and active citizenship required by American life.

What if, the doctor continues, rubbing his chin, stepping closer, speaking almost too softly in this part of the speech to understand. What if I were to snap my fingers like that at you, eh? But I won't, not today or tomorrow, but only when I'm sure that when I do you will go to the living room to play the piano—is that what you play?—not through healing, but through what I call the power of the wanting-to-do, and also the power of the pay-attention-to. What about you? Are you capable of either of those?

Virge says nothing. He has a sudden urge to whistle, which in fact is his only musical ability, one he likes to show off, but checks it.

Great question, says Stuart, snapping his mouth shut, whipping off his glasses like he's about to change his clothes.

You need my help, Flanig continues, speaking directly to Virge. You must let go and breathe and relax. Unclench your bones. Liquefy them. Can you do this for me?

Is this the beginning of the treatment? Virge wants to ask, but when he does finally speak it is only to excuse himself, he has to go to the bathroom. Wheeling his legs out from under the sheet, he jumps to his feet, as if practiced at it, and dashes across the hall, leaving them behind in alarmed silence, giving him an edge, a type of mastery over them.

Help him with that, Stuart, he hears the doctor command. The boy can't use his hands!

But, thank goodness, he has already latched the bathroom door, using his shoulder. And the only thing he can hear at that point is Almy's pen, scratching endlessly at the paper.

All right, frowns Flanig, a day later, perhaps a little peeved now, though smiling broadly, showing off his perfect but presumably false teeth.

People don't know everything, he says, and one thing they don't know is this news I'm about to impart to you. People think ossa are dead, and they are dead when we are dead but when we are alive they have a tremendous spark to them. A flame! Look at me when I'm talking to you, Virgil. It's not just red blood cells. If I could, with a great conflagration perhaps, a great forest fire, if I could just sear the flesh off a man as he walked, do you know that his skeleton would keep on walking? Just a step or two, of course, before it collapsed. But it would outlive the rest of the body by a moment that, in biological terms, is nearly an eternity. Oh yes, this has been witnessed, this has been confirmed. Recall how men have a dread of walking, living skeletons. Do you? That's because such things have been seen, have been confirmed, in wars, in fires. And this has given rise to legends. So as for you, Virge? As to what's wrong with you? Behold!

And the doctor pulls a black flash lamp from his bag and turns it on and holds the bright glass disk up tight against the back of Virge's limp fingers.

You see the bones? You see the dark cores in every digit?

Almy's pen goes on scratching.

No, says Virge, and it's true that he can't. He's not looking hard enough, and when he does, he's duly impressed.

A poor man's x-ray machine, to be sure, smiles Flanig, with a degree of charm in his eye. But it shows me what I need to know, and that's that your bones are heavy, overly dense, troubled. Ideally, our human bones have the lightness and delicacy of bone china. Do you have a bone china teacup? Have you handled one? Is it a wonder of strength and precision? So it is with us, Virgil. That's how we can stand, how we can proceed. Bone china bones! that's what we're going to give back to you before we're done here. And you are in luck, because I have brought along the perfect injection for that.

Virge can only concentrate on the musical brittleness of the doctor's voice. None of it sounds right, but then he's not confident that he knows what has been said. Injection? But the doctor is sure of himself, and handsome enough, in a way.

Handsome for a mummy, he says out loud, but no one reacts.

Almy, scribbling away, has stopped speaking at all, and Stuart stands peering out the bedroom window, hands in his pockets, moving his fingers around in there, as if ruminating on something, or perhaps just idly fingering medals, or coins. Everyone is as paralyzed as Virge's arms.

I apologize, says Virge after a while. It's just that I don't care for injections. And besides, my arms are slowly, I think, coming back to life.

Quietly, under the sheets, to remind himself that what he says could be true, he manages to twitch one thumb.

What?

Also, that I quite like cars, and I wonder what kind of car you drive, what you arrived in.

Get up and take a look yourself, smirks Flanig, obviously in foul humor, maybe from the mummy remark. His mouth is full, already eating something red and juicy, though it's not clear what it is or where it came from.

Turning to watch Stuart, Virge sees the young man wiggle his hands in his pockets, and makes an effort to do likewise, to move more than one thumb, and maybe so. More movement than before in the tip of one index finger, though the arms remains as heavy and immobile as fallen branches. So move the arms tomorrow, he promises himself, if for no other reason than to reject, with great nobility, the forthcoming needle.

A list of things he can't do without working arms includes, but is not limited to, brushing his teeth, which are beginning to feel decayed, and wiping himself after defecation. So who will wipe him? No one he knows. No, that's unimaginable. Excruciating. So hold it in, and it's been several days, but truly he's quite constipated, so no great effort is involved, and in truth he should probably have an enema, but again, who to administer it? Unimaginable. But of course it would be Stuart, wouldn't it, in his easily stained white clothes, kneeling behind him on the bathroom floor with mysterious instruments made of rubber and steel.

One of them is a hired companion, but whose?

The hands must be made to come back to life.

Late in the day by now. Time for the daily army train, he muses, and indeed he feels well enough to take the long walk out to the tracks, as he in the habit of doing nearly every afternoon, and watch the train rush by, but he's stuck in bed now, because the harder he tries to get out of bed the more he winds himself up tight in the sheets, and at length he becomes so immobilized that he thinks with some sense of perverseness that if his mother were to come in right now, and if he were to close his eyes and let his mouth go slack, it would fool her, and she would scream, and think he's dead.

But when at length she does come in, he doesn't do that, just lets her unwrap the sheets from around his legs, and what's gotten into her, she's so bright and cheery about it that he's tempted to yell at her, and ridicule her twinkle, just as Mont used to do sometimes, when she got a little too gleeful for him. But what has she brought Virge but a cup of hot black late-in-the-day coffee, and when she holds it to his lips for him to sip, and it even burns his lower lip and tongue a little, he is overcome with a twinkle of his own, a glow of gratitude for small sensations, for the hands that replace his, hands that are better and more expert than any hands he ever had.

Time for the train, she says, as if reading his mind, tipping the cup a little further.

The train, he burbles. And he smiles at her like an infant, reveling in his own sense of deep dopiness.

I hope you aren't thinking of taking any walks yet.

No walks, not yet.

But of course he thinks precisely the opposite, that if he can drink the coffee quickly enough, though it's scalding hot, she might go away and he could sneak out, since it's been a habit since childhood to take a walk and time it to the arrival of the train. But no, just as he swallows the last of the coffee he is sure he can feel the slight rumble of the room, meaning that the train is passing at that moment, and once again he will have to wait.

But the next day is different. All the conditions align: Virge is all alone at the right time, he's not stuck in the sheets, he is able to slip his feet into his shoes, he can walk in them and keep them on without tying the laces, he finds the house deserted, and he can easily sneak out because there's not even a car in the driveway.

So a few minutes later there he is, back in the great outdoors, back at the feast of life, breathing in the heavy and salt-laden air, the fibers in his hands and arms getting quietly rewoven, maybe, by some vast and natural loom. And look at me, he shouts, mentally, having gone all the way to where he fell, and beyond, to where he stands in his armless posture, planted at his special and accustomed spot, waiting for the train, though it's true that in that exact same spot he did stumble and fall again, due to the untied laces. It wasn't such a bad fall, just a stumble to his knees from which he was able to get right up again.

But never mind, because the train is on its way, and here it comes, the locomotive audible before it arrives, roaring softly, invisible until it emerges out of a nearby tunnel formed by inward-angled pines. In this part of its route, for some reason, it's a slow train, and what speed it has tends to diminish even more as it crosses the small steel bridge over the creek, but then the machine accelerates as it draws itself forward across the field, seemingly aimed squarely at Virge, who stands posed, firm as a pillar, at a crucial curvature in the tracks. The slight puff of wind that precedes things lifts up his hair to stand straight up at the crown of his head, and at the last minute the engine, always shocking in its size, follows tracks that curve off and away, forever just missing him.

If it is permissible to dote on what is modern, he does dote on this army train. It isn't of great length, composed only of two diesel locomotives, one facing forward, the other backward, and a string of khaki painted cars, boxcars mostly, their sides clad in perforated steel panels, translucent enough to reveal packing crates, stacks of mortar shells, even men dressed in battle gear. The cars themselves are decrepit, shedding particles of paint and rust like upswept leaves. But they are like living beings in that they stutter, in that there's a slippage in their forward motion, a way the wheels have of not engaging the track and sliding straight for a split second. Identifying, pitying, Virge would like nothing more than for the train to stop stock still one day, give him just one moment to walk right up to its face to caress and address.

But the train, a diesel beast, disappears in the same way it appears, heading north into a second tunnel of trees, as if this patch of open land, the bottom of their property, is the only place on earth this train materializes, coming up from the earth for a moment into the air, then descending back again, like a worm that's briefly visible after a rain. Virge doesn't move, his hair settles down, and after two minutes it's over, everything has passed completely out of eyeshot, then out of earshot.

Back home, Almy is waiting for him, holding the screen door open a tad.

Sorry, I'm sorry, Mother, he giggles, brushing past.

When that train goes by, she says in a neutral tone, I know it's slow, but still it rattles the teeth in my head.

What about your teeth? he asks.

Oh, I've got a condition, she says, rubbing her cheeks, where the roots of my teeth are loose in the jaw. You know? Did you ever rattle the toothbrushes in the cup? It's like that with my teeth. Deep down, they're loose somewhere. Did you never have that? I should ask the doctor.

Staring at Almy, listening to her accidentally harmonize with the birds in the sky, he understands, since he has heard her make this same comment a dozen times, that the past will never be gone, that he'll be unable to move forward beyond conditions that were created hundreds of years before him. Or that there will be a loop in time in which he advances forward at least a little, only to be drawn back, and all this without remedy or redress.

The next day, again, when he wakes up, the house is empty, not even Almy can be found. Did she go with them? Is he completely abandoned now? Nothing to do about it if so.

In the afternoon he takes yet another stroll out to the tracks, without falling, where he watches with the same emotions as the train lumbers by yet again, more troops heading north, same old story. This time, though, one of the soldiers sees him, salutes him, or so Virge believes, it's hard to tell, but in response he wiggles his fingers at his sides, and finds that almost all of them can wiggle within some tiny arc of degree. I am thawing, he concludes. Slowly thawing, from bottom, maybe, to top.

But it's not enough. Back home, he has a problem, in that the screen door is hinged only to open out, to allow escape but not return. No one to hold it open for him. To exit the house was easy, just nudge the unlatched door with a shoulder, but to get back in requires taking hold of the little iron knob and pulling outward, and though he practices the motion in his mind's eye there's no way it can be done under the present circumstances.

Some obstacles seem greater than others, with no relation to their relative importance. This seems like one for Hercules, and Virge surrenders, at that moment, to eccentric science. If someone were to come along with a medicine to treat the bones, turn them into bone china, now would be a good time for that someone to come along.

Or, alternately, if someone, one's father for example, were to return right then, bringing with him a real doctor, middle-aged and bearded, a thoughtful specialist, specifically licensed to work on causes and cures, a doctor who will make a house call, certainly, but won't move in, in the style of a boarder, and won't then put strange twists in the whole situation by disappearing for hours at a time, then now would be the time. A good start.

But no Flanig, no Mont, no specialist, and Virge has to stand there waiting for someone to come and open the screen door for him. So what to do? Let the mind wander. He starts thinking at that moment, for some reason, of Highway Number One, as they call it, which runs near the house and further on steeply rises and follows certain sandy cliffs on its way north. Virge thinks he can imagine how it works. At some point he pictures a surprise turn, it's like winding a huge clock to drive that route, with curves that alternate by veering out first toward the ocean and then veering hard back into a canyon. Nor does it fail to run at one point, due east, into a cleft between two hills, a canyon within a canyon. Here, it might be imagined—even when there's the certainty that this mental postcard of the highway is a fabrication—that here is where the highway workers simply left off construction, years ago, and so it narrows to something more like a regular unpaved rural road and then, as it curves up into the canyons, becomes a dirt path meandering through patches of prickly cactus, and finally, in a narrow cleft full of oaks, trickles away, lost, finally, in a jumble of dry leaves. If the traveler has chosen Highway Number One only to reach that surprise dead end, then he has no choice but to turn and retrace his steps back home.

There's more to the history of the train. Dismiss it, but no, why not tell it. Unable to move, stuck at the screen door, Virge goes on to think of a story he would like to tell, one of several stories he would like to tell someday to somebody like Stuart.

What happened is that one morning, when he stood so close to those roaring army boxcars, someone on board must have tossed out the contents of a honey pail at that exact moment because Virge got splashed with human excrement—not like a bucketful of paint, just a few drops here and there that washed away entirely when he got back to the house. But he happened to have with him that day a book called First Across Greenland by Jansens, a favorite from his collection that he often carried on walks, and the nickel-sized stain on the cover wouldn't wash off, and he could never get out of his head either the association of feces and Jansens, so that subsequent re-readings put him in an unpleasant mood. Not that it became an obsession, as he is already keenly engrossed in any and all stories of polar expedition, and nothing can undo that, but this one book, this Greenland story, might well have to be thrown out one day, but one can't bring oneself to do it, and he wonders if he might not get some advice on this matter from his hired companion. Paying companion. But Stuart isn't there to tell this story to, and in the meantime Virge can't get in the house, can't do even the simplest thing like that, can't turn his brimming anger into the strength it would take. At this moment it's like he's wrapped in chains, like the strong man in the circus, but everyone laughs to see how tiny his muscles are as he strains to burst the links apart. So don't strain, don't make a fool. Might as well stand there and continue to make a list of what he can't do with his hands, such as eat and drink and be merry unassisted. Urinate without missing the toilet bowl, that's a good one. Turn a page in a book, a book that one keenly enjoys. Pick at the scabs on his elbow, and watch them bleed. Wind his pocket watch too far. Comb his hair till it falls out. Worth repeating: hold on to the phallus in order to aim a jet of urine directly into bowl. Bowl of toilet. Row a neighbor's boat out around the cove, though he never did this before. Rub hair oil into hair for miracle growth. Play the piano, though he never did this before. Open the letters that may start arriving soon from anywhere in the world, and in that pile there might be one from the missing Mont.

The door creeps open then, and it's Almy, tentative, as if not sure who he is, then holding it open for him all the way, and he can see from her mouth and her eyes that she's been crying. Maybe? Is one able to tell when people have been crying?

The doctor had to leave for a while, she smiles, and then, after a pause, jumps as if bitten by something.

The doctor wants to really get started on your case, she adds, brushing at her dress, blinking hard. And he's on his way back here at top speed. Now let me take a look at your arms.

And she picks them both up by the forearms, unabashed to reach out and touch him, perhaps because she believes he can't feel any touch, and then lifts both arms gently up in the air, keeping the elbows near his face, as if to make him see them, to remind him to try harder to be well.

Oh, just look at them, she sighs, and it's true that they are white as potatoes, and starting to develop little bumps, like spuds starting to grow their eyes.

Don't do that, he snarls, backing away, because suddenly his hands and his arms, all the way to the shoulders, have flooded with something in between pleasure and pain.

And isn't that a good sign? While there has been some minor finger wriggling, the arms still haven't budged. Are they telling him something, suggesting some information to him, some secret they would like to share? His mouth wide open, making noises like a squeaky screen door, he lets his mother guide him back to bed, and the moment she's gone, while he's just lying there on top of the sheets, the pleasure and pain stop as suddenly as they began, and he finds that now he's cured. That now in fact he can move his arms, his hands, his elbows, his wrists.

Completely cured, by way of miracle mother's touch.

Virge leaps out of bed, and waves his arms around like a chimpanzee. Jumps back into bed, puts his arms under the sheets, and decides to keep this development to himself.

That night, at the dinner table, somebody—is it Stuart? No, Stuart's not there yet, it's just Virge and Almy—happens to mention Mont. In any event, when the name is spoken aloud, Almy gives a start, blushes, then laughs.

Funny you should bring him up, she says. I was just now getting the feeling that your dad was about to walk in the room.

It occurs to Virge then, staring at her, noting how her eyes close, and flutter, that she's in mystery communication with her absentee husband, just tuning in at that moment to some kind of dreamy or psychic radio transmission from him. Virge, feeling a chill in his head, gets it too, can hear something—and it's like a sudden rush of words coming from far away, like a distant conversation. He's always been good at hearing over distances, but this is preposterous, he has to admit. Preposterous if it's really from his dad, or more so if these voices he thinks he hears are the voices of faraway angels or soldiers congratulating him on the recovery of his arms.

Is that you, Mont, asks Virge out loud, so that Almy gives him a troubled but affectionate look, and it's especially tempting to stand up and go over to her and comfort her, lifting his beautiful new arms to lay them reassuringly on her shoulders. But better to wait, better to find the perfect moment of surprise. Accordingly, he opens his mouth to allow her to spoon in more food.

—

Next morning Dr. Flanig can be heard slowly clicking shut the door of his room, closing it with the nonchalance of someone very much at home but also with the polite attention to quietness, it must be admitted, of a good guest. And when sententious Flanig, whom they haven't seen for days, enters Virge's room a moment later, it's clear that the doctor isn't maintaining the miracle of youthful old age that he appeared to be at first, and is indeed slightly bent and even slightly hunchbacked, walking as if it takes a bit of concentration to avoid falling forward, or backward. What youthful spark remains somehow concentrates itself above the nose now, in the white hair and the bright eye. Below that, notable in the lips now, there is an eggshell frailty, a mortality, and perhaps this gets more advanced, even one minute later, than when he first walked in the room.

Pressing his hands together as if in prayer, Flanig steps deeper into the room, closer to the foot of Virge's bed, then, dropping the prayer hands and sliding back out into the hall, he returns arm in arm with Stuart, dragging him in sideways like a burlesque partner.

This one is studying anatomy, states Flanig, with a note of pride. Filling my shoes, and knowing what's in my shoes in the first place.

Stuart only nods, curls his lip politely. Flanig reaches up to tousle his hair and manages to knock the young man's glasses askew, so that one lens is magnifying his forehead instead of his eye.

What about you, Virge? continues Flanig. What are you learning?

Don't ask him that, groans Stuart, restoring his spidery, frameless lenses.

I mean what kinds of books do you like to read? And he turns to Virge's little bookshelf over the desk and closely examines the titles.

You mean right now? asks Virge.

No, I mean, over the years. Which of these books is your favorite? I am already refining my diagnosis by studying these books of yours.

Well, I did read, over the years, as you say, a book called First Across Greenland.

I have never.

Never what?

Never been across Greenland.

Yes, but do you know, Doctor, continues Virge, flattered by the old man's interest, that when my dad first brought it home I thought it was a book about a green land, two words, and thought it meant California. That Jansens was the first man to cross the state of California. Isn't that funny?

At this point, seeing as it's a diagnosis, Virge wonders whether to mention the stain on the book, if that would be relevant to the diagnosis, but asks the doctor instead how he goes about making medical judgments on the basis of one's books.

Oh, my diagnosis is that you are already taking your first steps on the road to full recovery, says the doctor. The titles of these books alone tell me that. How do I make the connection? I am going to tell you. I see that many titles refer to the Arctic, to expeditions and explorations and the like, and that tells me that you, like these authors, are constituted with great strength and endurance. A tolerance for cold and pain. At the same time I'm afraid it will be necessary to discard all these books.

I beg your pardon?

I say we must throw out these titles. Stuart, will you see to that? Imagine how damaging! Here one sits, in a state of relative and minor paralysis, surrounded by books on ice and other matters related to the permanent deep freeze of the poles. It's like putting a polio patient in one of those horrible iron lungs, when what's needed is the opposite—a lung composed of feathers or mist or clouds.

I don't know, says Virge, trying to follow this line of reasoning.

Could this be the appropriate moment to reveal his state of health, his cure? No. Better to wait and watch, as in fact he is starting just now to revise certain opinions.

Next time I come, continues Flanig, I will bring with me the next book you're going to read. Let me take charge of your library, and you will see the results instantaneously.

Then, as if on cue, Flanig and Stuart turn on their heels and march out of the room, leaving Virge just lying there, and it isn't until he's aware that they've sat awhile in the kitchen, the three of them having coffee and Utah scones, which Virge can readily smell, and lie there wondering why he isn't invited, or offered anything, thinking they must be talking about him, that they come back into the room, followed by Almy, but before he can get used to them again, before he can remind himself who the three of them are and what they are there for, Flanig goes immediately into medical action, shifting quickly, and somehow ends up right in Virge's face, cupping his palms over Virge's eyes, and the two become both quite still.

What on earth, says Almy. Be careful with my boy.

What did you see before I covered your eyes? asks Flanig, ignoring her, pressing down harder.

Nothing.

Why not?

Because I didn't get a chance to look, you old coot, he wants to say but bites his tongue. The doctor's hands come off, and there is his face up close, an inch away, where Virge can finally make out thousands of tiny wrinkles around the man's eyes, and it's like waking up in a sarcophagus, face to face with the well preserved.

You mean, says the mummified fellow, that you didn't choose to take the chance to look.

Choose what?

Then you've learned a lesson haven't you, Flanig says, triumphant for some reason that Virge can't fathom.

Always be ready to take everything in first, the doctor adds. Before something goes wrong. Memorize everything instantly all the time.

He backs away but then leans in and places his hand over Virge's eyes again, but without as much pressure. Then takes them away.

What about that time? Pay attention?

I guess not, Doctor.

Well. I am-a not-a sure, grins Flanig, putting on a bad Italian accent, gesturing broadly with his hands. I am-a not-a sure I can help a patient such as-a this-a one.

He's actually kind of a funny sometimes, says Stuart, flatly. Flanig makes a low whistling sound and tilts back, and holds onto a fold of

Virge's blankets, as if stopping himself from falling off the bed. Almy moves, sits at the desk and caps her pen, having neglected to take any notes.

There there, says the doctor, friendly again, hovering over Virge at a more comfortable distance now.

Come closer, jokes Virge.

Relax, says Flanig, and don't try to remember anything else today.

But Virge is thinking mostly about Stuart, and thinking that, if he is studying how to be this kind of doctor, he ought to be taking notes too.

Take a deep breath and let my hands take over like this, Flanig instructs, picking up the patient's hands in his hands. Virge experiences a moment of panic. Won't a doctor instantly recognize the lack of paralysis? Flanig does not, or does not appear to. He palpates the bony outcrops of the wrists and the knuckles, hums a little tune. Virge feels like an injured bird, and these are his wings, filled with bones that are not white, but spotted and stained, like little bird eggs. He's faking everything pretty well, he decides. He's managing to keep the limbs as limp as dough.

Stuart, my book please, says Flanig, and his assistant reaches into the black bag and pulls out an onion-skin pamphlet.

It's Flanig's Anatomy, the doctor smiles, waving it gently, letting it flop in his hand like a leaf.

Whose anatomy?

I'm going to have Stuart read this to you, after he throws out your unhealthy books. This will replace them. Stuart, start with the hands, and of course I've marked those pages for you. But then go on to read the whole thing. It will seem tedious and dry to you at first, but it begins to get most interesting after a while—it almost turns into a good novel, or a good adventure story, like your Green Land. And it's written by yours truly, and in it I tell you how the bones of the hand are remarkable in variety and number, and how it would be a great aid to the mind to memorize them all, like the scaphoid and the sesamoid. Have you heard of the sesamoid, Virge? Isn't that a marvelous name for a bone? Like sesame. It always makes me think of Ali Baba and his many thieves.

Virge keeps nodding, and nodding too much, keeping part of his attention on Stuart, who maintains his quiet distance, smiling perhaps, his hands again wiggling slightly in the pockets of his white trousers.

The doctor puts down the book and leans close in again, balancing for a second by grabbing the newel posts of the bed.

Let me try something, he says, again taking up one of Virge's hands, the left one, and he lifts it up, flopping, like a fish pulled out of a bucket.

Are you an observer, Virge? he asks, speaking at top speed. You led me to believe a moment ago that you're not so terribly observant, but look around the room now, yes, like that. And now look at your hand.

The doctor palpates the hand, hard this time, as if wanting to crack a few bones, and Virge has to stifle the urge to cry out, literally bites his tongue, while the doctor goes on to lecture on the metacarpals, those parts of the fingers that are never seen, he explains, because the adductor pollicis covers them like a pad of flesh tough enough to walk on, it's what allows acrobats to walk on their hands. Now get me the needle, Stuart, Flanig continues, turning to his assistant, who goes from languid inattention into action, and whisks out of the black bag a hypodermic already filled with a translucent and particle-flecked yellow fluid.

Oh, well done, laughs the doctor, and without waiting for a protest from the patient—who must use all his will power to keep from snatching the hand away—deftly flicks the long sharp needle point into the thickest vein of all, so that Virge cries out, not from pain so much as from surprise to see the colored medicine disappear so quickly under his skin as the plunger goes down without resistance.

Aha, says Flanig, as if having made a signal medical discovery. A complainer. An aristocrat. A grown-up Lord Fauntleroy, eh?

No.

No? he continues, mincing his words. Oh, but I think that's exactly what you are. But let's give his lordship's poor hand a rest.

And the doctor repositions the patient's fingers where they were, then pulls the sheet over the whole hand, as if he has just murdered it.

And dutifully, knowing somehow that it's required, or unavoidable, even though the fluid could be toxic and fatal, Virge slowly turns his head toward the other hand as if in invitation, and says nothing as the doctor lifts that one too, and makes a second and identically awful injection.

Remember the bone china medicine, Virge? It's working, even as we speak. It's a quieting solution as well. You'll sleep now, the doctor concludes, and immediately there is a feeling so blissful through his whole body that Virge is pretty sure he's going to die the blissful death he's always imagined he'd die someday, and as he sinks down into the soil-like sheets, into darkness, he can only watch the expressions of neutral farewell on all their watching, waiting faces.

But he wakes up. Who knows how long he slept. Is he fine? Yes, he's fine, there are then fingers, and they can be wiggled. There are two arms, and they can be moved. Are his arctic books still on the shelf? Yes. Virge lies motionless, remembering that he still hasn't had a bowel movement, but now at least there's the satisfaction of knowing that when the time comes, he'll be fine, he'll be hygienic. He remembers with satisfaction that he's in his room, the room in the world that he owns, that he has the deed to. The light has changed, and it must be evening now, with the shadows high on the walls. But what day is it? It's been harder, since Mont's departure, to keep track of things, because it was Mont who would do that, announce the days of the week and dates of the month as they passed, crossing each one off the calendar every evening as soon as Almy finished the dishes, making a little ceremony out of it, concluding the day with the stroke of Almy's fountain pen, and handing it back to her to screw back into its cap.

And Almy is there in the room with him, he realizes. There she is where he can watch her awhile, still sitting at his desk, filling out some form that glows white hot under the light of the lamp, not aware of the fact that he's woken up. She's perched on the edge of the swivel chair and rotating a little back and forth on its ball bearings, a slight and faintly gaunt woman in a thin print dress and apron, sinews showing in her neck, sharp collarbones that are presumably china-like, china-healthy, and unstained. Are his books still on the shelf? Haven't moved. And in turning this fact over in his mind, he can only conclude that something is wrong with everything, a major flaw in the system, such that there is nothing anymore to be afraid of. To be compared to.

———

I'm going to tell you something you don't know about your mother, announces Flanig next morning, when he's positioned in his regular spot at the foot of the bed and it's just the two of them in Virge's room. Virge, waking up to these words, sits up, alarm showing on his face, craning his neck to see if Almy has come back, because of course he would rather have the story from her own lips, but there's no sign of her, and the hallway looks deserted too.

What about my hands? asks Virge.

What about them?

Not quite cured, says Virge, hoping to embarrass.

Virge, Flanig continues, unperturbed. Did you know your mother and I met many years ago?

I didn't.

You may not know that we lived at one time in the same neighborhood, says the doctor, gesturing in a funny way, moving his thumb in pantomime as if practicing to give Virge another injection.

I hardly knew her, he continues. She was just a girl.

Go on. I guess, go on.

My point is, one day, years later, when I went back to visit the neighborhood, I saw her again, and realized that your mother had reached a level of beauty that is beyond age and aging, and had become a young woman worthy of appointment to her majesty the queen, if there were one. When your father married her, I was a step too late, or I might have been the luckiest man alive, instead of the second luckiest. What do you think?

Virge doesn't know what to think, except that it's a world containing elements provoking disgust.

Fueling a sense of sickness is the fact that doctor is looking more collapsed and mealy today than ever, his teeth a little moth-eaten, and who would wish to insult him?

Just think, Virge, it is I who could have been your father, instead of—instead of Mont. Is that his name? What a fine father he has been to his son.

It doesn't matter, says Virge, who one's father is.

Yes, good point. You suggest then that you'd still be the same Virgil if I, for example, were your father.

Unable to speak, unable to think any further in this direction, Virge closes his eyes and studiously puts on a show of deep relaxation, followed by sleep. It works. He hears the doctor tiptoe out, and gently close the door.

Later that day there's another opportunity to wander. The house is deserted again, and he gets the chance to try out every wonderful usage of the hands he had been missing for those several days. First and foremost, he urinates without missing the old toilet bowl. Nicely done, Virge. Defecates, then wipes, all to the applause of an imagined sanitation reformer. Returning to his room, he picks out one of his polar books and, without bothering to read, expertly turns, in succession, all the pages. And it's as good as if he'd read it again. The scabs on his elbow come to mind, and he rolls up his sleeve, only to find they have already healed. What time is it? Never mind for now he can wind his watch. Or twiddle his thumbs with greater and greater speed and precision, until his thumbs become a blur, and then altogether disappear. He does not and presumably never will row a neighbor's boat out around the cove. Rubs macassar oil into his hair. Doesn't open letters that have piled up for him in the mail, because there are none.

As he's wondering whether to try the old trick of chewing off fingernails to build things out of them, he hears the rumble of an engine, and steps to the window in time to see Flanig and Stuart and Almy pull up to the house in the doctor's car, and it is only now that he discovers that what the doctor drives is a splendid-looking Bellevue, just the sort of car that Mont and Almy spoke of buying one day, but the coincidence doesn't seem to bother his mother, who at this moment is tumbling out of the back seat, unknotting the scarf on her head, and laughing at the idea, it must be supposed, of being the kind of person who takes rides in open cars, wearing a scarf, laughing. They've been out buying supplies, it appears, and Virge walks into the kitchen, where he finds Stuart coming in the back door, stumbling under the weight of a great wooden crate that he staggers to set on the table.

Look, Virge, oh look, says Almy, coming in and clapping her hands. See what we brought. See what the doctor purchased for us, and you must say thank you of course, unless you want to bow down to the man, which would be awfully grand of you.

Oh, Mother.

Let's go shopping again right now! she exclaims when Flanig comes through the door, and she rushes to kiss him on the cheek, though her exuberance is too much for the old man, and as he pushes her off of him his mouth can be seen trembling a little, and his tiny ears strike Virge as being carved from ivory, and yellowing.

What do you say to all this food, Virge? Almy laughs, shrugging off the doctor's recoil, pulling treasures out of the crate: bottles of milk, tiny chargers of cream, a dozen red apples in a cellulose bag, radishes that look like apples because they are just as large, long European loaves of bread, a whole unplucked chicken with its head still on, carrots with their green floppy tops still on, a brown greasy bag that turns out to hold shortbread cookies, and a chocolate bar which she unwraps and offers him on the spot, holding it near his mouth, and he almost forgets his ongoing ruse, almost reaches out for it that instant with both hands.

A shame, he says, not knowing what the shame is.

Head hurting, heart pounding, halfway to the screen door, Virge remembers to drop his hand and open it with his shoulder. Everything is complicated. He's feigning paralysis, but what if the three others are feigning something just as terrible? Better to keep the mouth shut, and better to say thank you than to say to hell with you. There must be a way to move forward, some way to reach some figurative fingers or hooks down into one's depths and snag out the right person, but this technique has yet to be invented. What's worse, when he does slip back into the kitchen, and his eyes adjust to the light, he finds the three of them sitting around the table, crowded side by side on a breakfast nook bench, sharing the chocolate bar, taking turns, no one indulging in more than a single nibble before passing it on to the next. To Virge they all look more or less the same as before, and that's no help to him at all. If only they would change, and he could change with them. If only he could have less vertical depth to explore, and more breadth, more choice. Several alternative fellows to choose from. He looks again, though, and see that he was wrong. Stuart has changed, in that he's no longer blond but brunette.

The two young men, Virge and Stuart, could become friends in time, but it's too soon for that now. If Virge had a way of knowing Stuart's background, there could develop a greater interest in knowing more. He can't know, for instance, what awful conditions Stuart might have found himself in only a few years before, how he must have been at the mercy of things, before achieving his current tennis-court gleam. So far there is only a temptation to stare, at the gleam, then turn away, then, more coldly this time, more openly, stare again.

Give me the wig, says Virge bluntly, holding out his hand, then remembering his deception to let his arm go limp before they notice.

Why? asks Stuart, petulant, drawing his face back into the shadows of the breakfast nook corner.

It's my father's, and if anyone should wear it, it shouldn't be you. Not you exactly.

And with a shrug Stuart slips it off, or rather jerks his head forward so that it flips off his head onto the table, and then pushes it across toward Virge.

I'll just leave it there, says Stuart.

All right, I'll get it later. Or maybe my mother wants to wear it.

No thanks, shrugs Almy.

You've a right to wear it, Mother, stresses Virge.

No, I shall gaily place it on your head, she announces, and wiggling her way out from between the two men, comes up close to Virge and slaps the wig down on him hard and haphazardly.

Feels funny, mutters Virge, admiring and envying his mother in this new mode of hers, this madcap style, and finally relaxes, at last letting his body occupy its exact space, without endless adjustment.

Looks funny! she retorts, whistling, letting her hands for once rest on his shoulders.

I think, says Virge, that there were two of these things around a few days ago.

Your father took the other wig with him.

But why would he do that, Mother?

No answer. The Mystery of the Missing Wig. But why? Why would Mont need to disguise himself in town?

Almy goes on to tell the funny story of the wigs, how she and Mont purchased them years ago, when they were first married, and living down in Santa Julia, and had signed up to march in the Old Spanish Days parade, and were asked to get all dressed up as Indians or Apaches or something for reasons of historical commemoration. How they didn't have a chance to make real Indian costumes, and just wore their everyday clothes, but how the identical wigs, each with a part in the middle and long black braids on either side, made them look like a couple of savages, and how they were thrilled to not only get applause from the crowds along the route but to also get gently pelted, as was the custom, with eggs that had been hollowed out and filled with glitter, confetti, and an occasional penny ring or other gewgaw.

I don't know, concludes Almy. If your dad is wearing his right now, while you're wearing mine, the two of you are twins.

Two peas in a pod, agrees Virge sullenly, and in his turn flips the wig off his head onto the table again, where it lies twisted and flat, like an animal run over up on the highway.

I think, says Stuart, that your dad took it so he could disguise himself, and not be recognized by anyone in town who might have something against him.

So saying he takes up the wig and places it, this time, on Flanig's head, where its straight-cut bangs emphasize the old man's pharaonic qualities, but what is especially curious to Virge is that Flanig shows no reaction, just keeps licking the last of a chocolate bar off his fingertips, concentrating on this routine with a delicate yet slack-jawed sweetness.

There may be something wrong with the old man.

Next day there's no changes with the hands. They're both still spry and fluttering, as good for touching one's private parts as for eating a chocolate bar, but Virge lies on his mattress and maintains the fiction, and limply tolerates, the next day, another hypodermic injection in both appendages, despite starting to think that this sacrifice might be too ridiculous, and too terribly painful now that Stuart's in charge of the needle and fumbles badly with it, hemming and hawing in deciding which vein to penetrate and where, then leaving behind ragged punctures that leak a lovely green fluid, a mixture of yellow medicine and red blood.

Exit Stuart and enter Flanig then, with faintly shining hands pushing his hair behind his ears, planting himself on Virge's bed, returning to his acid style for a moment at least, smirking, his eyes up close to Virge's, but instead of speaking directly to his patient he tilts his head away, birdlike, toward Almy, who has followed him into the room and is leaning in the doorway, her arms folded behind her back.

Can you stand some bad news? he asks, smiling then scowling, inserting a finger between his collar and his neck, as if to let out some inner steam.

No, she says, steadying herself against the door frame, ready for whatever earthquake comes along. Well, I guess I am.

Then Flanig speaks forcefully, inflating his chest, recovered from any of the previous day's vagueness, filling his lungs to the point of stressing the buttons of his vest against their buttonholes.

All people get stronger all the time, he explains, with a sudden exhale. And, at the same time, all people get weaker all the time. The two tendencies tend to cancel each other out, and we end up, structurally, where we were. That's the beauty of it. We stay the same, automatically, anatomically. Science has spoken, and Science, when it speaks to the people, never lies.

Almy has no answer to that, just stays frozen at the sound of his voice, so he goes on.

I've been meaning to tell you for some time now, he continues, academically, that this young fellow has a secondary problem that I'm seeing now in the cranial area. Skull bones, you see.

And he removes a pen from an inner pocket and taps Virge on the forehead with it.

Did you know, he continues, that the skull has more bones when you're born than when you die? It then sheds the superfluities, like milk teeth, but doesn't always get rid of all the extras, leading to problems. Common enough, but temporary, though potentially fatal.

Oh God, groans Almy, embracing the door frame.

But hardly ever! Thank goodness for that, and for Virge's hardiness, and for maternal prayers and kindly hearts. What I recommend is a regimen of sturdy outdoor activities. With Stuart Sturdy's help of course. Oh Virge, what a grand time for the two of you!

But Virge can't help but react badly to the news regarding his cranium, because by now he has read all of Flanig's Anatomy, including the entries relating to extra cranial bones, so he thinks he knows exactly what the doctor is talking about.

So why, falters Virge, in a strangled voice, narrowing his eyes, but he stops there, and no one even notices him speaking.

And I've been wanting to tell you, says the doctor, since I arrived, that Virge is already gaining tremendous strength from our injections.

He glares back sharply at Virge.

Isn't that right, son? Quickly! Tell your mother the truth!

I don't know. Oh yes, great strength.

The doctor brings his face down close to Virge's, like a witch doctor in a crazy mask, but Virge won't allow himself to look too closely. What he does see, fluttering his lashes, is where Flanig's neck has a red ring of soreness where it rubs against the hard collar.

Tremendous strength, Virge repeats, robotically, and here Flanig abruptly stands up and spreads his fingers out horizontally in some kind of secular, scientific blessing.

Then he and Almy, arm in arm, withdraw, and, after an hour, which

Virge spends lost in bottomless thought, in chaos, Stuart comes in, cheeks flushed, something shifty and dark in the way he blinks.

I just passed them, he whispers, in the hallway.

Who?

Who do you think?

Oh.

I don't know you very well yet, says Stuart, keeping his voice low. But isn't it becoming kind of clear to you what's going on around here? Why I was waving warnings at you the other day?

What do you mean?

The doctor first wants to make you a little worse. Then he wants to make you better. Why would he do that? He's trying to impress your mother. That's it in a nutshell. Sorry, buster. But it's all about winning somebody's affections. Sweet Adeline, as the song goes.

You're talking about my mother?

Sure, but all the names with that sound *line* in them are so romantic. It's just something I've been thinking about lately. Don't you wish your mother were an Adeline? Or Angeline? Or Almaline?

But why, Virge asks impatiently, would the doctor want to impress her? She already likes him, I think.

You're not seeing the future, answers Stuart, pushing his glasses closer to his eyes, as if to see the future better himself, and frowning at it. You're not seeing the fact that the old and withered can get naked and shiny sometimes.

A farm thought comes in a farm season. Agriculture is sexual, but also inspires thoughts relating to the spiritual side. If beet plants have dark red flowers, and carrots have orange flowers, does that mean that the human soul is flesh-colored? If flowers wilt, does the soul wilt too?

Oh yes, concludes Virge, and his heart sinks. He gives up on life, momentarily. There's no one around, and the hands go automatically to where Flanig tapped him, hard, with the pen. Brain damage? Skull damage? Other questions come in their turn. If you're poisoned as a child, can you ever meet a big city girl, ever have a girlfriend of any stripe? Should looking into the future be more like watching for forest fires, or more like gazing into a well?

Nothing is simple. According to Flanig's Anatomy, some types of illness are transient, others eternal. Sadly, there are plagues caused by degenerate races, poxes brought on by carelessly cooked meals, agues attributable to one's mother experiencing a shock during copulation. No word on potential nakedness and shininess.

Virge lies alone in the house, thumbing the onion-skin pamphlet, lost in thought. No injections forthcoming, and it's a fact that the punctures in the backs of his hands have healed. The house is quiet as a far away barn. There's a smell and a warmth of wheat chaff in the air, soothing to the soul, and he hasn't any inclination to get out of bed and snoop around. So he spends the day on vacation, probably a waste of the life force. He's in a state of vigor mortis, he tells himself, only venturing to the kitchen once to snack on torn chunks of bread, some radishes and apples sprinkled with salt, a chocolate cookie. In short, everything that is more delicious when eaten out of the hand.

Finally, late that night, he hears the three other residents of the house come in, banging doors. Somebody falls to the floor, and, instead of weeping and gnashing of teeth, there is general laughter. Are they mocking him? He thinks maybe they are. Doors slam. Silence settles over all. Virge brings one wrist to his forehead to check for sweat, then fingers the eyes to check for tears, then slips one hand under the sheet to check for sexuality.

Next day, Stuart, golden and pale, his white breeches beginning to display the multi-colored dirt of the farm, steps into Virge's room bearing a tray of glass containers, rattling everything in a palsied and rackety way as he sets it down on the desk.

Just nerves, Stuart explains, sneering. I'm not used to waiting on people. I didn't think I was signing up to be a butler.

But to Virge, all the clinking and tinkling is calming, like the sound made by a box of Christmas ornaments. Meanwhile, Stuart begins to mix, and now there are new sounds: the gurgling of liquids as they pass back and forth from glass to glass, the slight fizz made by the chemical reactions, the release of gases. The effect is soporific, and without hearing a few soothing questions that Stuart the chemist puts to him during those moments of preparation, he drifts toward light sleep.

What wakes him up a moment later is the foul taste of something, whiskey and copper, like something you'd drink out of some old bottle found at the back of an abandoned barn, and Virge jerks away, recoiling from the glass that Stuart is trying to get to his lips again.

No thank you, he mutters, in tears almost.

Doctor's orders! barks Stuart.

I would prefer not to try it. Thank you very much for your concern.

Then I guess I'll just have to make it obligatory, growls Stuart with a sudden determination, and he feints and jabs, spilling more than a few drops on the sheets, leaving excrement-colored stains.

You have the nerve, yelps Virge, dodging, amazed at Stuart's new bossiness, but also impressed with himself, how he resists the impulse to throw up his hands to push away the medicine.

Well, it's not fair, stammers Stuart, retreating. It's my job you know.

No it's not. You're the one paying me. It's my job.

Well, I guess.

And you're the one who said Flanig was trying to poison me. To make me more sick.

That was before. The first phase. Now he's trying to make you better. Remember what I told you? This stuff is good for you. You've got to take it to get over the effects of the injections.

There were no effects.

Really? Your arms still don't feel a thing?

Really, I'm fine.

They stare at each other and manage, in the awkward silence, to maybe come to an understanding without speaking a word: that Virge need not heal, so Stuart need not nurse.

Do you want to hear a good joke? asks Stuart, his eyes softer now.

He looks sour but energized, like someone who's just been poked in the face to wake up.

I like jokes all right, says Virge.

Okay. How many girls does it take to give a guy paralysis?

I don't know. How many?

Two, but they both have to be named Alice. A pair o' Alices. Get it?

Yes. Yes I do get it, says Virge, without laughing. Now I've got one for you. Just a minute. Let me think. Okay. How many girls does it take to give a guy a sharp sting of pain?

How many?

One. But she has to be named Bea. Get it?

Where did you hear that?

I made it up just now.

You made that up? That's pretty good.

Here's another one, says Virge. I've got one more. How many girls does it take to hold a seance?

How many?

Two. A pair o' Normas.

I don't get it.

Pair o' Normas. Paranormal. A seance is paranormal. Get it?

Well that one's a stretch.

Let me think of another one then.

No, that will do, snaps Stuart, and he takes hold of the chair facing Virge's study desk, twirls it around 180 degrees, and straddles it backwards, so that he can cross his arms across the top. It's the first time they've had much to say to one another.

You don't have any medical training, do you? asks Virge.

That depends, shrugs Stuart, twiddling his thumbs expertly, maintaining an insouciance in all matters of importance.

Did you at least read all of Flanig's Anatomy?

Brother, I never read a word of it.

The coppery odor of the medicine lingers in Virge's nose and plays with his senses like a complex soda pop, shifting from bitter to sour to bitter, almonds and lemons, and he only grows more awake all the time, so much so that finally he fixes his eyes on his companion, who has whipped a kind of book or pamphlet out of a pocket and is reading, and asks him, shyly, to help him raise himself in the bed an inch or two. So Stuart gets on the bed and puts his hands in Virge's armpits and lifts, and Virge cracks up, silently, from the tickling.

Am I right in thinking, asks Virge, that reading something, reading anything, is a part of your companionable duties?

Sure. I guess you could say it is.

But only if you read your book out loud to me?

Stuart squints, more relaxed now. He turns the chair around to the proper side, puts his feet up on the edge of the bed and knots his fingers behind his neck for support.

It's a John Spark book. Now that you know, do you still want me to read it out loud to you?

Who?

To you.

No, I mean, John Spark. Who is he?

John Spark. Come off it. The famous John Spark or John Sparkle as he's sometimes known. He's a pretty great guy, and, truth be told, I was led to believe that he lives around here somewhere.

Around where?

You're good at pretending not to know much, aren't you? Sometimes I get the feeling that you're pretending about something else too. That both your hands are fine, but you're fishing for some sympathy.

There's no answer for that. Virge, struck dumb by the question, cautiously checks for any possibility of movement down there at the end of the limb to see if perhaps he can re-paralyze himself and make a liar out of Stuart. But no. Although he makes no motion at all, he can tell that things are just fine down there, and he starts to wonder if he could unparalyze other bones, say his skull, which, if it were pliable, could stretch to accommodate a greater brain size and therefore greater mental powers.

Not fishing for sympathy, he replies at last. Let's put up a sign in the room that reads No Fishing.

Outside the bedroom window, behind Stuart's head, he catches occasional glimpses of Flanig and Almy strolling out of doors, conversing, going in circles around the round, brick-bordered bed of tulips, flowers that come up blue and purple and yellow there every March. Flanig is going on about something, and sometimes he extends a hand to the horizon as if predicting the fate of the whole world, then uses both hands to push back the stringy curtains of hair behind his ears, then gestures toward the house as if to say something about his patient. Still, all the while his lips seem to blubber rather than articulate, and isn't there something empty about him? Something like the darkness you'd see at the bottom of a well?

Almy, purple circles under her eyes, purple the color of the tulips, nods and listens, listens and nods. Says nothing. Does nothing but attend and stroll, wring her hands at times, laugh at other times, glance toward the bedroom window, but it's presumably too dark in the room for her to see Stuart and Virge.

Here's a way I'll help you advance in your medical knowledge, says Virge, keeping one eye on the two external figures and one eye on the internal.

How?

You'll study my condition. First try throwing something at my face to see if I can't stop my reflexes—you know—the hand jerking up involuntarily to protect the head.

Yes, smiles Stuart. But now you've ruined the scheme.

What do you mean?

Better to let me think of that plan, invent it for myself. The rock or whatever it is would have to come at you unexpected, wouldn't it?

Virge can't answer.

I'll try it later, says Stuart, after I'm sure you've forgotten we ever talked about it.

Talked about what? asks Virge, blinking.

Okay. Very funny.

You know, I invented something a few days ago.

And Virge goes on to explain his idea about nails on hooks in the hallway walls and how, as you walk towards your bedroom, these hooks, strategically placed, help undress you if you walk deliberately, the hooks slipping into loops or seams in your clothes, and whether or not you had any life in your arms and hands or elsewhere you could manage to undress by simply inching forward each night and letting the hooks do their job.

Sounds like it ought to work like gangbusters, says Stuart, looking bored, but suddenly his right arm darts forward to toss a ball of wadded paper. It's a trick, an ad hoc reflexes test. Well aimed, it hits Virge under the eye, but Virge has already trained himself, and nothing is proved.

Seeing less of Flanig and more of Stuart works out well. No medicine gets taken, and this is their secret, their boyish bond. Days pass. No word from Mont. The name goes unpronounced. It's tiresome to get out of bed regularly, and Virge feels lazy, suspended, mattressed, the house still an iron lung. Well, more of a wooden lung.

Every day Stuart goes through the process of bringing in the rattling, glittering tray, going through all the motions of preparing the prescriptions, dumping spoonfuls of powder or drops of tincture into milk or water, which he then, at Virge's gesture, dumps out the opened window into the dirt.

Well, says Stuart, one morning. Today it's just you and me.

Same as always.

You're not afraid of Flanig?

No, answers Virge. Just wondering what's wrong with him sometimes.

There's nothing wrong with him. Don't say that.

Isn't there something? Something about his brain getting old too?

Don't say that. Forget it. In the meantime, your outdoor exercise program starts today. Get ready for it. Sunlight is healthier than limelight, and the latter's all you seem to get around here.

I beg your pardon.

You're the center of attention, that's all I'm saying, and it's natural, it's because you're sickly.

Uh huh.

Oh I say, says Stuart, affecting a British accent, that must be bloody nice for you.

I invented something once, says Virge.

Oh really? I think I heard about this.

Virge hesitates, but then goes on to describe, again, his disrobing idea, the installation of special hooks in the walls of the hallway that gently remove your clothing as you proceed toward your bedroom each night.

Now who's having brain problems? You told me that one before.

I'm sorry, says Virge.

Ever been to the talking pictures? asks Stuart.

In a way.

We should go sometime. I didn't tell you that I have some connections to the movie industry.

Virge is interested for a moment, if only in the idea of a film documenting all the great inventions, including Edison's, as well as his own.

Stuart takes Virge's right hand, then briskly rolls the pajama sleeve up to the elbow, like rolling away a bandage, and only then starts in on a finger massage, a vigorous tugging at the fingers, popping knuckles all the way across.

Let him do what he wants, thinks Virge. Nothing to me. Let him cure it, let him rip the hand off.

Any feeling at all, I wonder? Stuart inquires after a while, grabbing a bottle of what looks like lotion and Virge's first panicky thought is that it's another of Flanig's concoctions, and he draws away his hand—only realizing then that Stuart was working toward that provocation this whole time, and it worked, he tricked Virge better than Virge could trick him.

It started moving today but I can't much feel it, says Virge morbidly, handing the hand back to Stuart, letting him apply the lotion, which smells of rosewater and mints, and it's instantly clear how his skin soaks it up like a sponge.

Oh, well, that's great either way, shrugs Stuart, keeping a cool composure. Just to let you know what I know, I did notice the food missing yesterday from the pantry.

After a moment, Stuart speaks out again. You're not so bad off, so I'm not sure what I'm doing here.

You mean now or in general?

In general.

You're the doctor's assistant.

Well, it's more like I'm his amanuensis.

What's that? Teach me the new word.

I'm ready to quit the job, whatever you call it. I don't know.

I own this room, you know, says Virge. But without a thorough education what's the point? My vocabulary is full of yawning gaps. You could help me with that.

Stuart lights up at this news.

I can teach you some cinematic terms, he says. Do you know what the dailies are? The dailies are the key to everything.

Oh. Well, I already know that word. Try another one.

I'll tell you a story instead. Do you like funny stories? From the movies? It's about a robbery, and the robber has a gun and he's robbing a guy. Well, let's say he's robbing a farmer, like your father. So this farmer, a remarkably short fellow, hands the man a giant sack of money, the year's profits. But, when the robber gets to his hideout, and opens the sack, instead of money inside it's the little farmer, and he's got a gun now. I don't know which picture that was, but isn't that great? Isn't that priceless?

Okay, says Virge, squinting to think. I see how it was a good trick up to a point, but here's where it falls apart, where you have the problem of the farmer being able to find his way home. If he was in the sack, that's like being blindfolded.

Oh, pshaw, laughs Stuart. You really are an old man for your age.

How? You mean like a sage?

I don't know. Yes.

So Virge finally gets around to telling his own story, wondering if it could also be a moving picture someday. He starts around the age of nine, when his great grandma and grandpa died and so he and his parents moved from San Grande to live at the farm. At first it was a paradise for Virge, compared to the stifling city, with its bad smells and constant grinding noises, though the farm house itself was filthy at first, and they had to clean and clean. The way he remembers it is that one day Mont and Almy, tired of cleaning, told Virge they had something they had to do and while they apologized for the procedure still they padlocked Virge in the rubber hut while they went off somewhere else. And that was fine, there was no problem with that, he sat in the darkness as intended, detained but not really understanding what was wrong or right with being detained. He assumed it was a game, maybe Horse Come Into the House Now, and he had a head for games, or so he thought, and thus he sat as still as possible until such time as they returned. Their terrible mistake was to take him there a second time, days later, and this time he hated the game and became hungry and bored and resentful and as a consequence got elbow deep into the old cans of rose dust, and ate a modest quantity of it while his folks were gone, and by the time they rushed back, hearing his weeping and wailing from a distance, his face and hands and tongue were dusted and lemony with the stuff, like a bee with pollen around the mouth, but this was no pollen, it was a deadly poison, and of course the contents of the stomach had to be extracted in a hospital. But they didn't get all of it out because since then he's been a little on the sickly side, missing a year of school, for example, contracting more childhood diseases than others, and in addition there was a kind of lapse some years ago where his legs went to sleep, and it was a steady shower of mild pain, of pins and needles, days on end. All this to the degree that he was provided a chair, a wheelchair, the one that remains with him in a corner of the room, and it was only after the doctor said the legs might have to be made redundant, that is, amputated, that the blood started pumping robustly, as if the legs had heard what the doctor said, and he never needed the wheelchair again. Still, now he can't help but wonder if the dust might not be there still in some corner of his veins and cells, somewhere central, still an enemy of his whole system, dampening his inner fire, preventing him from fully participating in the feast of life, and wasn't there also the chance that the dust had stunted or at least misshaped his acumen, because after all he had spent a year out of school, fourth grade, just as he was making an impression, tall for his age, dressed in a nice school suit, reading a number of books about arctic exploration and now he could hardly remember anything of what he had read, as if the dust had weakened his comprehension, and also yes, to answer the question, his physiognomy does seem to be similar to that of older and more decrepit men.

Stuart seems to take all this in carefully. Makes no jokes. Appears to keep an open mind, taking his spectacles on and off, polishes the lenses with a special cloth. Jots down a word or two in a notebook.

Tell me again what you did that year—the year you didn't have to go to school?

What about your diagnosis?

This is my diagnosis. Just tell me what you did.

I did tell. I read books, and then I forgot what I read in them.

What is the one thing you do remember? What's one story you can tell me from your reading?

Virge truly can't recall at first, but one thing does come swimming oddly back to him, and he goes ahead and relates to Stuart this random incident, the story of how two of Jansens' men, out on expedition, got so cold and were laid so low by frostbite that they lost every ounce of strength. The reader first has to try to understand that degree of cold, a degree that is unknown in the life of the armchair traveler. A cold that first wounds you, like the stroke of an axe, then wraps you in a soothing but deadly numbness. In the end, only a slight distance from camp, even knowing where they were, they gave up trying, because while they had been crawling forward on all fours, even that pathetic means of locomotion was now beyond their abilities. What they eventually realized, with a flash of hope, was that they had given up right at the crest of the hill overlooking the camp, and that, with one more little effort, they could roll the rest of the way, like barrels. That's what they did, but by the time they came to rest against the outside of the tent, they were icicles, they were men who had rolled insensate through snow, like crullers through sugar, and they were dead.

Okay, replies Stuart. Good story. Very helpful. Now, here's my diagnosis. I have no way of determining what's wrong with you, or why.

—

Almy comes in one day with her hair cut completely away in a straight line behind her head, like she'd used a saw back there, so that now it's just a flat clump of hair, nothing hanging down, but he can't come to a point where he will know what to say to her directly about this new ugliness, or, for that matter, about Flanig, about the tulip patch, everything else. She waltzes in not just with new look, but with a new flair, holding before her the tray with the teacup of coffee and a single hot-cross bun made fresh, and whistling, which is odd, because she has never whistled before, and always complained when others did.

Sipping at his coffee through a glass straw that Almy has pilfered from the doctor's bag, watching her watch him, he gets the idea to ask her to take a walk with him. He's certain she'll wrinkle her nose in refusal, but no, she surprises him with a yes that is in fact only a half-hearted shrug, but a shrug nevertheless, and still it counts as a yes. So, after he's allowed her to help him dress, and let her carefully secure his hands, feeding the sleeves of his suit down into the pockets, throwing a single stitch there as if to prevent anyone from pulling them out, there they are at the tulips, standing awkwardly, facing the same direction, away from the subtly stinky wind off the ocean,

Almy, in her cardigan and cloche, squints into the distance, her face light brown and blurry, like a mirror of his that won't stay still. He squints in his own turn, bending toward her, staring hard into her for greater focus, for signs of how she feels regarding him, his exaggerations and, if only she knew them, his lies. If he were certain that Flanig had been trying to hurt him, he would tell her that, to undo the hypnotic effect, but he's not sure of it, not sure of anything. What he sees in her without her saying a word is a sturdy and flaxen complexity, which is reassuring in a way. She has always had watery blue eyes and rosebud lips. Flaxen hair. A grimness.

Watching her blunt-cut tresses blow above her neck, stepping up close to her and letting her link one arm into one of his, he understands in a way, not for the first time, what mothering is, and how mothering ends when the only child at last departs the home.

He could make a speech, write a book on such evaporations. It's not unlike polar exploration, after all, where you conquer the pole and then you are finished conquering it. That's just how it goes. His own mission, hands in pockets or not, will be to leave, and Almy will have to fend for herself and her guests.

My departure will make for a wistful occasion, he muses, and wants to explain to her exactly when this will come to pass. But wistful for whom exactly is not exactly clear.

Remember Jansens? he asks.

Yes, she smiles. I remember him in a way.

Well do you or don't you?

Good old Jansens. Yes, indeedy. Jansens of Jansens' Sea. Isn't that correct?

And Virge brightens to hear her get it right, and goes on to explain how he read a book or books by Jansens, but how he can't remember much about it, and it's funny but he always gets Jansens mixed up with Hanson, because he shouldn't have read them all in such quick succession, although he's certain that it is Jansens and his men who are shipwrecked and have to spend a polar winter, eleven months long, confined to one tiny island. To survive they build a little hut, then bury it in snow, one iron stove pipe sticking out of the snow like a periscope, and they gradually burn as firewood certain expendable parts of the ship they came in, but at last comes summer and they are able to sail away in what remains of the ship, though Jansens has died and they have a new leader by then. And the part of the story that amazes everyone who hears it is that years later this hut, still buried under snow, is discovered by modern explorers, who start digging a cave in the ice, and there is that hundred-year-old hut, still intact, even a tin of frozen sprats left behind on a wooden shelf. But even more amazing is that, there in the hut, tucked away in a cracker chest, is the body of Jansen himself, skin the texture of crackers, as if left there for future shipwrecked sailors to dine on. Or perhaps he'd folded himself in there, moments before death, as a way of disappearing without hurting the feelings of his men.

But did any of the others make it back home? asks Almy. Back to their wives and homes?

Yes, I believe they did. I'm pretty sure they all did.

Almy frowns, leans over, and gives Virge what can only be called a poke with one finger into his cheek, as if checking his density, then walks away a few yards to wrap herself a little tighter in her sweater and stare out toward the trees.

It's almost time for the train to come by, she says, surprising him.

But the poke in a way had made things worse, as it didn't feel especially friendly, and now he focuses his mind on the whereabouts of the train, and gesturing without words to point the way, he walks with her silently up the long path, then down, all the way to where they can stand by the tracks and wait, and indeed the first thing she does is to squat down to put a hand on the track to see if she can feel the vibration, as if she is a practiced watcher and follower of trains.

Remember your teeth, Mother, he yells, wheeling out of balance slightly on the gravel slope, stepping back, almost falling down, and at once there comes the train poking its nose out of the trees, strangely less noisy than he remembers, like it's been tuned up, though it's been days since he's been down here to watch, and maybe his memory isn't as good. Definitely it's a degree slower, and has lost its hesitations, its little stammerings. And this time also he hasn't brought a good train attitude with him, so simply he has to plant his feet and watch, first the train, then Almy, and when he sees her holding her jaw with one hand and waving languorously with the other he realizes that she has perceived, through the perforated steel panels, the ranks of soldiers in the boxcars, and that her first kind thought is to salute them and welcome them as they slide sadly by.

There are always soldiers in the cars. It's impossible to count them, it's too hard to see, so he has never included them in his reckonings and records, but it's always been reassuring in the past to glimpse their patriotic silhouettes, rifles on shoulders, and if you wave you generally get waved to in return. Sometimes, if the men stand up close enough to the panels, it's possible to make out characteristics, such as particular height or shortness, or especially sunburnt or especially ghostly complexions.

But something is wrong, something is different today, and as Virge stares into these interiors that pass and dissolve away so quickly, it's clear that while there are men in these cars they are on the short side, not in uniform, not carrying rifles. It's clear that, for the first time, these aren't soldiers, but in fact civilians. Virge has entertained the idea in the past, that since the army trains all are heading north, that maybe they are heading up to northern latitudes and beyond, to the arctic regions, that maybe there's a war up there that nobody knows about, and all he can hope is that they'll have a care not to wreck the arctic landscape, not to soak the snow in blood, for example, or leave equipment behind to rust in the drifts. But why, today, civilians? Could they be recruits, or even prisoners of war? In any event he wants to acknowledge them, to wish them luck no matter who they are, and would prefer to join Almy in waving, and actually he does do so in a way, crooking a finger inside a pocket as the boxcars move by, especially slow today, as if weighed down by such unusual and slouching cargo.

It's a longer train than usual. When the final car goes by Virge's gaze is drawn toward one fellow who presses right up against the perforation and who stands out because the smoke from his pipe escapes through the screen and traces a horizontal line backwards as the train moves along. The man is there and gone, familiar and unfamiliar, glimpsed for a second but not in much detail, other than a mane of long and coal-black hair.

Virge thinks he knows who it was.

Therefore he runs along with the train for a few seconds, keeping up with it as far as he possibly can, before it's swallowed by the second tunnel of trees, but he never gets a good second glance at the pipe smoker.

Still, with a painful thumping going on in the heart area, he thinks he knows who that fellow was.

None other than his dad.

The hair wasn't the right color or length, but could it be that he was wearing the second and up till now missing Indian wig? Maybe he's a prisoner, and all the men are being transported north to some kind of penal colony. So many questions, but yes, it seems to Virge in retrospect that their eyes met briefly through the perforations just as the car slipped into the trees, that there was the slightest possible nod of recognition.

But what now? Virge glances sharply back at Almy to see if she's thinking the same thoughts, but no, it doesn't seem so, she's still just waving passively, automatically, and given that the train is gone, she seems to be only waving to him, to Virge, head tilting with pleasure, though when he approaches her again he sees only the expression of someone who in fact has little of consequence to think about.

So then come the doubts. The things we see are not always the things we see. Evidence before the eyes, even a tangible object held and hefted in the hands, is sometimes chimerical, spit out by factories of desire. Therefore it may not have been Mont. But it could be someone similar, or, because of the black hair, an actual Indian or Mexican. Now that the episode is over it is already receding, regrettably, into fog, receding in just the same way, he realizes with a pang, as the sound of his father's voice, turning thin and powdery, a thin cloud of dust, a sneeze. Either way, whether it was him or not, the one thing that's clear enough is that Mont, one way or another, dwindles. Mont wanes.

3

Meanwhile there is home. Virge seldom leaves the property, and maybe never can for good, but imagines he will. So what of sunshine, exercise, sociability? All these come recommended, so Stuart persuades Virge to get out. To go to a movie.

They end up taking Flanig's car, the Bellevue, which Stuart can and often does drive with the doctor's permission, as long as it's running well, and it's something tremendous just to sit like a dummy in the passenger seat, headed toward some nearby small town, where Stuart is pretty sure there is a theater dedicated to the presentation of moving pictures. While his companion maneuvers the many curves of Highway Number One, some of which run so close to the edge of the cliffs that the ocean is directly below them, Virge stretches his arms out into the rush of wind, flapping his hands like paper, ecstatic that he does not to have to hide his perfect health around Stuart. It's April now, still cool, and the two of them agree on all sorts of things, such as the beauty of the light that falls on the water from between scattered clouds, and the importance of maintaining a reasonable speed around frightening curves.

Arcadia is where they are, in a sense, and Arcadia is the world's greatest medicine for the ailing and the well. Stuart teaches Virge the glance-and-glance-away game—how to make quick twisty movements of the head to left or right to catch a snapshot of something as scenery sails by. If, for example, you happen to steal a look at just the right time, just as a crow is about to land on an overhead wire, it looks like the crow is frozen there, like taxidermy, in mid-air, bird claws stretched out ahead of it to grab the line, wings held up tip to tip, an oily butterfly. Or a quick look at the Pacific and, look, the guy casting a line from the beach down there has his bait frozen in front of him, his fishing line curled like a lariat in the air, his tongue sticking out between his lips. Then Virge, relishing the game on his own, goes further with it, and begins to get snapshots of things that aren't really there, not in a psychic but in merely a creative way. Glance once, and the landscape is covered with ice. Then, glance again, it's green land, green California again. Look again, and wait, har de har, it's Mont, on the side of the road, with his thumb out. Look everyone, let's swerve and run him down, and another thing they agree on is the plot of a new movie, and in this movie they stop to pick up the hitchhiker, but he runs on down the road at triple speed, in oversized shoes, and they can never drive fast enough to reach him, although they can see that his hitching arm is mangled, almost frozen looking, as if injured in some northern and unromantic war, while his other arm seems stretched nearly to snapping point by the weight of his shaggy leather suitcase. The good part is that you can see, whenever he glances back toward them, that there is still a sarcasm to his expression, a sneer that suggests nothing has changed, he's still the same impatient and owlish old dad. On his head he wears in this scene not a wig, but a tattered felt hat, like what a hobo would wear. However, as he goes on running, the brim of the hat lengthens in such a way as to cast an ever darker shadow, so that in time the dad underneath the hat disappears, though the hat itself sails on, parallel to the ground, like a pie plate someone has spun above a shadow. Then quick cut, quick chop of the editor's guillotine, as Stuart explains, and he's gone, no Mont, not even the pie plate, or the shadow.

Why would a doctor hire you? wonders Virge after a moment, changing the subject, sticking his nose in the air.

Then, after a moment, he continues, ruder still.

You don't seem *professionally* companionable.

The doctor, says Stuart, orderly in his speech, has me here for a reason. I'm not sure what it is but that doesn't mean there isn't one.

Flanig needs you because he doesn't like me, or vice versa. Will he like me better when he has no mind left?

He likes you because of that thing. What you said once about Greenland.

The what?

About how you thought California was Greenland. That made him think highly of you.

Really?

He's appreciative of such things. He has an aesthetic side no one sees. I did it once too, and he hired me right away.

Did what?

When he told me about bones being made as healthy as bone china, I thought he meant the country.

What country?

I thought he meant that Chinamen were especially healthy.

Oh.

A few miles later, Virge had another question.

How is that aesthetic? he asked.

Oh, the doctor likes you all right, said Stuart. He told me so, in so many words. He said to me that first your health was failing, and now it's unfailing. Making a joke of it. That's how he likes it. That's how you know he likes somebody. That and the accidental geography. Green land. Bone China.

All right, says Virge, softening.

All right, brother, says Stuart, brushing at various stains on his pants, never able again to present himself as gleamingly white as he did the first day on the job.

When my mother first mentioned the doctor to me, continues Virge, she called him Herr Doctor Flanig, and I thought that meant he was a hair doctor. A doctor who fixed your hair. So there's another one for the collection.

But Stuart doesn't seem too interested.

In time they reach the beach town in question, but it turns out they are way too early to see a movie, since there is no movie theater. And it turns out there's nothing to do there at all. Later, back home, lounging in Virge's room, patient in bed, Stuart working on a drawing at the desk, the whole day has nearly been forgotten.

Someone like you, says Stuart, haughtily, putting down the pen, ought to get himself a job. It's much better to have a regular employment than not to have one. Salary keeps up style, even if it's a small salary, and not much of a style.

I'm too weak to work, protests Virge. No company would accept me.

Weak how?

In the core. In the vigor.

Well, but there's your style.

I didn't know I have one. Do you?

Brother, don't you see it? Watch these cuts.

Stuart stands up from the desk chair and dances a little with his eyes closed, kind of a lumbering motion with the legs but with quick cutting movements of the hands. Self-taught, deems Virge, though aware that this could be the latest dance craze without him knowing, and really he likes what he sees, and thinks Stuart would look good dancing after this fashion on the roof, where there's a little platform, almost like a stage, and Almy could watch and enjoy dancing while the doctor sits below, too feeble to climb up. Why hasn't he been suggesting dance on the platform all along? But it goes out of his mind again because Stuart's dance is a brief one, and he drops down into his chair, feigning exhaustion, fanning himself, impersonating his companion.

I'm too weak in the gut, he groans.

Your style, says Virge, choosing to ignore the mockery.

You have one too, Virge. Everyone has one.

Ha ha. Name it. Name mine.

Your dance is better than mine. Part of it is you falling down. I'd like to paint a picture of you falling!

How do you mean? An advertisement?

No, no, no, there's this kind of painting I'd like to do, with you in it. I admit I don't know how. In French it's called plein air. I prefer to call it Plain Air. *Virgil in Plain Air.* That's our title. What do you think?

Do you just leave that part of the canvas blank? The air part? Or is it blue?

Joking? smirks Stuart, then goes on to explain more about his style of painting, pacing back and forth across the room, gesturing, explaining the idea of landscape, coastal scenery, trying to get Virge to see in his mind's eye a variety of California colors and forms as they might appear on a canvas, with beams of light angling from the clouds, and seagulls veering.

But today I'll stick with the kind of painting I've done before, he concludes, and paint you in an indoor scene.

So Stuart comes back with a bag of painter's supplies, filling Virge's room with the smells of oil and turpentine, then makes a second run, this one to Almy's garden for purple tulips that will give the painting, as he explains, arranging them in an empty coke bottle, more color and genius and *joie de vivre,* or as Stuart translates, joy of revival.

What I really want, he explains, as he begins, is to be a scenery painter. For the movies someday. What I'll do with these flowers is make them beautiful enough to be in the movies. Our movie.

Well in that case shouldn't you paint them in black and white? asks Virge.

Is that a joke, because it's not always obvious if you're kidding, says Stuart.

But the conversation doesn't go anywhere, and over the course of an hour Stuart just paints, standing at an angle that lets Virge watch from bed as the whole picture bleeds itself out on the canvas.

The tulips come first, a disappointing cloud of blue, not purple, muddying up the middle of the picture like something has been spilled there, and Virge starts to think his companion is a little ahead of himself to be termed a real painter, but then the rest of the picture is entirely out of his imagination, a concoction of arches, frames, fleurs de lis, and pine trees, as Stuart can't seem to avoid landscape elements even in a still life. Finally, included at the last minute, and not painted too well, comes Virge's head, half visible in a corner, made to seem older than it already is, a picture of Virge in twenty years maybe, with purple jowls and bags under the eyes, the robust but exhausted face of a sea captain. Then, below that, not at the very bottom as one would expect but halfway down, comes the signature, Stuart Duquesne, all capital letters, in seasick long hand.

There's definitely a panache to it, anyway, judges Virge, not wanting to also mention the muddiness.

Yes, replies Stuart, confidently. And see, this is how I would design sets. Like this. Movies have these great background things, painted with, you know, pines and tulips like what I'm doing here, with landscapes, Roman aqueducts, Arab fountains. That's one reason I keep working for the doctor, because one of these days he's bound to have a patient who works in the movie business, and I can introduce myself. Meanwhile I can practice on you.

And what would I do in the picture?

What picture?

You said I could be in the movies. Okay, but how?

You could be . . . and Stuart thinks about it for a minute, absentmindedly tapping a brush to his forehead several times and leaving a gorgeous blue flower there. Why, I guess you could be the star.

I want to play the role of the cigarette sultan, Virge announces, then, embarrassed, realizes that Stuart has no idea who that is.

Paranormal messages begin arriving from the distant but focused brain of Father Mont. The first of them arrives while Virge is wearing the Indian wig, having achieved something like a dream state. Somehow he knows that for his theory of the wigs to work, he must stare at himself in the bathroom mirror and remain absolutely without expression.

And, after a while, the message arrives. Too bad that this first one is so depressing, but what else could be expected.

You're a grown man. I speak frankly to you. There's a lot to see and I don't want to see. Picture oil stains everywhere, oil pooling on the ground, but the ground is cement and linoleum everywhere you go. Smoke from towers a million feet tall. Though it would be nice to have a helper here, just helping me out at times, don't do it. There are lots of us here, an army of guys, so we are always moving in groups. Just look at me. What's the difference between one in a million and one of a million. Far from home, but otherwise nowhere. I'll be just fine.

And Virge, still looking in the mirror, wonders why the transmission ends, wonders if indeed it has ended, or if it ever really began. Considers the propinquity of it. Whether it would be appropriate to rise to the occasion, and make some kind of formal reply. Dear Father, my bathroom is adjusting itself, what about yours.

But there really doesn't seem to be any room for response. It's just a connection, a message in a bottle, in a wig. When nothing surprises, that's how you know you've become an adult. So he exits the bathroom with solemnity, still wearing the wig, feeling priestly, moving by degrees down the hallway. He can't stop celebrating, or rubbing his tongue like sandpaper over his back molars.

Later, in bed, doubts overwhelm. Why only with the wig? In front of the mirror? Why not, if you're Mont, just write a letter on a piece of paper and send it? The theory, if you buy it, is that father and son are synchronized, though miles apart. But the wigs aren't even made by Indians, they've never been near a medicine man, they're just manufactured goods, cheesy costume pieces, so adjust the hypothesis, because there's more likely something scientific, maybe technically the same as two men communicating over the wireless. It could be so simple and mundane as radio. If so, he wants to count this as his latest invention.

No matter. No matter what headaches to be put through trying to understand, trying to understand. The thought of Mont being where he is, that thought is a burden to have in one's keeping, and Virge is further ground down by the idea that he's required to make the journey himself, to retrieve and redeem the family member who is lost but at least now known to be alive. Try this movie: Virge walking door to door through the entirety of the city, perhaps tilting as he walks but making great strides, ringing the doorbells of bungalows by the millions, taking it day by day, standing motionless, as he sees himself, in the round clouds of bugs that pulse under the porch light, handing over a photo of Mont to fingers that outstretch cautiously from behind screen doors, cautious due to the rise in crime, because in big cities there is always a rise in crime.

Yes, they'll say. We've seen him. But you are nothing like him, you are skinny as a crane and highly strung, and why would we say where or when we saw him without proof positive that you are the next of kin?

Afternoon again. Again a series of empty days. No wigs, no masks. Virge and Stuart spin away the hours in reading and desultory talk. Doctor Flanig's voice wafts to them from the living room, delivering what sounds like, from a distance, another lecture on bones. Perhaps delivered to no one. A yellow cab arrives, appearing in the driveway, framed by the window over Virge's desk, surprising him, as he hadn't heard it crunch down their way along the driveway path.

It's for us, says Stuart, looking up from his drawing pad. It's for me and the doc.

What's wrong with him?

Not him. The Bellevue. It broke down. Happens a lot. And I'll tell you a secret about the old man. With the money he spends on cab fares he could afford to buy a new car.

But where are you going?

Can't be told. Secrets of the something. There are stupendous mysteries, you know. Not meant to be solved, I guess.

A warm interior wind sweeps down out of the canyons, somewhat blustery, and it picks up dust and dead eucalyptus leaves with it. In the slight depression in which the house sits, it speeds up, and whips Almy's tulips nearly flat to the ground. There, near the bent flowers, trying to open the door of the cab into this wind, without success, is the driver of the cab, who, when finally the door gets opened, turns out to be a girl. She is small, especially small in the eyes, head topped with a red beret, one hand holding the beret from flying away in the wind. It's the official uniform of the cab company: cropped wool jacket and smartly pleated slacks. To Virge she looks terrifically modern, streamlined, a new invention, and he is especially surprised by her short stature, as it seems she would hardly be able to drive such a car, but he is also struck by the luxuriousness in her, the attracting factors, the way she at one point leans backwards over the front fender, head back almost the to the hood, though it's unclear whether this is a kind of fancy sexuality pose, as in automobile ads, or part of being blown over.

Finally, straightening, the girl looks like she's had enough of the big wind for one day and simply gets back in the car, not bothering with the door, just lolling behind the wheel, serenely rocking back and forth a little, no idea she's being watched, snappily honking the horn at intervals, giving it a rhythm, a musical twist. For the two young men inside, watching her, the window is like the screen of a sharply focused film and they gaze with an increasing sense of excitement, mixed with discomfort, at least on Virge's part, as she takes a rag from an inside jacket pocket and wipes her nose, leaving a comical smudge of black oil under the nostrils, a monkey's mustache. Perhaps because he's never stared at any girl for so long, Virge warms to it, feels a heightened degree of illusion dissolve inside, even puts his hands up against the glass and ends up holding this driver in high esteem, and what he admires is how she has turned the taxicab's horn into a jazz trumpet, how she looks rounded and foreign in her droopy beret, and other features, too numerous to list.

And then here comes the doctor, venturing out to meet his cab and cabbie, leaning into the wind as he makes his way down the gravel driveway, handkerchief tied in a clever way around his mouth to keep from breathing the sand. That's funny, says Stuart, not laughing.

What's?

That he's going to town without me. I wouldn't mind going, and he knows it. You could come too. He's got it in his head that for two people to go in a cab costs more than one person.

Why do you let him treat you that way?

What way?

You know. Sort of . . . airily.

Airily? As in plain air? I told the story already, about how he took me off the streets, when I was only a newsboy.

I thought you said you were a bum.

Newsboys are bums. Working bums. Look at me now. Notice the difference?

So now you're a hired companion—being paid to be somebody's friend. Or paying, I should say. Maybe that's also being a bum.

Virge amazes himself that he can say all this.

I disagree, says Stuart slowly, blond and beautifully unperturbed.

How so?

Listen. The cab driver doesn't mind getting paid a few dollars to be a driver. She gets paid like I get paid. Look at her and tell me she's a bum. You can't. And I'll also mention the fact that her name's Natalie Sandra, and that I know that as the result of her liking me.

What?

And she doesn't dislike liking me, Stuart adds, thrusting his jaw out, pointing toward her.

Are you saying you know her?

Like a book. We're like bookends, with one book in between: Flanig's Anatomy.

How could she know you before, squints Virge, new to jealousy.

Stuart stammers, and tells the story of how he really only met the girl once before, on a previous cab ride, and the two of them, Stuart and Natalie Sandra, sat up front and chatted on the way down the coast. That they hit it off, got to like each other, became sweethearts without anyone saying so. That she doesn't know yet that she will be the star of his first picture.

All this being difficult to swallow, Virge stays quiet, and stares at the girl's neck intently, watching how she brings her rag up there at times to wipe something away, like a biting insect or a rash, but not leaving any more streaks of oil. Then, looking hard for a reason to dislike her, he sees that the way she brings her hand up to her neck repeatedly is like the way a girl with a guilty conscience would do. Can you tell if a girl has engaged in sexual intercourse, he wants to ask Stuart, but thinks better of it. Look beneath the surface. Underneath the clothes are no clothes, in her case as in his, but shadowy to think it through from there.

Also, continues Stuart, Natalie Sandra's an organist in a church around here somewhere. Flanig says he'll take me sometime to church sometime to hear her play. But you and I could just go without him.

Is it an in-commonist church?

Oh, that's rich. Maybe that could be your newest invention.

Look, look, interrupts Virge. This is good. Look out the window. The doctor can't get the door open with those withered up old hands of his.

So Stuart presses his face to the glass next to Virge's. If anything the wind has picked up and insubstantial Dr. Flanig can't pull the door open anymore than Natalie Sandra, who's crawled inside the Ford, can push it.

Come on, says Virge. Let's go help them.

But by the time they get outside, the wind has died down, the tulips are straining upright again, probably taller than before, and they can just see the rear of the cab as it drives away on the dirt road that leads right up to the coast highway.

Next time, we'll go with them, says Stuart.

All right.

We'll get out of the house in time to catch a ride with them, you watch. Or better, we'll play a choice trick on the doc and end up getting a ride with Natalie Sandra and not him.

And Stuart, speaking these words like someone who spits or smokes cigars, strikes Virge between the shoulder blades, but too hard, and Virge goes down, catching his fall by getting his hands out of his pockets in time, but ending up on all fours, like a farm animal.

I see things differently, he informs Stuart, mildly.

I'm sorry, Patience. Do you mind if I call you Patience? Do you get the joke? Tell me what kind of treat you'd like me to whip up if we go back in the kitchen?

Cookies.

Cookies, then. Do you get why I called you Patience?

I guess so.

No you don't. You're the doctor's patient, and with me, to me, you've shown a lot of patience, and I appreciate that, and there's the reason.

—

Later, back to the mirror. Swimming in words.

All right, says the wig, *It's time for you to start being less fragile. You fall down way too easily. I just don't want you to get hurt, that's all, or wander away, for example, and fall off the cliff. Does anyone owe anyone an apology? Can he who thinks he can, do what he thinks he can? Questions from the world's greatest authors, but sure, you're thinking how can Mont talk to me, when he doesn't know how to manage his own life? So I'm asking for wisdom. Notice that it's me who comes to you this time! Over and out.*

—

Almy gets into the habit of lecturing the boys on conditions around the world, issues which never seemed to interest her before. Circumstances are ripe, she explains, for all of them to hole up here while the outside world falls apart, with the idea being that the sooner it does that the better. But they need to help bring some day of reckoning to pass, she says. Even little errors, such as the state of the bathroom now shared by four, the way Virge stacks things sloppily and precariously in his room, the dirty handkerchiefs she pulls triumphantly from under his bed, the crumbs his friend Stuart leaves on the kitchen countertop when he eats his toast over it and not over the sink—such errors will only lump them all together with folks who are falling apart all around them, and in fact in her own comportment she has become precise beyond reproach.

Don't touch my hair, she screams one day, for example, when walking in the door, fresh from a visit to the beauty parlor, hair cut even shorter than before and quite different, a marcelled wave in it, a style stamped permanently into the hair, like it's been poured into a mold, all this courtesy of Flanig, and his car, which she is learning, courtesy of Stuart, to drive. And who else would walk in just behind her but the doctor, rubbing his hands as if he is the one who's been beautified. They come in through the front door, into the parlor, as if they knew that there they would find the two young men, and there they are, Virge lounging on the divan, Stuart pacing back and forth across the living room, reading out loud, but only to himself, the tinted funny pages.

How do you like it? she asks, transformed from screaming to kindly, pausing to pose, patting the waves in her hair without touching them, pouting her lips to show off lipstick the color of beefsteak tomatoes.

A work of art, to be sure, mutters Virge, actually not liking it much, and so working on a tone that's rare for him, hardly lifting his eyes from staring at his trouser creases, adjusting them with thumb and forefinger, no longer maintaining the fiction of paralysis, having judged, correctly, that the change would not be noticed.

You'll see, she snips back, understanding his tone. Stuart will compliment me, she says. Stuart appreciates style.

Well, he is the artist around here.

And Virge realizes, or just theorizes, that while Almy and Stuart hardly speak, and don't seem to get along well, they do approve of one other in so far as they are the two better looking and aesthetically conscious people in the household, the ones who pay each other compliments, she being praised for, of all things, the bones in her face, her neatness, her hair, and Stuart getting kudos for the cut of his clothes, the creases he irons himself in his pants, his frameless glasses that sit on his face like fine jewelry, his squared-off posture. There is the potential in both of them, despite the age difference, to be more than they are now, and here is Almy, very much aware of her expansiveness, and who wouldn't be struck by such a freshly minted demeanor? As she crosses the room toward where Virge lies on the divan she seems taller and sharper, like a woman on a Christmas card, and for the first time he realizes that she is out of her element here, that she's the sort of creature who ought to be seen strolling down Broad Avenue or at the corner of First and Main, one arm loaded with Christmas gifts while with the other she leans smartly backward, tugging on the leash of her little Scotty dog.

But what difference does it make, he thinks again, what Stuart sees in her, because even though it's Stuart who may have brought all this out in her, who, without intention, remade her, it's only Flanig who is conceivable as a suitor now, who is the one she spends time with, who is the one who suits her. Should anyone care? That is the question. Should a missing husband care, if he's missing? If you don't receive a real letter from someone, only wig transmissions, does that someone exist? If your father abandons you, is it all right to suppose that you were only intermittently fond of him in the first place? Et cetera.

Flanig after all this time has become a sad tale and a hollowness.

That man Flanig, says Stuart one day, apparently coming around to Virge's point of view, is a parade without marchers, an envelope without an address.

But Flanig continues to pay for things. He's a doctor, after all, and he seems to be fond of cold cash, and he is a fountain of it. Pays for everything, and pays for more. There's all the food of course, but also there are gifts. A pair of velvet slippers for Virge, trips to the parlor of beauty for Almy. Flanig has a new silliness to him that could be disturbing, but instead it's entertaining and endearing. He laughs in the act of giving, and then seems touched by the gratitude, nearly moved to tears. Around the house, he floats, freed from some kind of gravity. Doesn't have much to say anymore, but cocks his head and peers into your face in a way that is infectious, so that sometimes they all seem to be floating and laughing.

Almy, however, at this point frowns, waves a dismissive duchess's hand and, with Flanig in the kitchen now, extends the conversation, pulling cans of food from the crate Flanig has brought home from the grocer, lugging it in himself in a peculiar and frightening show of strength.

Look, Virge, your favorite, she smiles self-consciously, framed in the doorway, holding up a can for all to see and squint at. Creamed carrots! I picked up a couple of cans of it because I remember what you like.

It's odd to see her speak of food when wearing lipstick. He thinks of a young magazine girl selling carrots with erotic flair. Then he thinks of a housewife pretending that her absent husband is dead and sparking things up sharply with a much older man with cracker skin and questionably acquired wealth.

That morning, late, nearly noon, remembering the need for sunbeams and vitamins, Virge and Stuart go to town again, this time by bike, after Mont's old three-speed is found in the back of the barn. The doctor's car is still dead, but that's not going to stop them. There's still no movie theater, so Stuart tells the plot of one he remembers, a Western about a father and son, one who becomes a sheriff and one who becomes a criminal. At the climax of the picture, not recognizing each other, they shoot each other to death at the same time.

The ride back is slow, as the bicycle rides roughly and out of line, poor excuse for transportation, unridden for years, and there are difficult puddles on the shoulder of the highway left over from an earlier storm. A crossing of green land. Tilting wonderfully at the edge of cliffs. Stuart is not adept, pedaling drearily on the uphills and coasting on the downhills with the expression of a victim of something, cars speeding by inches away, Virge all the time teetering on the handlebars like a vase about to fall.

A movie about us would also be good, shouts Stuart into Virge's ear, with extra wobbling.

A movie about us wouldn't be about good and evil, quips Virge, pleased to be cast in an upcoming feature. It would be about bad and not so bad. Failing and failing again, though not so much the second time.

When they get back a little after dark, exhausted, disgusted, there's no sign of anyone, though the car's still in the driveway, and when Stuart gets inside he flops down on the divan and falls heavily and noisily asleep, arms sprawled out on cushions and floor.

Rest, rest, pronounces Virge solemnly over the body, and then slips away.

A check of the other rooms as well as the outside of the house reveals nothing. The tulip garden is deserted, but he feels that Almy and the doctor have to be around somewhere. They could be nearby, secret, malign. It's a bad feeling, like being locked in the rubber hut again. Moving stealthily about, looking for any note that his mother might have left, he ponders how it would be if, once he finds them, he'd give Flanig more credit, sit with him, follow his daily routine, whatever it is, and listen to him carefully, agree with him, buck him up, encourage him.

There is the sound of a voice at last, someone singing, but it must be Almy's, not Flanig's, he supposes, because it drifts to him unsteadily, out of tune, as if on a Victrola, coming from behind the closed door of Almy's bedroom.

No, not singing, but crying, or strangled sentences of some sort, heard but not comprehended.

Or would that be the sound of something amatory, something dirty.

And, if it is, and yes, he thinks, it probably is, Virge, who has heard and properly comprehended such sounds before, jumps to the possibly ridiculous conclusion that Mont is back, and that his dad is in there with Almy, and that settles that, and why consider any other possibility.

There's something wrong, however, with his thinking, but without stopping to examine the grounds of this idiocy, Virge sneaks up close to the door in question, realizing at least that to burst in would be inappropriate, despite a strong desire to do so. What remains, then, is to drop to his knees in order to apply his eye to the keyhole, not to watch of course, but only to glance, to get a snapshot, to verify.

But sometimes what we see is not what we expect. In this case a man is involved, and he appears to be naked, partly naked, shirtless, with pants pulled down in such a way as to show off two tiny brown hairy coconut halves that turn out to be buttocks. But it's not Mont, of course, of course it's not Mont.

What further proof do any of us want than what our eyes tell us? These are the buttock halves of the doctor. So there has to be a medical emergency here, thinks Virge, his perceptions messy and haphazardly structured. Someone else is there in the room, or, there's a good chance of it, because after a time, after many blinks and rubbings of the eyes, he sees a hand, and it's not Flanig's but one that is almost artificial looking, refined, an aesthetic hand that rests on the small of the old man's back, like a plaster decoration, solid and white, glued on there. Whoever or whatever belongs to this hand must be shrunken to a size where she readily disappears under the trembling body of the old doctor, because nothing else is visible, at least not from the keyhole. But it's not necessarily an instance of sexuality, it could easily be a treatment or procedure.

Don't certain doctors routinely get on our beds, hover over us, palpate us, then diagnose and treat? And look, of course, the evidence for this is that there's a handful of cotton swabs sticking out, in some cases falling out, of the doctor's trouser pocket.

Then comes Virge's awakening, that is, the procedure of disabusing himself of his troubling naiveté and his misperceptions. Then comes what? The act of reacting is a puzzle to him. Rage would be conventional. Yet, yanking his eye away from the keyhole, standing up straight again in the hallway, mentally bent, then unbent, he can't say that what he feels is rage. Better to call it philosophy. Didn't someone, Jansens maybe, say that it's not the act of pleasing, but freedom from wanting to please, that the wise will strive for? That what pleases one is painless to all, that all men are wise, so there's no occasion to envy or to judge, and therefore Almy is wise, and Virge is wiser still?

He hunches his shoulders then, and because he can use his hands so eloquently now, he lifts them, palms up, making an exaggerated shrug, a gesture of worldliness and resignation. If it were the old Flanig, the philosophy would probably be different, no shrugging or measured wisdom in such circumstances, but this is the new version, a mooncalf who exists somewhere beyond what is common and right. Here Virge lifts his hands high above his head and feels that this is a holding up of rounded shapes of air that show the weightlessness of his examinations.

Good, he whispers. I sit in judgment, and I am one who tilts toward the forgiving of the damned, and the damaged.

Dismissed, dismissing himself, he turns full circle and tiptoes down the hall, slowly straightening to full posture, full stature, a state of statueness, as he strides forward on monolithic legs. There is an acid pleasure, he finds, in growing up, a thrill in handling all the dos and dross of adult to elderly existence. At length he finds himself walking out the back door and into the sun, till he's in the old field, crunching stubs of stubs underfoot, relapsing a bit, burning and dizzy in the harsh dust and sunshine, suddenly down on his knees in a furrow of dirt, holding one hand over both eyes.

From a distance, it would be possible to view him and wonder about him in that position, folded up in the empty field, picking up dirt after a while and pouring it out on his head. He is active enough for any who see him to realize that, wait, that man may be on his knees, but he is nothing if not vital and active. These are bad times but that man there, just look at him, he's one who, in some ways, compared to many of us, is wealthy in his own personal way.

Virge will build on this wealth someday, and yet, in this new condition of fitness and non-illness, what is he? He's the same. Subject to miracles, but the same. There are distinctions—no more apish shoulders that droop and twitch, no more teetering asymmetry—but not much else about him looks that different now. The face in the mirror, bewigged or not, is still oldish and troubled in the way it appeared before the attack. His cheeks look like they're swelling, like batter rising in a bowl. Rising, but then sagging. Pressing his hands together, intertwining the fingers for special concentration and velocity of thought, he feels beneficially distorted, perhaps mentally superior now to the others, if only in a minor way. It's worth repeating that those who lose eyes or tongue gain in other realms, not growing a replacement but growing an alternative, so that an evolved tongue replaces the eyes, or vice versa. But lose and then regain a body part and there the compensation comes in the form of evolved humility, sensibility, friction. When Virge was weak as wet paper, his thoughts were distributed into separate compartments, a series of envelopes, each smaller than the next, a series of shifts away from and not towards conclusion. Now everything is the opposite. Now to proceed from small to large, he might say, and now to un-gather and un-father ideas. Now to shape, with shaping hands, a sense of grandeur.

At the same time, sometimes the initial reaction to progress is to feel a sharp nostalgia for the preceding misery. Jansens feels most cast down, he writes in his account, whenever the weather clears, the sun beams on his expedition, and the crew has the prospect of warmth and speed. When finally the shore of Greenland is achieved, the crew celebrates, but the captain can never get over the feeling that the storms that nearly foundered them on the way were his only authentic experience. Later, when he folds himself up in the big biscuit box, Jansens must believe that all is lost, but that the box is as comforting as a mother's smothering embrace.

Virge, rather than bask in the return of feeling to his limbs, keeps wishing it might have returned a few days later, to give him the opportunity to prepare for the new entity that he understands himself to have become. Like those who need a blow to the head to recover from amnesia, Virge got what he needed: a testimonial, a witnessing, a vision through the keyhole, to serve as a pick to the ice in the mind.

Back inside, it's as if nothing has happened. Flanig, Almy and Stuart are gathered in the breakfast nook, chatting with some animation, as if they had been there all day. The thought comes to him that the hand glimpsed in the bedroom belonged to Stuart, and he stares for a while at all the hands in the room, his own included, only to reach the conclusion that his mother's are the ones that are refined, the ones carved from ivory.

His own hands, even stuffed in his pockets, convey a sense of innocence.

Swallowing hard, Virge steps up to the edge of the table, straightens his spine and speaks over their heads, beginning with the announcement that he has an announcement, and that's as far as he gets until the others encourage him to go on.

Unbeknownst to you, he says, keeping his eyes on the ceiling, removing both hands from both pockets, I've been experiencing an inner frostiness, that's all I want to say. But it's over now, it's finished.

And he reaches his arms straight out and flexes his fingers for them, playing an invisible piano.

After the delayed oohs and aahs, after Almy's perfunctory kiss that she plants on her palm and blows in Virge's direction, he's not a topic for their discussion. They go back immediately to their lighter theme, whatever it was. So he sits down there with them, next to Stuart, not able to concentrate on what's being said, hands in pockets, rolling his eyes around in his head, feeling a degree of disappointment, a degree of freedom.

And yet the next day there is a mood of laxity and turpitude. He can't help but notice it. Almy bakes a cake for no reason, and sets it on the table before him, like a birthday cake.

Now just look at that, says Virge, when he sees that it's a production of multiple layers and flavors, decorated on top like a French stage set, full of fleurs de lis fashioned from gold foil and little pillars carved into the sides from stiffened frosting, and of course it is no great surprise to learn later, just before the four of them dive into and ultimately polish the whole thing off, washing the crumbs down with cups of coffee, that it is Stuart who designed the confection, sketching it out on paper first but, knowing nothing about baking, left the purchasing of fancy ingredients to Flanig and the actual kitchen work to Almy.

Make another one for tomorrow night, is Flanig's comment as soon as they finish it off, but, sadly, he says it in such a whining way, juvenile way, that all the air leaks out of the celebration.

All right, all right, snaps Almy. Give me time to finish enjoying the first one.

And Flanig, at that, sniffles, Raggedy Andy style, like he's about to cry.

———

The next day, there's always the next day. Almy and Stuart get straight to work on a second cake, while the other two sit up straight and silent in the kitchen chairs and observe the sticky preparations, Virge keeping one eye on the doctor and one on the bakers. It seems like it would be a good time to talk things over, get everything out into the open, if such is possible, but he can't or they can't manage it this time, and Virge takes to flexing and cracking his ten spidery fingers, along with other operations combating boredom. The doctor's neck, in these moments, becomes an object of fantasy, where he can picture his hands wrapping around the windpipe, though under different circumstances. If the doctor were all there, if he were less wattled, less brown, less neutralized, God knows what might happen. As Virge watches more closely, Flanig's face sags beyond sagging, and the doctor puts his own fingers to his skin as if to stop it. What a creature,

Virge thinks, is an old man. What a wrinkled bean pod, but where are the beans?

Unaware of scrutiny, Flanig clicks his lips together slowly and savagely, like an animal licking its chops, and Virge, ashamed of himself, hides his hands under the table, and ties his fingers into elaborate knots.

If we eat dinner early enough, and get to dessert early, observes Stuart, perhaps Virge and I will take our cake outside.

But Almy, face made up with yellow flour, gives him something like a dirty look.

What did I say? he pleads, but then shuts his mouth.

Stuart's right, says Virge, primly. We will take our cake outside, Mother, since we hardly care for the opinion of the world.

But things don't work out as planned. A little while after Almy has set the unfrosted disks of cake on the window sill to cool, Virge happens to glance out the window in time to see a man's head rise up there, like a puppeteer peeking up above the stage. It's no great surprise—just a man daring to trespass on the property, it's happened before, nothing to be alarmed about, except that this fellow, sporting long black hair like an Indian, but very fair of complexion, eyes them all as coolly as can be, even ends up smiling at them, unabashed, even entertained, as if having purchased tickets to a show. Hello and what do you make of us, one wants to ask. But in the end Virge only clears his throat, quietly, just casually enough that the others turn slowly to see what he's looking at. And, as they all watch in fascinated silence, the fellow winks, shrugs, grabs both the layers of yellow cake, one in each hand, and dashes off and out of view.

What to do? They all stare at each other in calm bewilderment, but it's Virge, reborn Virge, who is the one to jump out of his seat and burst out the screen door, full of a previously unguessed-at vitality, not so much hoping to catch the thief as to talk to him, since he wonders if the man might be a soldier from the boxcars, or somebody extraordinary from the boxcars, because you never know who might be familiar with and hungry for one of Almy's luscious desserts. But when Virge has run twice around the house, there is a mystery: the fellow has vanished entirely, as if some hidden trap door known only to trespassers had opened, revealing a flight of stairs that descends deep into the earth. Or ascends into the clouds? Out of breath, Virge leans down to rests his hands on his bent knees, to loosen his tie a little, and it's at this point that Stuart catches up, using language Virge would never have expected, where is the fucker, where is he, and all Virge can do, voiceless from his burst of speed, is point down to the ground, and, with two of his fingers, try to imitate the motion of someone running down a flight of stairs.

You mean he ran out to the train tracks?

No.

Then where?

Do you know about the men on the trains? asks Virge, finally, when he gets his wind back.

What men? You mean the engineers? The brakemen?

No no.

Then who?

Oh, never mind. You have to go close up to see them. Tomorrow I'll show you. It's soldiers and such. Maybe Mont, I mean my dad, or someone like that.

But they don't go down to where the train runs by. They also don't go the next day, or the day after that, and in fact it turns out Virge can't bring himself to go there again for a long time. Not because he's afraid.

That night, after Almy says grace, a prayer that's harder to follow than usual, with references to the hungry thief, ending with some few words in Spanish, more fluent this time, as if she's making progress in the language, they eat in silence, and afterwards Virge and Stuart grumpily wash the dishes while Almy and Dr. Flanig sit close to each other at the table, Almy reading a section of the newspaper out loud, transmitting it slowly and gently to the old man, as if they are just a bland and sentimental couple, and nothing is said about anything or done about anything except that for Virge it's elementary to see that everything has altered in his world more quickly than he could have imagined, while on the other hand he might be better off worrying about the dour headlines he can read on the front page and the equally dour ads that appear on the back, than worrying about his own future dourness, or lack thereof.

My boy, my boy, says Flanig, taking the newspaper from Almy, folding it neatly, a skill he retains, and motioning to Virge to come join them at the table.

Virge wipes his hands on a dish towel in response, while Stuart glides out of sight, into the dark cave of the living room.

Listen, says Almy, casting sidelong looks at the doctor, who blinks his eyes back at her with a melting and remarkable kindness in his gaze.

It's about me? asks Virge.

Doctor Flanig thinks you're not well enough for him to leave yet. We all know you're much better, but better is relative.

You're saying I'm relatively better.

Don't you agree? asks Almy, poking Flanig in the ribs, but whether she is trying to get him to laugh or to get him to say something is impossible to tell, as he does neither, just reaches out a hand to gently hold Virge's elbow, and it's the warmest and softest hand in history.

I don't know. Yes that's fine. It doesn't matter.

Sympathy and symmetry, pronounces the doctor.

Virge is about to say something, but shuts up, feeling nothing can or should be changed right now, and nothing will be changed. Let it go on. Let's see where it leads. There are at least a thousand stages in life. A thousand shakes of a leg.

I don't think I'm missed much. Am I? Does your mother miss me? She get a new boyfriend yet? Ha ha, just kidding. Remember my palm, and that patch that's got hair growing out of it? Remember? I used to tell a story when you were little about people the size of fleas, crossing the desert, my palm, almost dying of thirst, until they reached the oasis, my hairs. But where's the water you'd say, and that's when I'd spit into the patch of hair and I'd say, Allah be praised it just started to rain. How did it happen? I burned myself grabbing a radiator and they grafted skin from my leg onto my palm and it just kept growing leg hairs in its new spot. Did I ever tell you that story? San Grande is a kind of desert. No oasis though. Hoping to see you soon.

Grandma was famous for her black and white pies, the story goes, and didn't Almy learn to make them too? Whatever happened to black and white pies? Once, while they were on the roof having pie, years before, Mont picked his son up by one leg and one arm and spun him, and joked about throwing him right off the roof.

In the middle of the night Virge stumbles across this memory, and wakes up, can't sleep, thinking about the roof, how they haven't been up there in ages, how he hasn't had black and white pie in ages. Kill two birds with one stone, he thinks, and drifts off.

Then wakes up, and it's so quiet he can hear the waves crash, and then he starts thinking, not wanting to, about the keyhole.

About what he might see if he crept back to it. What he might see or not see. And he has to consider that if he sneaks down the hall, crams his eye up against it, what if Almy should appear, sophisticated, posing like a nightgown model in the middle of the floor, arms held out and fingers around one wrist, as if taking her own pulse?

But it's not her, just Flanig that Virge desires to see, desires to expose, and what he wants is to pull the doctor out to the open, pry the hermit crab out of its shell, just to see what's wrong with it, since so much of it is hidden, and it's the hidden part that must be the sickest.

Sleeplessness sets in, and Virge twiddles forever with the top button of his pajamas until it pops off and, holding it aloft to look, it slips and drops halfway into a nostril, and he bolts upright to sneeze it out.

Silence. Then one sound comes along, but it's only a barking dog, far down the coast, and it whimpers and shuts up, as if strangled.

Virge thinks of Stuart then, who is sleeping, or probably sleeping, on the sofa, and he has a mission now, to spy a little, maybe wake up his friend and talk things over. Interview Stuart about the doctor. Ask if he believes in people staying where they are or moving on, or is there a third alternative, something that combines a little of both, something that gives one a sense of home when traveling and a sense of traveling when home. Life comes in black and white to the less intelligent, but in gray to the superior intellect. In the end Virge gets back in bed and succeeds with sleep, only to jerk awake from a dream where Flanig was floating outside the window like a sheet of paper, body not naked but fully clothed, and everything bathed in dull colors, not quite electrified but glowing phosphorescence, with the problem to solve of the doctor's death, and the doctor is angry in the dream, reaching out a bony finger to tap at Virge's window, as if banished, and shaking his fist to be let back in.

The roof, the roof, let's get everybody on the roof, says Virge still talking to the ceiling. In this case he's alone still, in bed, and it's still dark out.

Before I go, he continues, I ought to have one last evening on the roof, as in the old times.

Certain forward motions can't be kept under wraps, they expand beyond the mind of the philosopher in all directions, and because this is the case with Virge, he swings out of bed, and this time pads right down the hall, quiet as a mouse as he tiptoes past the door with its tainted keyhole, walking right past it without perturbation. It's Stuart he wants to talk to, and when he gets to the living room he stops for a moment near the divan to observe his companion, the sleeping Stuart, so shrouded and covered in a crazy quilt that Virge can't see any part of his body sticking out, just an inert formless bundle, though it's dark to see details.

I've got something to tell you, he announces, coming closer and directing his hissy whisper at the bulk.

But there's no response. Sleepers like to stay asleep. It's dangerous to speak so loud for fear of waking the others, getting them involved, and he clamps a hand to his mouth to stop himself from raising his voice. If there's to be a plan, let it first be his, that's all he asks for, and then it can be Stuart's.

The roof, Stuart, the roof, he pleads. It's wonderful news. Come on, wake up, Stuart, don't mess around.

No answer, but Virge is not deterred and sits down on the edge of a nearby chair.

It's Mont. I mean it must be my dad. He's up there. I guess that sounds crazy, but I don't know what else to think. There's a platform up there that Mont built years ago. You follow? So I had the notion that Mont and the guy who stole your cake, well they're one and the same, we just didn't get it because sometimes he wears a fake wig, I mean a wig, since all wigs are fake. Remember how he disappeared so suddenly and we couldn't figure out where he'd gone? It's because he climbed the ladder to the platform! You see, although I didn't mention it before, we do have a platform on the roof.

Silence, but he can't be asleep by now, it must be that he's just rude, showing off his lack of interest in a crackpot.

Okay, I was dreaming. Of course it wasn't my dad. I happen to know he's in the big city. I don't know what's wrong with me. Sometimes I feel smart and sometimes I feel not so smart and I know you're wishing I'd just shut up.

But Virge can't shut up, and goes on to explain how there was a fad years before, when they first moved into this bungalow, a craze for building patios, terraces, verandas. The outdoor life, it was called, the western way. And when Mont saw some plans in a magazine for building on your roof, he went nuts, and despite a lack of funds he borrowed some money and did a fine job, and all through subsequent springs and summers and falls and even occasionally in winter they would sit in patio chairs, sometimes huddled in the cold, sometimes enveloped by mosquitoes, and Virge tells Stuart the story of how Mont would wake up in the middle of the night hungry for ice cream, and he'd get Virge out of bed and help him up the ladder with a flash-lamp, and there they would crank out the ice cream by hand and Virge's job was to hold a hurricane lamp aloft to keep a beam on the surrounding halo of ice and mention whether it needed another dose of rock salt or not.

Perhaps, at this, there is the slightest hint of stirring under the quilt.

In the kitchen cabinet, asserts Virge, rubbing his fingertips together, his habit lately, we still have the electric torch. Get dressed, Stuart, and I'll get it and come back.

But in the kitchen, in the darkness, he feels overcome by weakness and uncoordination. Something isn't going right, in his legs this time, and maybe the roof, any elevation, feels like a mistake, because if his dad really is living up there, spying on them all this time, then how awful to discover such betrayal and how awful to risk falling off.

Enervated, struggling to open the top drawer near the sink, the drawer that is always a little bit sticky, his hands not quite themselves, he pulls too hard and the whole drawer pops out of its slot so unexpectedly, and so heavy with all its miscellany that it just drops straight to the floor, all the contents spilling out with the sound of a terrific automobile accident.

In the circuslike silence that follows, Virge assures himself and the world that no one heard the noise.

The boats are in the harbor, someone comments from down the hall, and hearts sinks. Someone's slumber has been ruined, someone shattered awake from the deepest sleep.

And, within seconds, there are rustlings, footsteps slapping down the hallway, and rather than wait for whoever it is to come in and switch on the bulb, Virge walks over to the wall and does it himself, just in time to throw a spotlight on Almy and Flanig, one ancient, one fresh, in gray night dresses, rubbing their eyes under the electric light, then rubbing again at the spectacle of Virge still holding the drawer by its handle, and, scattered everywhere, the junk that has spread slowly across the linoleum: pennies, penny nails, enema bag, salt shakers, souvenir thimbles, batteries, the wig again, funnel, jar lids, balled rubbers. No flashlight.

Sorry, squeaks Virge, not wanting to look either of them, Almy or Flanig, in the eye, but even so, taking them in from the neck down. There's the sorry sight, the not fresh gowns, their bare arms, Almy's nipples protruding very frankly under the cotton, Flanig's chin more concave and stomach more convex than Virge imagined, because of dentures and girdle during the day. Nightcaps for both, but it's a kind Virge never knew of, with brims and ear flaps, like hunting caps. Everything, dress and hat, made of cotton too thin to give warmth or block out noise.

Better not to stare straight ahead, or down. Better than standing here waiting, he thinks, it would be better to get down all fours, a familiar place to be, and gather and restore. A moment later, crawling on hands and knees, sometimes at their feet, comparing ankles: two wizened, two sturdy. Everything goes back in the drawer in a nicer order than before, with categories invented on the spot, pencils next to ball of twine in the linear category. Virge finds he can't utter a word when he's done, and keeps his head down, though not able to stop looking at keep his eyes off his mother's bare feet, and her toes, white as garden snails.

Some can categorize and moralize at the same time, and Virge decides that this is one of his talents The concepts and customs having to do with inferiority are all relative, and even age, beyond the numbers, is artificial. Feet can show heavily veined ankles, nets of blood, skin ivoried like plaster. Or be curtained away, cloaked under socks, curtains held up by garters, a kind of stage rigging. But old age is always younger than some other age, so nothing in itself.

By the time Virge wrestles the drawer back into its slot, he feels strong enough to step forward and engage Flanig eye to eye. No blinking or backing down, best possible posture, waiting for the lecture, but instead steps an inch closer, and sees only a vague oiliness or congealed fluid in the eyes, as well as a stuttering of the pupils, fits and starts, as if a great excess of thought races through the knotted mind. No sign or risk of weeping and wailing, and this lends a gravity, plus a poetry. Flanig's eyes go round and dark. He is all kindness at times, all kindness now, so his hand lunges forward to hold Virge's elbow. From that perspective he becomes a figure for Virge, and it could be said that at least his hands are warm and wet, like buttered biscuits.

What happened? yawns Almy, coolly enough, rich to look at in her lopsided night cap and perfectly pillow-creased cheek.

Oh, he says, straightening into military posture. Nothing. Nothing happened.

Almy shrugs, and bares her teeth. All kindness, too, or it's more that nothing about him matters as much as many other concerns.

Why think only of Virge? He'll be better off, is her conclusion, the one that everybody reaches.

You worry me, Virge. Not a care in the world, but it sounds serious.

Worry no more, Mother. Go back to bed so as to see you in the morning.

And to his surprise she takes the cue, and moves off, Flanig in tow, glancing over her shoulder as they disappear into the cold of the hallway. They're always descending. He perceives it with dread, a kind of kind of marching into the underground interior of a tomb.

But what about Stuart? Surprisingly, he still hasn't burst into the kitchen, and could it be that he's that sound of a sleeper, that dead to the world? It's the next drawer down, it turns out, that holds the torch, and with the item in hand, revived with new batteries found in the first drawer, Virge moves with determined step into the living room, keeping pace with the tenuous circle of light that precedes him across the floor.

So here's the divan and the cone of light falling on the divan isn't strong, but it's enough to show what couldn't be seen in the dark, that the bundle in it isn't a bundled Stuart. His companion has pulled one and disappeared, but not before plumping up the covers, inserting cushions and little bricabracs, creating a Stuart that's a rich compromise, Virge reflects, between being home and being away.

Next morning, the phone rings and rings and Virge, despite a headache that makes his head feel twice as large, and perhaps twice as intelligent, feels he ought to answer it. Not in too great a hurry. He also has lately experienced a general reluctance to touch trembling and noisy objects, his hands themselves often feeling noisy and trembling, but he finally lurches forward out of bed, pads down the hall, into the kitchen, to snatch up the ear piece.

Whoever you are, he mumbles into the horn, unable to finish the thought, though he hopes he comes off as one who is dangerous to awaken.

Yes, may I speak with Stuart Duquesne please? says the voice pointedly, the girl or woman on the other end, pronouncing it dookeznee.

I'm afraid Stuart isn't here.

Then I'm sorry.

Why?

Are you sure? He's not asleep? Say, on a couch or something? Could you just take a look for me? If you could be so kind, kid.

Or did she say kiddo? There are notes of both sweetness and sourness in this tete a tete, this ear to ear, femaleness dripping like wax through the telephone line. And where, he wonders, knowing the answer, where did he see the face he associates with a candle-wax voice, once? Natalie Sandra is where. He is ardent about her, in a way.

Oh please be she, he blurts out.

Who is this? Is this the house of the crippled boy?

I'm sure Stuart's not here, barks Virge, now as rudely basso as he can make his voice. But Miss, hold on to the receiver at your end, while I have an employee check for you.

Back in the parlor, it's sad and surprising to discover that there is the actual Stuart stretched out on the sofa, wrapped like a great tube, midsection tightly rolled in the crazy quilt, but authentic sleeping face half buried in a pillow.

No, he's not here, he snaps when he finally gets back on the phone, and, without waiting for reply, hangs up.

Occupational peril of a shut-in: Erroneous judgment of what is shut and what isn't.

An hour later, Virge revisits the living room, and there Stuart is stretching, wide awake, yawning, then hopping up, shedding the blankets, breaking into some hearty calisthenics, shouting out the count.

Join me, Virge, he shouts, high spirited. It's unpatriotic not to maintain good health.

So Virge does join in, no amazement there, and Stuart shows the moves of several jumping figures and leg procedures, and then the Chinese art of weightless weight lifting, Stuart announcing higher figures as they proceed.

But Virge, after a hundred repetitions or so, can't keep up, and plops on the floor, politely watching while Stuart continues.

It was your girlfriend, says Virge after some time, who called this morning. Did you hear the phone ring?

Oh?

She told me to tell you that she's thinking of getting married soon.

Is that right?

Yes, to a man.

I'm not quite used to you this way, Patience, beams Stuart, moving slowly like a priest, arms over his head, and clapping, or as if cutting the air with a big pair of scissors.

What way?

So Hollywood.

After a time, there's a clap of thunder not at all startling, one that comes on gradually and eerily.

A sharp smell of ammonia, explains Stuart, precedes lightning.

It's the pantry, answers Virge. The vinegar.

Add in the smell of rain. Initial drops tapping the roof, massaging its head, water boiling in the corners of the sluices. Virge turns his head to look outside. Later, turning back, he sees Stuart far across the room, displaying the top of his skull, peeping at the tips of his shoes, which Virge notices for the first time. Fancy and pointed!

All right, he breathes, letting go of a degree of electrical tautness.

The storm brings the denizens out of their dens, says Virge out loud when his mother and doctor loom in the hallway. Flanig is especially scrawny this morning, a suit of clothes on a wire hanger, and he stretches out on the banquette in the breakfast nook in much the same way that Virge used to do when paralyzed.

In time the other three sit down at the table with him, in silence. Stuart lights up a cigarette, but then more amazing is how Almy too selects one from Stuart's proffered case, and together they stand up and move over to the sink, where they can talk in whispers and flick their ashes down the drain. This time the other two join them there, at Virge's instigation, not to smoke but to gaze out the window, watching with collective boredom as the heavy rain turns to light rain, turns to mist, then turns to nothing at all. Finally there comes an intense and theatrical sunshine, a spill of pure heaven through the kitchen window onto the blue countertop tiles, which shine like real diamonds now. It's only California, but today the light is as sharp as it may be in the Arctic, and it doesn't gather on surfaces, but cuts and shatters everything it touches.

I returned, recites Flanig, more animated than usual. I returned, and saw under the sun.

Saw what? asks Almy, scowling. They are all at the table at this point.

That the bread is not to the wise.

Chew on that for a while, says Stuart.

I'm chewing, says Virge, nudging Stuart in the ribs. But it's a serious moment of insight for some, for anyone who cares to really listen. Yet it all falls flat in a moment, and it's easy to see that neither Stuart nor Almy is too affected by the passage, and even the doctor, afterwards, lies down and stares with moist eyes at the ceiling, and Virge sits next to him and twice pats his hand.

We should tell these two gentlemen about the roof, Virge announces, swallowing hard, turning back to Almy, blinking, wishing he didn't have to speak to her in order to convince her of things.

We should tell these two, he repeats, about the roof.

Almy stares and stares, maybe stupefied by her second cigarette, letting smoke run out of her nostrils like she's been at it all her life. She's wearing a new dress today, in a fabric printed up with little repeated fruit clusters.

Tell me, tell me, says Stuart, childishly. What's on the roof? I prefer roofs to houses.

You really want to hear the story?

I prefer to, yes.

Mr. Bingham built it with his own hands, says Virge.

Oh, a long time ago, puts in Almy, as if to dismiss further interest.

So at that time, that is, when I was a little boy, continues Virge, gesturing, he was building it, and I remember he worked on it all the time. So much so that he barely lived in the house, and preferred living on top of the house. Right? It's a platform, is what I'm trying to say. We could go up there and sit and, this is the best part, it's the one place on the property to get a view of the ocean. Everybody's going to love this particular experience, especially when we turn on the radio and dance, or something.

It's dangerous, whines Almy, stubbing out her smoke. I don't like heights.

So one day, Virge continues, Mont came inside and said, it's finished, and the three of us went up. But. You should see it for yourselves. I don't want to spoil things.

Go back to the part about the radio, insists Stuart. Doctor, did you hear what they're saying? That there's a radio on the roof. Did you catch that?

Oh, I'm so glad of such blessings, beams Flanig, rubbing his eyes, sweet as a child that has woken, gratefully, from a frightening dream.

The only conclusion you can come to, Son, is that things aren't going well. Violence has been done to me. Oh yes. Be careful upon arrival. It's something about a big city like this, there are lots of ways to get trapped in situations here and the same could happen to you. I don't go out anymore since they have it in for me. Everywhere you go you keep your wits about you, focus hard not on your feet in front of you, but on all the other feet, you need to see who's coming at you, consider yourself warned, Sylvester. Sell something that everyone else needs to buy, such as medical equipment. Bandages, hypodermics. Everybody's sick most of the time. Look at me, I'm sick right now. Strike the right note the minute you get here. And you are coming, aren't you? When and who should I expect?

Almy is opposed to the whole roof idea, but goes along with it heroically, and even goes ahead and prepares a few things to eat, and they all gather a few minutes later on the lesser known side of the bungalow, and up the built-in ladder they climb, even shaky Flanig, until they all stand huddled up together, tightly knit at the height of the frightening platform, and their backs and necks interlock and veer against one another so that each ends up with a separate view out over the world: the fields and houses, the river in its frame of bent trees, and, as promised, not so far away as it seems otherwise, the solid ocean and part of the beach visible past the top of a palm, and with that touch the view turns almost tropical.

God, what a pandemonium, declares Stuart.

Panorama, corrects Virge.

Hey, Virge, your dad's not up here.

What's that supposed to mean? asks Almy. No answer to that.

Virge grabs hold of the edge of a tarpaulin and whips it away, like there's someone under there, but instead it's a nest of battered patio items: painted steel chairs, a stack of tiny tables, a plywood radio that looks nothing like a radio, more like a kitchen cabinet, but does have a single steel dial in the middle.

Your dad must have been a genius, says Stuart, with one of his rare notes of sincerity.

I do love a good cabinet, puts in Dr. Flanig, coming up so close, smelling of talcum and excrement, and they all look at him, expecting some additional comment, but maybe he doesn't understand the radio part, because he simply lays his hand across the top of the wood and lowers his head in thought, or prayer, or bewilderment.

I think the doctor needs a sit down, says Almy, fussing, patting at the waves in her hair, then stooping to similarly pat the seat of one of the chairs. When the two younger men make no move to help, she guides Flanig in such a way that he glides smoothly like a manikin across the platform, and she folds him expertly, instantly, into a rigid sitting position.

Now we'll turn on the radio, announces Stuart, raising his voice, and he crouches next to the radio, and, peering over the tops of his glasses, starts working at the dial.

I'll get it going, he drawls.

I bet you will, says Virge.

Let it warm up and it'll go, states Almy, suddenly involved, and it's true that after a few minutes they hear a crackle of static followed by gongs, then finally the strains of something, of syrupy violins, but the music only trickles from the speaker, so they all have to bend down and angle one ear forward.

Ah, the old melodies, smiles Flanig, leaning closest of all, shuffling his feet in some semblance of a waltz step. Later, sipping at a glass of wine, he's almost himself again, and Almy, uninhibited, demonstrates how to drink straight from the bottle, like a man, then seems ashamed of herself a second later, and moves on quickly to a new phase. There is always a new phase for her now, this one a complaining stint about the occasional gusts that mess her hair, and when Virge jokingly cups his hands around her head to feign protection, she snaps, and claims she'll push him off the platform if he does it again.

Mother, says Virge, recovering on the spot, becoming adept, finally, at the banter. Mother, tell us the funny story about when Daddy almost threw me off the roof.

It's a true one, she nods to Flanig, returning to her more country accent.

He was a man, says Flanig, of tremendous strength.

Yes, beams Almy.

A muscular dad all right, puts in Virge.

Once your father finished putting all this up here, Almy goes on, then pauses and looks around, blankly.

Go on, Mother, urges Virge.

Well he took some rope and hauled up the chairs, but he carried the parts of the radio up the ladder because he wanted to put it all together up here. All the little electrical parts, in buckets.

But tell about throwing Virge off the roof, says Stuart.

He also told us, she responds, that kings in ancient times would sit on the roofs of their own palaces. Do you know that story, Doctor?

King David, mumbles the doctor, more frightened looking than ever, his hair so long and straight, despite the wind, that he has a royal presence himself.

Yes, that's right, agrees Almy. King David spied Bathsheba in her bathtub, and fell in love with her on the spot. And wouldn't you do the same, Virge or Stuart, if it was you? Virge, are there any bathing beauties on the beach this evening?

Mother, he hisses.

Wasn't King David in a baby tossing story too, Stuart interrupts, winking at Virge.

One time, when was it, in June I guess, when you were little, Virge, we all climbed up here to watch a sunset, and your father got it into his head to pretend he was going to toss you in the ocean. All the way. Throw you off the edge of the platform so you'd land in the water and learn to swim. I was scared he'd do it, of course, then not scared, and I was able to relax about it.

Well, did he do it or not?

No, but he picked Virge up by the arms like a suitcase and swung him around and around, and Virge started crying, and I almost died from watching it, at first, and that was it, I guess I got used to it.

To what?

To him being . . . a monster. And that's the end of my story.

Almy tips over toward Flanig then, as if to check something about him, or maybe she's just a little unsteady in her chair.

Doctor, she grimaces, we're going in now. Dios nos bendiga.

In this moment of commiseration for him or for herself, her permanent wave gets finally undone by the wind, and her hair turns into a fright wig.

Oh, look, begins Virge, but stops. At one time he would have been so embarrassed to see her like that, but things are different now, and in a moment of rooftop ascension, he forgives her everything.

In days to come Virge and Stuart go frequently up to the roof, making it into a kind of boy's clubhouse, but, once there, Virge usually tunes out and hardly hears a word Stuart offers about the colors bleeding in the sunset or the light draping on the ocean, or any word of Stuart's poetry at all, since he spends the time thinking through problems, and most often he lights on what he calls the gress problem. Regress, ingress, exgress. It's his word for the way his brain has of falling on its hands and knees before a handful of mental snapshots familiar since childhood, along with a few of more recent vintage, without any apparent ability to dismiss the familiar and summon the new. This repertory persists, hour after hour, no matter how much one would prefer, really, to break off completely and come up with what would maybe amount to an entirely different life. The book about, or was it by, Jansens, is the worst example of all the failure that has often accompanied true striving. He ends up folded in a cracker chest, after all skin turning to biscuit. Better to obtain and read some other books, of course, as Flanig suggested, but for one reason or another that never works out. Better to get new experiences, better to be elsewhere, but that's not happening today either. This is how it must be for some. He's examining the juncture where various portions of his mind dovetail. First he has the severely compressed and constrained memories of the past, such as rose dust, iron lung, beautiful ocean view. Second he has the wig transmissions, probably bogus, still oppressive. What's third? No, there are only these two. If it were all a movie, there would be a small black yapping dog in each corner of the screen, angrier and angrier as they watch what's going on, unable to shut up for even a second.

———

It's summer, and the green has seeped out of the hills, leaving the foliage sometimes yellow as wheat, sometimes brown as butcher's paper. The heat masses at knee level, a transparent fog hugging the ground, and in that fog all you can hear anytime is the buzz of huge black bees. So it's the roof then, every day, where it's a tad cooler, and one evening Stuart starts in right away about the glories of the sunset and the fake majesty of the little creek, but in time gets around to making a start at telling a story about himself. Watching him, not listening, Virge smiles and says to himself, Now speaks the golden man. It's the hair the color of dry pine needles, the glasses. The sunset bathes them both in light, but it's Virge who turns orange in it and Stuart who turns golden.

I'm planning on the getting of a job, Virge remarks, in the middle of a small pause in Stuart's telling.

What for?

To pay bills. Share the burden.

But the bills are paid, laughs Stuart. The doctor's a good egg, there's no denying that.

But maybe he could use some help.

Let's see, let's add up the whole household income. How much have you brought in, Patience, from previous jobs?

No one likes to live on charity.

But Stuart just lights a up a golden cigarette, shrugs.

So I'll be getting that job, insists Virge.

Well, I'll help you with your classified advertisement. Young spark seeks employment. Will accept post as arctic explorer.

Maybe. I have my ambitions. And in your case, you have Natalie Sandra, but let's not talk about her right now.

What do you want to talk about then?

I want to hear how you met her. No, first I want to hear how you met the doctor.

So there on the roof, luxuriating, easy in his golden skin, Stuart tells that story, not a long one, at least not in the way he tells it. It's simple to relate how he grew up on the west coast like Virge, but further south, in the small town of Rio, pronounced Rye-oh, and how he also, like Virge, had an incident in his early childhood of poisoning, although it wasn't nearly the same, because all he had was just a taste from a bottle of witch hazel plucked from the medicine cabinet, fatally drawn to it by a lithographed label, the glowing face of a little female angel with the pinkest and creamiest cheeks. For him, at the time, it was an act of drinking the girl, the angel, to absorb her and let her enter the soul by way of swallowing. And while a healthy tablespoonful of witch hazel counts as poisoning, he barely had a third of that, two sips or tiny swallows at most, and besides his parents got him to a doctor and had his stomach pumped so promptly that there was no danger of any lingering effect.

I should have had my stomach more thoroughly pumped, says Virge. I still should.

But Stuart isn't listening, and goes on to explain how by the age of twelve he was in outstanding health, but turning out to be a bad and rebellious child, undisciplined, not willing to abide by his parents' customs and discipline, because after all, living in that household was intolerable, militaristic, getting up so early, hours before dawn, the constellations out, in order to put on an itching school uniform, locking your hands behind your back when speaking to superiors, polishing your boots with your own saliva. That and much more, that's just the tip of the iceberg, and at age fifteen he simply left, went off to the city, and it's no Horatio Alger story there, as you might imagine, no industrialist or banker crossing against traffic whose life needs saving, though it's a fact that up north, in the streets of San Grande, where he ended up, it was a kind of grimy Oz, a green but not-so-emerald city, with some bright towers and Italian tiles above, up where no one could get to, but a dark place below, thick as lead and down there in the streets where he was it was mud and dust, and the smell and feel of wool and saliva because he had no other clothes than the school uniform he ran away in, and a heavy stack of fresh stinky pages, ink turning his hands from white to black, and this because right away he got a job as a paperboy. Corner news vendor, town crier, this is how he made do, earning a pocketful of nickels every week for a year or two, sleeping in the backyard of some guy, a Mr. Molieri, a news boss, who carried a golf club with him wherever he went, but didn't play golf, it was only for beating off stray dogs and in the city there are always dozens of stray dogs, dogs that when they came up to you smelled like urine, not dog but human urine, like people had been peeing on them, or worse, so you felt so sorry for them, but Molieri's approach was always to take a swing at their heads with the club. In short he was a bad boss, a bad egg. But his back property was a beautiful green yard after all, a paradise of banana trees with little clusters of fruit, inedible, or so they were warned, and figs off a tree that they were commanded to eat, as part of their salary, though they sometimes made the boys ill with such an overdose of sweetness. Molieri gave him a blanket and a place to curl up under a potting table, and in the winter he was allowed, with several other paperboys, to cuddle up close to the backyard incinerator, where they spent the cold nights with the newspapers they hadn't been able to sell that day, twisting them, one boy at each end, into the tightest possible paper logs, and, with their shirts off, casting them into the incinerator, like true laborers, stokers throwing logs into a locomotive. In the morning Molieri would knock them all awake with a firm tap on the head with the heel of the golf club, and off they'd march into the brick and oil and asphalt of dark downtown, or Tar Town as that neighborhood was called. And then, and then. Virge doesn't want to be rude but his attention wanders from such a long and detailed story, and he finds to his annoyance that all he can think about is how the story must not be true, though presumably, it is true. True enough.

He looks out, aware that Stuart is still speaking, aware that the words aren't getting through to him, across the landscape, and realizes that an actual marine fog is coming in, maybe the first tentative finger of a storm. Over the ocean the clouds are gelatinous and dove gray. It's not a pretty evening. When Mont built the platform he didn't square it up quite straight, so it sits at a pitch, slight but noticeable, so that things can and do slide off if they go unwatched, and even the chairs they sit on shift downhill a little at a time.

Surprisingly, Stuart continues, and Virge is listening again, his story turned into a Horatio Alger story after all. One day he was approached by an elderly man wearing a fashionable suit, but also a black and formless hat that sat on his head like it had been melted there. He was coming up to Stuart in the middle of Tar Town, outside the hotel, to purchase a paper, and after standing reading a moment, not yet paying his nickel, taking his hat off to scratch his head and letting fall a mane of cold white-yellow hair, this old man turned to Stuart the newsboy who stood there holding out his hand waiting to be paid, and said something to the effect that the newspaper kid shouldn't be standing there gawking but unafraid of him, as he was a person children ought to be afraid of. He was a doctor, he said at last, and could afford to pay, and that he was one of the last good ones. And Stuart was surprised because it was so odd that anyone who bought a paper would bother to speak intelligently to the boy, take time out, say a word, and it seemed more peculiar because the doctor talked on and on, obligingly, almost as though to an equal, mentioning what an impression it makes to see a boy working and not begging, as self-confident men must always have an aversion to beggars, and wanted to know what Stuart thought of the news in the papers he was selling. Here was a chance question that changed his life, it turned out, because Stuart realized with a rush of embarrassment that he had never actually read more than a few words of any of the hundreds of papers he'd had in his possession over the months, he'd been so fixed on the selling, as well as the twisting into logs and burning, and also there was the fact that he was not the greatest reader in the world. Well of course he'd noticed the dramatic and exclamatory banner headlines, and recognized certain names under photographs, such as those of presidents of countries, or actors or criminals or so forth, or all of the above, but now he could only regard himself with shame, confronting the fact that he had never for a moment felt that the story might have some value or meaning to him, and how sad to think of those words burned up in Molieri's backyard when what he could have been doing all that time was lifting his mind to a higher dimension, through the process of constant reading and review of the world's grandest and/or most scandalous developments. And perhaps because the embarrassment was so acute, he suddenly felt inclined to insult the old man, and told him to kiss off, to take a hike, some words to that effect. Yet what ended up happening was that the gentleman, who naturally was none other than Dr. Flanig, seemed intent on overlooking the insult. His next action was to pull out a crisp dollar bill, buy all of Stuart's papers on the spot, toss them in the back seat of his car which was parked a few steps away, and drive the two of them home to his house in the hills, where he let the boy spend the afternoon alone in a large echoing room, playing records and reading, at last, every word of that day's San Grande Examiner.

This went on for several days, interrupted by decent meals and discussions of what it was that appeared in the news. But then a difficult decision had to be made, on whether to play along with the scheme that was unfolding here—the notion, already strongly hinted, and quickly understood, that the doctor was willing to groom him, teach him some part of his medical knowledge, and so bring him into the business as his assistant, at terms superior to those of a newspaper boy. The other choice was to give a succinct no to any such proposal and keep his freedom, because Flanig could readily be viewed as just another form of authority waiting to take command, to rob Stuart of his soul, to turn it into grist for the medical mill somehow, et cetera. But after all, in his current state, he could count himself as little more than Molieri's serf, or worse. In the end he took the leap. He went to work for Flanig, thinking that one form of boss always follows another, and you just have to be careful to be on the lookout constantly for better bosses. Isn't it the case always that the only solution is to find the best boss possible, until you are the best boss possible yourself? Or the worst.

In another way, what it boiled down was the choice between hardness and softness, of sleeping in Molieri's yard and waking up to the harsh urban dawn, or sleeping in an alcove, just off the consultation room, and waking up to the urban dawn filtered through a little stained-glass window that cast a pair of blue and blood-red diamonds on the bed.

So, concludes Stuart, I opted for the luxuries of the life of a doctor.

But you're not a doctor.

I know.

I mean Flanig isn't a doctor, either.

Oh, but he is.

I mean he's also, what do you call them, an in-commonist. Didn't he try to convert you to that point of view?

Oh but you see, he never converts boys, smirked Stuart.

Well, politics are beyond me. My dad kept me from it.

My parents, muses Stuart, raised me with detailed values. But I threw all that off when I left home, so I don't know. I guess the doctor and I never felt we needed to say much on that point. Whatever you were, whatever he was, that's not how either of you are now. You mean how Flanig is weakening? How he's gone rotten inside? He's not much to look at now, but he was a dynamo back then, when I first knew him. And so what that he's an in-commonist. You could say that these days about almost anybody with a big mouth.

So who will cure the doctor? Virge inquires, after a long pause.

You mean, who wants to make an effort to get his mind back to him? Or him back to his mind? I'm not sure we'd want that. We have to figure out what we want.

The next evening, Stuart picks up at the point where he had left off, the point of the story where he had moved in to Dr. Flanig's apartments, had decided to become an apprentice, and how it was that he started this new life with no more than the clothes on his back and a sturdy masculine urge to succeed. It's a long story, the way Stuart tells it, and during one pause, where there is time to contemplate the sunset again, Virge gets offered a cigarette. In fact Stuart has been offering cigarettes since he arrived, and Virge has consistently refused them, but here at last is the moment of surrender. He takes one, Stuart lights it, then Virge adjusts the length of it between his lips, as if measuring it.

Naturally, a moment later, he starts in coughing, but not violently, and soon takes a few more puffs, only to cough again. As for Stuart, his smoking is debonair, and, even more debonair is how he pays no attention to Virge's noisy inauguration into this vice, and begins his account of his first days as the doctor's assistant, tending to a stream of patients in Flanig's consultation room. It was a gold mine of illness, given Flanig's high rates, and Stuart, paid well, learned to perform his assigned tasks, such as weighing and measuring patients, learning the multiple switches of the x-ray machine so that the doctor could linger over the films, tracing the bones again and again with his fingers, the diagnosis always focusing on the skeleton, no matter what the complaint. It was at this early stage of his career that Stuart became a disciple. That is, he fell under the spell of Flanig's striking features and theatrically draped white hair, the electrical smile, the teeth so bright they seemed shellacked, implying genius, since if the doctor's own bones, as expressed in the teeth, were so white and straight and sound, he could surely straighten and whiten everyone else's bones as well. And the patients, unanimously, swore that he did.

In time, Stuart's adoration moderated. But he did settle into the belief that he was lucky, that he'd taken the proper path in life. And all was fine until one day poor Stuart discovered something awkward—the nauseating spectacle of Flanig up on the examining table with his pants down, a female patient underneath, bringing under his spell a woman he had cured, through bone work, of hysteria. The husband, however, filed suit for reckless philandering and alienation of affection, even though to hear Flanig's much more serenely told side of the story, it was her, the hysteria patient, who had first spoken of passion, and not the other way around.

To Stuart, the whole episode was disillusioning. Eighteen years old by then, he was called on to testify in court, and couldn't in the end forgive the doctor for pressuring him to state, under oath, that the woman had also made romantic overtures to him, Stuart, which was patently untrue. From then on things were markedly more formal between the doctor and his apprentice. Stuart could no longer think of himself as something like a son to Flanig. He could remain a dutiful worker for an employer who, in return, would overlook Stuart's occasional mistakes, but never offer praise for moments of hard work and cleverness.

Look at my hands, interrupts Virge.

What about them?

So dry. They need lotion. Some of that nice stuff you used before.

Don't interrupt me for that, please. I'm just going on with my story.

Sorry.

Oh, but meanwhile there's something funny I can tell you about your hand. Do you know there's a part called the snuffbox?

No.

Here, go like this.

And Stuart has Virge flex and hold his right hand out in the air, palm down, and flex the thumb in such a way that the two tendons that run up into the thumb from the wrist become prominent, and there, in the space between them, the skin sinks in such a way that a little natural depression is formed. This, explains Stuart, is the so-called anatomical snuffbox and it is one of the many proper labelings you learn when you learn the parts of the human body.

Can you sit there and recite them all? wonders Virge.

Not much! The hand, for example, is a tough study. All those muscles and bones would give anyone, except the doctor, a headache. To mention just a few, there's the trapezium, the trapezoid, the trapecarpal. All those and many more. Still it's true to say that I know the names of many. I like to give recitals like that, and I'll give you one someday.

You said you never read the pamphlet.

Well of course I've picked up a lot of things, from just hanging around.

What do you call—what do you call a girl's sex part?

Ah. That one I also know. You call it, if you want to be polite, her geranium. Impolite, her peony.

Next morning, after Almy and Flanig go off on a walk, Stuart concludes his story over coffee and more cigarettes, relating an incident that took place only a few months previous.

An attractive young woman came in to see Flanig, and Stuart's first thought was oh, no, here we go again, but in fact she turned out to have an interesting condition, something not dissimilar to Virge's. Her name was Phoebe, like the little black-headed bird, and she wore a black veil to complete the association. In her case, her hands, not unlike Virge's, were paralyzed, but actually it was only the fingers, meaning she had lost the ability to move or flex her fingers in any way, and what was more peculiar was that, although she seemed under the veil like a beautiful and healthy girl, none of her ten fingers could be uncurled, but all stayed strongly clenched and retracted into the palms, like clams or some other types of shellfish retracted into their shells, and this one small detail, though you'd think it wouldn't, pretty clearly ruined her beauty, and made her whole comportment vaguely molluskan and retiring. In the consultation room Flanig called in

Stuart and assigned him the task of soothing the girl's nerves to the point where he could take her hands in his and try to physically pry the fingers away from the palms, so that they could at least be examined a little before they had a chance to retract.

So what did you do? asks Virge, on the edge of his seat, selfishly more interested in this story than in any others he's heard.

And Stuart goes on to explain how he, with great effort, did manage to gain the girl's confidence, did manage to unpry the fingers, the girl groaning and protesting all the while, and it was like pulling a nail out of a board with your bare hands, and finally, with some help from Flanig, who up to that point had seemed fussy about touching the girl, Stuart got her palms down flat on the desk, fingers spread wide, and went so far as to grab a pair of bronze bookends and place one on top of each hand to keep a solid pressure there and prevent a recoil. Flanig then did something unusual. Instead of palpating her hand, feeling each individual bone in its turn, he only took a large syringe and injected his famous yellow fluid, one shot into each finger, and after a few minutes the girl relaxed, and dried her tears, even gave a hint of a smile, and reported a feeling of vitality coursing through the tissues of both hands, and when they took the bookends away she smiled and lifted her hands and artfully danced her fingers in the air as if playing the piano or performing some Greek dance. Then, with clear expressions of gratitude, she paid the bill, took her leave, and when Stuart looked out the window, suddenly attracted to this beauty as to no other, the girl was gliding down the drab sidewalk, still playing her invisible piano or harp or whatever it was, all the way to where he could see her no longer.

What do you think happened when the fluid went into the girl's hands? asks Virge, anxiously, perspicaciously, taking a drag off the remains of his cigarette and holding in the smoke as if an answer must come before he can exhale.

I mean, he whispers, through clenched teeth, was it designed to make her better or make her worse?

I don't know. It didn't do anything to her at all. You have to shut up and wait for the end of the story.

Virge blurts out the smoke, and follows it with one more terrific fit of coughing, his last, at that moment becoming a jaded and bona fide smoker.

And here, says Stuart, is the end of the story. This young woman, graceful, lovely, alabaster in complexion, whose name was Elmwood, Phoebe Elmwood, came back a week later, and what do you suppose? Everything had reverted. Her hands were just as wound up and all folded in on themselves like before, probably more so, and she showed up in tears, which could nearly break a guy's heart, because, in a way, I had fallen in love, but only with the version of her that was healthy, the one I'd seen walking away down the sidewalk, not the new one. So, and by this time I'm sick to my stomach, I went back to work, and got a good hold on the fingers to try to uncurl them, like before. But this time she seemed to be in much worse pain, and she screamed at me, like I was pulling her fingers right out of her hands, tearing them out at the roots you would have thought, and all the while she was clubbing me on my spine with her other fist, hammering, because her fist was like a hammer, and I only got as far as seeing that her nails had cut her skin, that there were pools of blood in her palms, and I was in tears by then too. And then Flanig came in the room and told me to let go of her and to fall to my knees to pray, which he'd never asked before or ever mentioned even. So there I was, praying in any way I could imagine, the give us some daily bread part, and so forth, whatever came to mind, and then he ordered her to pray as well, but she wouldn't, she just went back to cowering, saying that she couldn't pray because she wasn't a believer. Then it was Flanig's turn to turn on all his charm, all his hypnotic powers, saying he was an unbeliever too, just trying to calm her down I suppose, because it was the first time I'd ever heard him say that. And she did calm down. But then he went to her and started touching her elsewhere, as if diagnosing her, but I already knew he had different intentions, and he even started speaking frankly about romance, as if his touching her in that way of his would be a sure if dirty cure, but this made things much worse, and she started screaming again, only this time it was the word assault, the word battery, and unfortunately the doc laughed at her, and insulted her, which was a terrible mistake because our Miss Elmwood turned out to be the daughter of a big deal family, the kind you're not allowed to insult. And that was that. The arrest warrant, and so on. Just when things looked pretty bad, we got the phone call from your mom, from Almy, and here we are.

Did he change his name? asks Virge. I mean, is Flanig a new name for him?

No. No! But I guess he didn't need to. So far they haven't come after us. Out here in the sticks nobody knows who you are or where you are.

But you're sure Flanig didn't change his name? When I look at him I get the feeling his name is, I don't know, Albertson or something.

I don't know about that, shrugs Stuart. But no, he didn't change his name and neither did I. I guess we felt we could start over just as ourselves. And now look! We're here because we don't have anywhere else to go. He doesn't, at least. I don't know about me. I need the job.

Nowhere else, ponders Virge.

And it's especially important to Flanig, as a married man, to get back to having some sort of a practice, and bringing in fresh patients, such as yourself.

As a married man.

Yes.

You're saying he had a wife? I mean, has a wife.

No. Yes. In San Grande, living up there now, I think. I never met her, since they lived apart. In that sense they're really not married. Like you. I mean like your mom and dad.

California is not Greenland and no region of China is scattered with bones. Standing before the mirror, sporting the wig, Virge is not an Indian, and appears to himself, expressionless, more like a heavy lidded and jowly girl, who has poured black hair dye everywhere, the wig so light-absorbing and dingy that it looks like something found on the highway, half alive.

He stays put though, even feels a transmission coming on, but loses it. There and gone. It's like a tingling at the crown of the head, and he waves his hands above his head in an effort to snatch it back, whatever it was. There and gone. And he has to wonder if it's the most crucial message of them all, and whether he can get it later, in a retransmission, or is it lost, and that's the end of that. Or if the messages are the fruit of his own imagination.

Which is more likely? he asks himself, emphasizing each word. It's true that if he's not in front of the mirror, and not wearing the wig, he hears nothing.

Whenever asked if he will join them on the roof, the doctor reacts with pleasure, followed by an ambivalent grumbling, followed by an interval of nasty spitting.

No, he'd better not, says Almy. I can just see you two having a laugh at his expense.

But one day there are no objections at all, and Flanig himself petulantly insists on making the climb. As it turns out, it's their last night there, the final night on the roof. Almy consents to join in as well, and even offers to provide certain hot drinks, called cinnamon sloops, which she has recently learned the preparation of, and Virge and Stuart are to bring up other snacks and refreshments, just like the first time. Virge goes up early with a bottle of pickled eggs, and fiddles with the radio again to see if it might be possible to tune in something. Stuart and Almy and Flanig climb up a little later, Stuart with bread and Almy with the tray of cinnamon drinks in jelly glasses, along with, coincidentally, a jar of jelly she made the year before out of blackberries growing wild down the road, though at this point it's impossible to associate such kitchen arts with the woman Virge finds sitting across from him, this sophisticate, this farm flapper, perfumed, laughing in tiny chirps like a parakeet and slurping at her drink, like someone in a shabby downtown apartment. She's not, Virge notices for the first time, wearing her wedding ring. How long has that been the case? Answer unknown. The ring of pale finger skin revealed by this absence stands out in contrast, and so the paleness alone must signify her status to the world, like a missing arm testifying to war.

But then silence reigns in every mind, so Virge just flops back in his chair, as do the other three, and they eat, mutely, out of a long hunger, and peer out bug-eyed over the edge of their jelly jars, no one actually drinking after they've had the first somewhat overpowering sip, all leaning and looking, not at each other, but in the same direction, to the west.

The ocean turns one color after another. For a while it's a brilliant silver green, and then, as if another liquid gets poured in, it fades to gray.

California is a paradise for everyone who hates their past, says Stuart.

Isn't that a song? asks Virge, but then the air smells for a moment like heavy truck exhaust, an odor which sometimes drifts all the way down from the highway, and when Virge wrinkles his nose Stuart says no, don't, wait a minute, don't be such a fussbudget, because that's the smell of progress, the smell of civilization coming to our part of the state.

And, speaking of civilization, look what I've brought you, says Stuart next, not missing a beat, holding up a big urn of skin lotion, like a tennis trophy, over his head. It's clear to see that he's ripped off the original label and replaced it with one of his own design, a piece of paper he's inked up with clunky fleurs de lis and the words Sturdy Patience, in gothic letters, and though it's not too skillful, still he's gone to so much trouble that Virge is touched by the display of friendship, and then thinks, but how good a friend is he if we're paying him to be my friend? But then remembers, for the umpteenth time, no, they're paying us. All of it, Virge can't help but note, all of it is a muddle and a mare's nest.

So he takes the jar and with a twist of the lid opens it on the spot so he can dip in and work some into his hands without waiting, and of course he proclaims to all how great it feels, though all along he has the feeling that it's a different brand—it just doesn't have that same perfect smell as the other stuff, which was so pepperminty, like stomach medicine, while this is more along the lines of petroleum jelly, which would be all right but that it goes onto the skin in a cold and lumpy style, not absorbing and therefore able, like the other one, to plunge straight from the pores to the bloodstream.

Oh, says Almy. I hope that's something to rub on my forehead for the headache.

Sorry you're not feeling well, simpers Stuart, acting the dandy.

No, I mean I'd like it for when I do get a bad headache, she explains with a sigh and a pursed, doll-like smile, reaching over for a dab of Sturdy Patience. Virge has rarely seen her so content and can't help but think it's because she has become what she always wanted to be, a dame on a roof, a floozy at the pinnacle of success.

Crows fly by in a V formation, as if they are mocking or perhaps learning from the ducks. The ocean is a different color now. The sun is on its way down, apparently, but at this point is just a smear of bright mud, high over the water. The staccato yawps of the birds fracture the evening silence in a friendly way.

Almy sings in a quiet way some snatch of song: There is one future for those who live, duh duh duh, in the past, she sings, no past for those who live, dah dah dah, in the future. It's an interesting choice of words as far as Virge is concerned, the ones he was trying to remember, because they bring up images out of images, pictures burned into his mind, woodburned if his brain were wood. He steals a glance at pensive Stuart, and swells his chest and neck so much as to almost be choked by his tie, suddenly convinced that his companion will hear those lyrics and calmly deduce from them Virge's discomfort, and so by that route come to an abrupt understanding of human nature. Or a human's nature.

I can't help but remember, says Almy, how we used to have bonfires. That's back when I was a little girl, I'm saying. It's when I came here to spend time with Grandma. That's not to say we built the bonfires ourselves. No, but the kids would come down alternate weekends and light fires on the beach, and so we'd walk on down there and just watch from a distance and that was all we did do. But there was something funny and wicked about it too, I guess, because Grandma wouldn't let me get too close.

What is it? croaks Dr. Flanig, and Virge's first impulse is to laugh at the poor man's deafness, or obtuseness, until he realizes that he's not sure what Almy's talking about either, or at least doesn't understand where such bonfires might be, or have been.

Stuart, for his part, seems impatient with the way the evening is going, and starts squirming in his chair, shifting in it in a way that the arm of it, given the downward slope of the platform, starts to lean against his companion's chair. Stuart won't or can't stop and finally his body is pressing down hard against Virge's arm, like the arm of a fat man, or a bully, and both chairs begin to tilt, to the point that there's danger of one them tilting right over, which, if it were to happen, could mean both chairs going over the edge.

Help help, squeaks Virge, half as a joke, half as a real plea.

It's just like that other time, snickers Almy, when your father pretended to throw you off the roof. Now Stuart wants to push you off the roof it looks like.

It's more serious than that, replies Virge, emphatically, and he goes quiet for a moment but then barks out all kinds of orders, until Stuart stands up, grabs Virge's chair, and semi-heroically slides it and heaves it up, with one hand, out of harm's way.

Well, it is kind of funny what happened, says Stuart smoothly.

How do you mean? asks Almy.

Well, I certainly didn't plan to keep pushing him. I was just trying to make myself comfortable.

But Virge takes it badly. He's never raised a hand to anyone, but the time has come, he believes, to be forthright and violent and not open to interpretation. So Stuart then is the one to get one of those not-very-hard punches in the arm that men give each other, sometimes in a friendly way, in this case not.

Virge does no more than that, and is surprised at himself for having done that much. That's all he does, or perhaps will ever do. Although he does then accept a cigarette from a grinning Stuart, and smokes it serenely, expertly, quite aware of the delight he brings his mother in doing so.

Oh my boy, she says, shivering.

Enough, enough.

When you're jake you're jake, she laughs.

I'm more bumpy than all of you, jokes Virge, mishandling the current slang.

The result is silent disapproval.

And afterwards I'll just throw myself off the roof, he continues, finding them unbearable, and this inspires Almy to go on to tell another old story that, however, isn't too different, of how Mont once played a falling-off-the-roof joke on her. It was while he was hammering and sawing away at his roof patio, and she came out with a tray of sandwiches and found Mont lying on the ground at the side of the house, unconscious or dead and with his tools all around him like he'd fallen off along with everything he was holding. Naturally, she just about lost her mind. But just as she dropped the tray and rushed to help him, he jumped straight to his feet, and pointed at her, and doubled over, and basically just whooped it up and laughed her to scorn. Oh what a funny guy, she has to admit now, but she has to say that she never really forgave him for it.

Still, you can't help but wonder about that man, she concludes.

A roof, says Virge, brings out the best in everybody.

Still, in private, he is desperate to get away once and for all from the roof, from the house. From all sameness. The stories are thick bland substances that forever circulate and twist about him like mud or cotton or hay, and what's most galling is that his father has escaped the sameness, and his mother too has escaped it, in her way, yet he has gotten absolutely nowhere.

Events will intervene to separate the three of them. In this moment, one of their last together, the four of them go under the spell of the sea breeze. Stuart puffs up into straightest posture in his chair, and his hair in the late light takes the color of peanut shells. At one point he does a little trick in his chair, jumping vertically while gripping the arm rests, and locking his elbows so that he can quiver, like a minor gymnast, a couple of inches above the seat, arms rock solid but then not all that strong, then close to collapse.

Stuart fits in here, says Virge, done with his snit, edging toward equilibrium. Unlike us, Mother, he belongs to the beach. You could find Stuart or someone like him washed up there, living like a castaway, with his eyeglasses to use as lenses for starting fires. A Robinson Crusoe of California, that's what he is, and who would be surprised.

Gosh, thanks, says Stuart, looking pleased with himself and everybody.

Then the more serious smoking begins, and they all end up inhaling meditatively for a while, tossing their butts over the edge of the platform, then savoring both Almy's and nature's perfume. Virge spends some time studying the sliver of silver moon, trying to remember something interesting to say about it, but when he looks down, discouraged, Stuart has yet another surprise for him, produced from nowhere. It's a little iron dumbbell that he lays down on the platform at Virge's toes, a five-pound weight, or less, a weakling's caliber. It's an heirloom and an antique, Stuart explains, that must have belonged to Virge's dad, because look here are the initials DB nastily scratched into one of the spheres. It's something he came across in a closet off the living room while poking around, and now Virge, at Stuart's urging, stands up straight as he can manage and slowly lifts the thing from waist-level, lifts it with one hand up to the area near his chin. Lifts, and resolves to duplicate the action.

Uno, dos, tres! laughs Almy.

And so on.

It's something to see, says Almy, how well you two get along.

Meaning what? inquires Virge, suspicious of certain things she says.

We're the picture of health, puts in Stuart. And smart too, he adds, lowering his voice, as if to share a secret.

That's partly what I mean, adds Almy. How beautiful the two of you are.

But did you know, continues Stuart, that we're in the habit of inventing labor-saving gadgets?

Where's Doctor Flanig, asks Virge, raising his voice. I need my doctor. Where is he? I wanted him to see me engaged in this. In this muscle activity.

But the doctor has slipped away, and this now becomes cause for some alarm.

Oh Lord, says Almy. Did he fall off?

No, no, is Stuart's reply. He went down the ladder a few minutes ago. I thought you saw him.

I thought I did too. I mean I thought I saw him stay.

Virge, disappointed that the doctor isn't there to see his exercise routine, decides he'll just toss the little dumbbell over the edge of the roof, but then thinks better of it, given that the old man might be down there, so he waits a while, till his eyes can clearly make out the empty tulip bed, and then, aiming carefully, heaves it precisely there, where it lands among the flowers with a thud. But no one is paying the slightest attention, so Virge sits down heavily, forgotten, full of the dispiriting notion that the roof magic has evaporated forever. That they won't be back.

A colder wind off the ocean hits them, the sky starts to turn a little purple and ocher, and the three of them shudder simultaneously, watching each other shake, then nodding with knowing smiles.

A time for telling secrets, says Stuart, but no one takes him up on it.

Spread out below, designed for their private delight, the scenery seems as if it has been transplanted there from some alternate, colder continent, especially when you look at the way the trees stretch north for miles and miles, like those of some forest surviving from the first days of the world.

Virge explains, and is pleased with himself for finally remembering something he knows, perhaps culled from Jansens, that once all this area, or perhaps somewhere further north, was home to none other than the woolly mammoth, and sundry other prodigies of primeval times.

Gracious, repeats Almy. I mean gracias.

But she's yawning and on the verge of leaving.

Then, as if to throw the glare of present times on Virge's observation, a group of people just then comes into view, traversing a beach that's visible where the cliffs curve to the west, and it's possible to tell, even at this distance, lit as they are by the orange sunset, that they're mostly teenagers, or older, young people in orange skin and sleek black modern bathing suits, each one grasping a log or length of lumber as big as each can manage without falling, though some of them waver and stumble kind of comically on the terrain that is really more rocks than sand. Virge, still full of the urge to talk and observe, states how this is a welcome development, a tremendous coincidence, given Almy's previous mention of bonfires, and that he's going to stay right there in his seat on the roof, as long as it takes to watch how things unfold.

But Stuart is barely listening, or watching, and just sits there puffing on a cigarette, having assumed a posture of slouching luxury, casually acclimated to the rolling cold, while Almy stands, wobbles, wishes all a good night, and starts down the ladder. Still, her departure doesn't seem to have anything to do with the young people, because at the last minute she raises her head back up above the roofline and explains that she has to go attend to the doctor, make sure all's well down there.

She can be so annoyingly sweet, says Stuart.

What's wrong with you tonight? asks Virge.

I'll play along. What is wrong with me tonight? Nothing, I guess.

I mean that . . . you're good at . . . doing things for me. You found my dad's dumbbell and that was generous. Not to mention the lotion, and that sort of thing.

You're the only dumbbell I see here. You're in a fine fettle, I must say.

What's that—a fettle?

I don't know, it's just what you say when things are fine. So look what else I found in the closet, says Stuart, as if to change the subject. They're your dad's too, maybe.

And Stuart produces from under his chair a pair of binoculars, heavy and black, the largest possible aperture and power, and raises the lenses to his eyes in order to peer out at the folks on the beach.

Stuart, do you suppose that paralysis recurs? Is recurring?

No.

Because I think it is. I think it's hitting me or going to hit me in a minute.

It's just the cold. Here, let me put more Sturdy Patience on you, if that's what you want.

Stuart puts the binoculars down in the seat of his chair and bends over to work on Virge's hands, but after only a moment of this application of the inferior and smelly product, Virge folds his hands into his stomach.

No that's all right. I'm all right I think. I was wrong. There's nothing wrong with me now. I have to stop worrying about it. To the untrained eye, I'm fine. To the trained eye, I'm really close to being fine.

Later, the first glimmerings of a beach bonfire appear, and it's so quiet, with the wind blowing just right, that they can catch snatches of the voices, and, it seems to Virge that he can hear even the whispers of those who have broken off from the group to tell secrets or arrange assignations. Finally the fire roars up like an explosive device, turns into a blaze the size of a house up in flames, and ringed all around it now are the teenagers, holding hands, and they are singing a song with lyrics that, as far as Virge can tell, are in a foreign language.

Well, Patience, what do you think? That's gotten to be quite a fire down there.

What? Oh yes. Frightening people, really. Sickening to more civilized folk.

Now who has the fettle?

Suddenly Almy is back, clambering back on to the platform with a paper bag that turns out to hold a thermos, and a couple of old china cups, and she proceeds to pour steaming cups of hot cocoa for the two of them.

What do you think of the bonfire, Mrs. B?

Well I never like to see the young people up close.

Why's that?

Their bad behavior. Their clothes. Their destiny on the day of reckoning. His lips are near the trumpet!

Come on now, urges Stuart. Bad in what way?

Bad and worse, she continues, cheerfully. You know, in olden times, the Indians here built bonfires in order to throw white people right in the flames. Then they'd take the ashes—ashes from the poor pioneer's bones—and make bone china out of it, and make nasty little cups and saucers for their Indian rituals.

Ah, Bone China, says Stuart, winking at Virge. We're back in that country.

It's a shame that we aren't really, Virge answers back. I'm sorry that we never made it there. To that part of China.

In any case, maybe that burning people business works out all right in some ways.

But Virge is lost in thought, staring at the way Stuart holds his cup of cocoa, then imitating it with his own fingers, making them hook perfectly around his cup like intelligent worms. Hookworms.

Patience?

What? asks Virge.

Oh I don't know, answers Stuart, so slouched in his chair he seems half-melted. Given that we're going to hell anyway.

Speak for yourself, snaps Almy. You boys are too much for me.

Mrs. B., says Stuart, straightening himself. What I'm thinking of doing, really, is climbing down and going over to investigate this bonfire, or bone fire, or whatever it's called. Maybe join in the fun. Maybe, if they're real Indians, they'll toss me in the fire. Or maybe I'll play the Indian, and I'll do all the tossing. What I want to know is, who's coming with me?

I don't know, says Virge, throwing a sidelong look at his mother. I'm not sure.

Stuart doesn't move, but after a moment pulls a little flask from somewhere under his sweater. First there is some unscrewing to be done, and then he trickles some of what's inside into his cup of cocoa, and smiles broadly at the other two, and Virge thinks, this is good, the alcohol is Stuart's way of joining the beach party without going to the bother of walking down to the beach. And for a while it seems true: no one gets up or stirs in any way. The three of them just sit and watch the distant fire burn and burn.

They're not Indians, says Almy, finally. They're just kids. I don't mind it, not really. And the two of you ought to go down there and be a little more sociable, if you ask me.

This is what Almy says instead of what Virge would prefer her to say, which would be something like, Don't go down there, my darling boy, because it's dangerous and it looks like they're raising hell down there and think what might happen to someone who doesn't have as much vigor or vinegar or vitamins as the others.

And then, because nobody makes a move, Almy visibly relaxes, and, after taking a tiny sip from Stuart's flask, opens up, and talks and talks, and tells a story of her own, one Virge has never heard before. It's all about how she used to come to the farm as a child when her grandparents owned it, and how she was their guest, not to mention their darling, and their pearl of great price. How every day she was allowed to go out riding, because of course they had horses then, everyone in the world had dozens of horses then, and the one Grandma and Grandpa kept there for her was a gelding named Dime, and she could ride old Dime, best horse in the world, along the beach, clapping up the water into froth, his hooves nearly silent in the damp spongy sand. But then comes the sad part of the story, about how the farm failed one year in a drought, and the crops died and the horses, even Dime, had to be sold to the glue factory, and how then there wasn't much to do at the place for years except mope around, though Almy kept coming, summer after summer, trying to recapture the good times of the past, splashing in the waves as if she were a horse, but it was never the same.

And then there's the much sadder part about how her grandparents got to be old aged, and infirm, and finally it turned out that both of them passed away on the same day, which happened to be Almy's sixteenth birthday, dying from the same run-in with the flu, a day when it wouldn't stop raining and they had to take both coffins to the cemetery in the downpour in the back of an open wagon, and how the two graves were so full of water by the time they got there that the coffins, when they went in, just bobbed there like wood canoes, until somebody drilled some holes in them, and they sank. And it's interesting, she explains, how a year later, after getting married in San Grande, and moving permanently into the old house with Virge's father, she found a box all wrapped up in gift paper in the back of a closet, a birthday present they'd hidden there just before they died, and when she opened it what did she find but an old German chocolate cake, now turned to nothing but a collapse of dust and hard candy, her name still spelled out in icing on the top, along with the vague and broken image of what might have been a horse. And she still had to wonder, was the cake supposed to mean that they were going to get her a new horse, or was it just in memory of the days when she did have a horse? Or was it a horse on the cake at all, or maybe a dog or nothing at all?

Well you've bent like rubber and stuck like glue, says Stuart, waving his cigarette in the air, and seems to mean it in a less than sarcastic way.

In any event Almy doesn't hear it at all because by the time he gets these words out she is already slipping away down the ladder without a sound. Hare go down the foxhole.

Did you hear that? asks Virge, a little later.

Hear what?

How she suggested that I'm the type who doesn't know how to snip the apron strings.

Didn't hear it. I don't think she did say that. I think she may have said the opposite. That you know how to tie them.

Sometimes it's wiser to remain in of doors than out of doors.

Aw, you're crazy. What about how we went to the movies. We tried to go to the movies and you had the time of your life.

I mean I know what I look like. Not beautiful, not like she said. I'm sad and ugly or something. Melancholy. Man in the moon man.

Okay. Maybe so. It's not so bad as you think. And why bring it up now?

I'm just thinking how Indians would throw me in their fire. When they see how I look.

Nah, the Indians I know are swell. They welcome you. Feed you. Befriend you. And then throw you in the fire.

Neither of them moves. All actions, Virge thinks, are equivalent, and all actions, given enough time, are doomed to reach a similar inconsequence. So why start something new, like meeting new people? Opportunities will only display one's limitations, one's silences. Opportunities will only rise, and then fall.

Look, says Stuart, just close your eyes for a minute.

Is this something you learned from Flanig?

No. And again, no. Remember on our car ride, how we played the glance-away game? Do you remember any of your snapshots?

Mm hmm.

Okay, so close your eyes and bring one image to the top of your mind. To the platform. Okay. You got it?

Yes.

Now this is what I do. It's what I taught myself when I was a paperboy. I get that picture clear in my mind, and then I move forward from there. It's like all the paths cross there, at that moment, and you can choose a different path. What's your image right now?

A crow landing on a wire.

So you see, you don't know what happened next. You control the crow. What happens next?

It lands on the wire and gets an electric shock. It falls to the ground on fire.

Choose a different future.

Okay, it changes its mind and swoops back up. It flies out over the road and follows us, flying just behind the car.

Better. Much better.

And then it flies ahead of us. It's leading the way. It wants us to follow.

Where to?

Over the cliff, says Virge, his eyes squinted shut. It flies out over the ocean. The Bellevue breaks through the guard rail and does a swan dive, falling for a long time, turning, spinning, honking its horn, then it slips into the ocean quietly, hardly a splash. Then cut to you and me, hanging by our fingers from the cliff edge.

Beautiful, Patience. It's beautiful.

What about you? What's your picture?

I'm borrowing from yours. I'm freezing the scene right where the crow flies out over the ocean. But I'm changing it a little. It's Flanig at the wheel. He's the one hypnotized by the crow. So it's him that crashes through the guard rail, and there's no hanging on to any cliff edge.

The hot cocoa is all gone, and Stuart sips straight from his little flask. The breeze feels to both of them, without their saying so, like cold spirit hands flitting around them, brushing them on the face, the arms. Staying on the roof becomes more of a task than a pleasure. The moon comes out and sits directly behind their heads, where they never see it. A swarm of wasps, out late, sweeps by low over their heads but the three on the roof are only aware of a passing warmth and buzz in the air above them.

Look at it, look where I'm pointing. Virge follows Stuart's finger and there finds a light falling down from the sky. It's a comet, isn't it?

No, impossible. It's a shooting star.

No look, we're both wrong, it's just a little thing, it's not part of astronomy at all, it's lying on the beach.

Excuse me?

It's fireworks. Maybe they've got some little rockets. Ooh, there's another one. And another.

The voices of the teenagers still drift at times to their ears, despite the distance, and Virge, is sure he hears one of them say something about him, about Virge, but he can't catch what it is. Maybe he could hear them, he thinks, if he were wearing the wig. But it shall never be donned again. Well maybe not too often. The sky above the trees is punctuated now with flames that are more painful to the eye than beautiful. In this case no, it's not fireworks but instead, as Stuart describes the scene now, peering through the binoculars, the kids on the beach have brought bows and arrows with them, that they are holding the tips of the arrows in the bonfire until they catch, then shooting them into the sky, like ancient archers trying to burn down some walled citadel. But most of the arrows land in the water and some kids splash out to grab them before they float out beyond reach.

It looks like fun, says Stuart, but Virge reminds him that there is always the peril of fire, though as soon as he says this he regrets that, once again, he may appear too timid, too neurotic, at least compared to Stuart, who seems so adult and jaded this evening.

Name one thing that you're really just dying to do, says Stuart, taking a last noisy drink from his flask, then peering down with one eye deep into its interior.

I mean that one of the arrows could drift back behind them, says Virge, worried in spite of himself, not wanting to be worried in the least. It could fall. Into the trees. Not the pines right there, but back toward us, back into the gum trees. Think about eucalyptus trees for a second, how flammable those things are.

And he thinks of a cedar he has thought of before, a tree that is deep within him, narrow, nervous, on fire.

Stuart, these kids are idiots, stresses Virge. You don't know what I know. It's eucalyptus. Oil-soaked rags. Carboys of gasoline. You surprise me. I mean it surprises me what you don't know sometimes.

Oh, now, I shan't have any patience with you. Get it? Patience? Anyway, kids today know what they're doing. They're fine young people, I'll wager. I happen to know some of them, you know.

Okay, let's say you do, admits Virge. But that doesn't mean that maybe one of them can't turn out to be not terribly good at the arrow shooting. And that would be a shame, to lose some of those trees. Not a shame, but more like a crime, more like natural assault and battery.

I'm not thinking about fires at all. I'm only thinking that we go down and ask to join the idiots club. To mix and mingle. See, then we could get them to stop.

You go. I've got a phone call to make. I'm going to call Natalie Sandra. See what she says.

Stuart glances at Virge, smiles vacantly, and then, surprise, lifts himself out of his chair, first using the gymnast's lift and elbow lock to get up, and then, like someone climbing down into a swimming pool, dips out of sight down the ladder.

Then it turns solitary and cold as Greenland, mercury dipping, he thinks, into the fifties. Fifty below? There are a few mosquitoes that buzz in his ears but don't seem to land among the dark fine hairs on his forearms. How do they stand the weather? Virge wonders, getting up, opening himself like a compass, getting colder, and standing for quite a while. Looking out toward the bonfire, he judges that the arrows have stopped, but just then he realizes that his fears were not so absurd, that a fire has really and truly started in the eucalyptus grove, but no, his eyes have been fooled by something else, everything is all right.

Then he takes note of the fact that Stuart has left the looking glasses behind, and he gives them a try. At first, he can't focus the lenses, but then, as in movies when the pictures moves from blur to clear, the faces of the teenagers abruptly fill up the whole of the round frames. Of course he meant to take a closer look at the trees, but now that he's watching the party he can't pull his eyes away from it. For one thing, there's his friend Stuart, already all the way down there, very visible in his dirty white tennis togs, already an idiot at his ease among others, already cutting the rug, whatever that may mean, it's only a phrase he heard. But somehow the impression that Stuart projects, even over such a distance, is a false but fiercely focused bonhomie. His frameless eyeglasses reflect back the bonfire like a pair of brass coins, masking his eyes, but what a smile, and it's easy to tell that he's playing the phony with a girl in a white top, a girl Virge thinks at first he's never seen before, but then recognizes with a stab of regret as Natalie Sandra. But never mind. Behind her it's striking to see how, out of focus, three or four arrows are floating, dreamily bobbing on a wave, still lively with their little squibs of flame. Virge can't hear what Stuart and Natalie say, not quite, but watches their mouths move, and after a while Virge finds himself filling in the missing dialogue, inventing the banter.

Don't you look lovely tonight, and I wonder where the moon has gone, says Virge out loud, knowingly, cracking himself up, but stops there. Meanwhile, they begin to dance. Not just Stuart and Natalie Sandra, but all of them, and it's not a real dance, but just everybody wheeling around without purpose, hands raised to the sky, as if the plug has been pulled on civilization, but after all it's rather wonderful to see the way Stuart spins solemnly, holding his hands at his waist like someone trying on trousers, while Natalie Sandra reaches up to balance one finger on top of his head.

Then they all stop dancing, and talking, and he can see that they're all pointing at something. Finally he swings the binoculars in the direction they're indicating, only to find, to his horror, that the lenses are completely filled with blinding fire, and when he rips them away from his eyes it's to discover that this time, without a doubt, there is a fire in the trees, and now, too late, it has engulfed the whole of a small grove on the cliff's edge, so that he can already hear the terrible cracks, loud as gunshots, as the trees break apart, already smell the odor of what? Of cough syrup. So, are those dopes happy, now that they've made a bonfire to eclipse the first one, now that they've set fire to the world? And yes, when he swings the lenses back to take another look, it's to find that they have all only amplified their rites, taking their inspiration, it would seem, from the fire, all of them, including Stuart and Natalie Sandra, dancing more frenetically than ever, bowing to the flames as if to glimmering and cracking gods.

4

Wishing you were here, I guess. Because you're more of a man now? And how I pray you could come to me soon. You know I could use a helping hand. I don't mean I've got chores for you. I mean a partnership. Please work on your speaking skills so that when you go door to door, like I do, you'll know what to say to people. I suppose you've never been too good with the sparkling side, the gift of gab. Always a hungry onlooker at the feast of life? But I do believe you could work on it and make a big improvement before you come, or while you're on your way, because the oil is selling really well now, and I need a partner, partner.

That night, in the wee hours, long after the marine layer moves in to smother the fire in the trees, and scatter the party goers, long after Virge, after waiting forever at the screen door for Stuart to come back, has gone to bed, he wakes up craving a long drink of cold water from the kitchen sink, never mind that he'll probably have to prime the pump, and, in dead silence, he moves out into the hallway, where it's dark as deep water, and where he begins by taking the slow, thick steps of a man walking in a helmet on the sea bed.

His arms are held out straight so that, teetering back and forth a little, his fingertips can just brush the opposite walls. In that way he inches forward and, as his eyes adjust to the light, he comes to realize that there's someone else in the hall, a few steps ahead, and of course who could it be but the doctor, also navigating the hallway, moving along at the same snail's pace, but for some reason clopping and clicking loudly on the floor, as if his feet have turned to hooves. Virge rubs his eyes and sees more clearly the back of the crouched figure as it slides one shoulder against the wall. Flanig's got on his baggy nightshirt, and his long white hair's been styled by the pillow into a cowlick, a mystical flame leaping from his head, and all in all he comes off like a ghost of a father in a stage play, or a dream.

Watch out, Doc, murmurs Virge in a helpful way, but Flanig starts at the noise. Who're you? he hisses, not turning around.

It's Virge.

Oh, hello.

But the old man sounds angry, sepulchral, medieval.

What's the matter, Dr. Flanig? asks Virge, solicitous. For heaven's sake.

Here would be a good place to begin the new and often called for personal charm, by making friends with the old gentleman. But Flanig doesn't reply directly, just keeps moving, perhaps craving water too. I wish the house had rubber floors, he says at length, finally turning toward Virge, one eye closed and the other dark as a drain at the bottom of a sink. He holds on to Virge now with both hands, and Virge draws the doctor nearer to him, realizing for the first time that the poor old fellow is as light and rustic as a basket of dry leaves.

Why rubber? inquires Virge, politely.

Because I hate the shocks. I keep feeling like she's going to come out here and I just wish I were grounded, that's all. Don't let her touch me!

Virge has never seen the doctor this agitated, and he lets go and moves away, stepping backwards in quiet, giant steps, finding his way back somehow, without incident, into his room.

It's raining, then raining hard, and the sound of it reminds him of a mistake he's made, that only occurs to him now, that he left his shoes outside, because they were muddy, and now, judging from the sound, they must be filled to the brim, a pair of matching leather vases full of rain.

And no they never go on the roof again. For Virge it is too painful to look out and see the scene of crime, the little burnt area. Admittedly, it could have been much worse, it is just one thicket of trees that got turned into a sad stand of charcoal, of desolation, but the effect is that of a tumor on the horizon, a fly that has fallen into one's bowl of oatmeal, a shit stain on a page of favorite reading, and without Virge's leadership, no one else bothers to climb the ladder for the view.

July is when the air gets humid and dull, and one morning Almy's bare feet are heard sticking and slapping along the hallway tiles, though it's unlike her not to put on shoes. Stuart, forever the smart aleck when possible, can be heard imitating her, smacking his lips or something to produce a similar sound, from wherever he may be in the house.

She pokes her head in Virge's door, as she often does. Then, a moment later, there they both are, Stuart poking his head in after Almy's, so that his face appears above hers, and this way both of them have the air, to Virge's amusement, of actors peeping around the edge of the proscenium, hardly aware of one another. They're both wondering, he bets, if and how they can be of service to him, but it's Stuart who wins in the end, because Almy, finally perceiving that Stuart is hovering over her like a giraffe or something, retreats, and a second later there comes the sound of her bedroom door thrown shut, a terrible boom, probably not meant to be thrown so hard, and a lock of Stuart's hair flops forward into his eyes from the puff of hallway air.

So what to do today? asks Stuart, with a nonchalance, running his fingers through his hair, adjusting his glasses, fingering his squared-off jaw, though his face is stained with traces of some recent snack.

What do you say, he continues, to some sport, old sport? What do you say to tennis?

What do I say? asks Virge, going for a comical British accent, not too good at it. I say, I say, tennis be damned.

Say instead that there's nowhere to play. Say that we don't know how to play.

But that's what I meant by damned. Would you like me to say the word again?

Fine, Stuart groans, but disappears, then comes back a moment later, face clean, drops of water dripping from his chin, to tell Virge to get up anyway, that today's the day they definitely will do something, the day he's definitely going to earn his companion's salary, he just doesn't know what, just not a movie again, and he comes all the way into the room, sits next to Virge on the bed and leans down to put an ear to Virge's chest to check the heart rate.

Still fast and still strong, is my diagnosis, remarks Virge.

Thank you.

And what about those hands of yours?

Heroic, I guess. Godlike. I wouldn't mind six fingers on each. Do you suppose the doctor can add digits, or does he only do subtractions?

No, no enhancing. But, I'm the doctor now, at any rate, and I'll do all the diagnosing and surgery from now on.

Well I was kidding, adds Virge. And you're not a doctor at all.

I'm Flanig's apprentice, and so it makes sense for me to take over the practice.

Okay. Okay. But you don't have a medical degree.

Neither does he. But we call him Doctor. He is a doctor. He has a degree in, I don't know, the classics or something.

And this is what qualifies him to work on people's bones and what-not?

Correct. He read Dante's Inferno, or something like that, something all about bones. But, Patience, I ask you in all seriousness. Do you want to file charges?

Virge doesn't know what to answer, or what follows, or what to expect from such a world, thinking only that none of this matters as much as the idea he has formed at that instant that he and Stuart will escape from here, borrow the doctor's car and drive all night up to San Grande, the town that acts as a central depository, where things are recovered, where he could at least stare at his father for a while before deciding whether to recover him or not. Virge swallows.

And? Stuart repeats.

Virge throws off the covers, gets dressed in silence, sits down at his desk, and, thinking it rude to say such a thing out loud, takes up the fountain pen and writes a note for Stuart that reads, What say we take the car for another ride?

—

We'll at least drive to the top of the hills, says Virge, after he's sure Stuart has read the whole note.

Oh yes, says Stuart, I like that, because, see, it parallels your progress, this going to the top. Do you see what I mean? It's like following the line of your chart, if you had one. It just goes up, and up.

I need to seep out of the house, Virge thinks of saying out loud, but doesn't. Not into the ground, but seep all away from here, just disperse from here altogether. Not sleep walk but seep walk. Leave but leave in all directions.

It doesn't take that much to pull it off. Stuart's the one who knows how to finesse the Bellevue, and push the right button out of many on the dashboard, the one that immediately combusts the gasoline with a clean American roar, and soon enough they are sailing up out of the driveway in this luxury car that they immediately think of as theirs, and soon enough they are turning, their bodies leaning with the arc of the car, on to the flashing black asphalt of Highway Number One. Open road. California here I come, except they're already there. From Virge's neighborhood it's a quick climb up a slope to get high above sea level, and soon, with a brusque turn, it's suddenly a different view, they're all of a sudden in a hot brown canyon, still rising away from the ocean, even losing sight of it sometimes all together.

What they've found, not for the last time, is that famous shift in all geographies, west to east, that transitions from thin to syrupy. The plants alter too, and they shoot past iron-gray oaks twisted as wreckage, and stretches of orange flowers the size and shape of teacups, and, to Virge's amazement, they sometimes make hairpin turns right out over the ocean view without slowing, as if they are about to crash through the guard rail, but then veer right back into the darkness of the oaks and foliage, Stuart at one point zooms past a patch of prickly pear so quickly that Virge has to shout out, slow down, slow down, I've never seen this plant known as cactus before, but I know it, Stuart, I know it when I see it.

Roll down the window and smell your cacti then, snaps Stuart, unhappy with the way the car is handling, appearing to battle a bit with the steering wheel on the curves, as if the axles, or the tie rods, or even the driver's hands, are on the verge of snapping in half.

Then he does have to slow to a crawl because the road narrows, loses its shoulders, turns extra hazardous. For a while, engine coughing, they chug and lurch through somebody's garlic farm, the two of them breathing deep, holding their noses, alluding to bad breath, the kissing of women, Virge not amused but pretending to be, at the low humor.

Then there's a little waterfall that splashes right onto the road, but mostly under the road, and Virge wheels in his seat to see how the water shoots out symmetrically on the other side.

Later there's the strange, edifying sight of some carcass of something at the side of the road ahead of them, hemmed in by prancing turkey vultures, and one vulture that's about to land, and Virge glances away to keep the mental snapshot, but when he looks again the dumb buzzard has merely landed, just as it promised to do, but Stuart gets to show off the doctor's horn and scare the birds away, then proceed to run the right wheels right over the beast, though it's already flattened down by other cars.

Further up the canyon, they take a sharp turn and enter a black hole in the earth—a mountain tunnel. Entrance to Inferno? It's dark as night, cool as Greenland's great caves of blue-black ice. Stuart turns on the headlamps, yodels expertly. But only a new distinctive sound under the hood echoes back to them, along with a smell of mechanical burning.

It's probably the engine. Stuart slows down and wrestles with the gear shift stick like it's wrestling with him, trying to yank his arm off. But to no avail. The car wants to break down and does. No more power. The Bellevue drifts, coughs exhaust, then pointedly halts. Even the headlamps go out, and they are left sitting there like saps, alone in their now motionless and meaningless seats in the silence and absolute dark.

What happened? asks Virge.

To hell with it! says Stuart, vulgarly, incompletely. So they get out, and lean against the car, and try to pierce the darkness to see some speck of light at the end, but the tunnel curves here, so they're out of luck. Maybe we could just live here, says Virge, smug with himself for not being all panicked by the incident, for transcending the lowness of Stuart's language. But something wet is meanwhile dripping on him from the ceiling, which makes for an unpleasant sensation in his hair, and in edging away from the drip he moves away from his companion, with the result that, because of the dark, he gets lost.

I think there are evil ghosts in here, says Stuart from somewhere unfathomable.

Oh, tell it to the Marines.

But that's just it. What I'm seeing over here is the ghosts of dead Marines.

Yeah, sure. Oh goodness, Stuart, you're frightening me.

I can see them all before me when I squint my eyes, their heads dripping with blood.

With what?

All the ghosts in here. Don't you see them? They're not Marines after all. They're the ghosts of all those who died when their cars failed them in here, and they were never able to find their way out. Or others I see—the ones covered in dripping blood—they're the ones who were run down by cars that barreled through here as they tried to walk out.

Step closer to the wall, at least, if you don't like disasters. You're the one worried about cars not seeing us.

Oh they'll see me, says Stuart.

And they'll see me, echoes Virge. And there is some sense to this, as he's wearing a brilliant tie of a yellow hue, while his suit seems to have darkened in hue, so that the tie is the one thing Virge can see, looking down at himself, and maybe it would light up in the headlamps like a flare. Like a cedar in flames.

Next his eyes adjust a step further, and he can see the wall in front of him now, smell (now that he can see it) the damp cement, and reach out a finger and touch a bright bead of clear water about to fall, so that the bead, like a drop of mercury, slides down his finger into his palm and stays round and complete there, a perfect sphere.

Hey, what's this? laughs Stuart, and Virge turns and can see his friend clearly now, just inches away, leaning over to pick something up off the ground. It's a day of odd discoveries, and when Stuart holds out his find it turns out to be a heel that's come off a shoe. Could it belong to Mont? As likely as not. Stuart holds it up to Virge's nose to sniff and then pushes it right into his face, despite the potential injury from the nail, and Virge recoils in disgust, and as he spins on his own intact heels an impulse makes him keep going, keep walking away.

Where are you going, Patience?

Back home.

Don't be silly. Don't you know how far it is? You'd never get there. You'd melt. You'd go all soft and waxy in the heat. I'd have to scrape you off the road, like a wad of chewing gum.

But Virge keeps going. It's all the same to him. He has hands, and can use them, and could crawl on all fours if it came to that, if he were to lose the ability to stand. Never doubt the magnificence of human limbs. I can do this and this and this, and it's the case that there is more in them, more power than before. While he walks he employs them, just to spite those who may not be aware of his dexterity, placing hands on top of his head to adjust his cap, holding the lapels of his jacket, interlacing fingers behind his spine, placing a finger in each ear.

But also, at that moment, walking as fast as he can, he proceeds under the assumption that he'll never see Stuart again.

But then slows down, having discovered something, a feature of the tunnel, an interruption, that brings him up short: it's a niche or slot or something that has been carved or rather cast into the middle of one otherwise plain concrete wall, a kind of alcove, and this alcove in turn has a window that opens to the outside and lets a single beam of light pour down straight into the darkness, like light for archeologists in some monarch's tomb.

Virge, craving light more than he ever has before, moves right toward the window, and once there, finds that his body fits in the space just right, as if it were engineered for young men lost in the tunnel, seeking refuge. In the niche he's safe, precisely out of the way of any car that might come along, and just tall enough to turn around and lean on the window ledge with his arms crossed and stick his head out and relax, and he might as well be a permanent resident of this tunnel who suns his head there like a grampus every afternoon, and easy to imagine years of such afternoons. He can and does stand tiptoe after a moment and crane his neck and peer down into a canyon, a crooked gully not too far below that he is the first explorer to discover, perhaps. At any rate, it's dotted with green oaks and some other kinds of trees and the heat of it wells up to him like bread dough, along with the thickly sour smell of sage and general leaf litter and the wet black mud at the very bottom.

Good view, he says, speaking only to the view, thinking he might as well count himself the owner of this place as well. This room with a view. If there were a way to know the distance down, a way to count the layers of air that he senses but can't quite see between him and the bottom, that would be knowledge specially known to the proprietor. But the floor of the canyon isn't visible, it's hidden as it is below the canopy of trees, and when Virge follows his instinct and spits, his bit of human fluid drops slowly, hangs, trailing behind it a long thread that stretches all the way back to his lips and, when long enough, bends in the yeasty air like a spider's silk. All the while, almost magically, there drifts up to his ears a bland and fricative music, or speech, and after a moment he understands that it's the sound of the stream, speaking to him from behind the curtain, unintelligible.

All rooms are escapes from other rooms, but if you find yourself for the first time on the edge of a room, a stepping off place, an emergency exit, where the stairs haven't been built yet, you contemplate, can't help but contemplate, the extension of the right shoe into space, the slow tilt forward. Elevator going down. Picture the Bellevue smashing through the guard rail. Scrawny Virge could hoist himself up on the sill, turn his body like a screwdriver, and insert his body into and through the slot, and in this manner worm himself out into the green void. It could be considered an experiment, that's all. There could be a book of exploration devoted to that one trip alone. To fall slow, then fall fast, to fall feet first, then face first, perhaps descending so rapidly in the long run through the perpendicular layers that he might catch up with that tiny ball of saliva he already let fall, go after it mouth first, reach it, become the first to spit a wad and then recapture it, reswallow it.

The cartoon believability of suicide. Stuart—where is Stuart?—would laugh, light a cigarette, his hands shaking somewhat when striking the match, would take a drag, relax, lean out of the window in just the same way, and Virge, plummeting clown, would look over his shoulder in mid flight and meet his friend's gaze, but no time for a nod or a salute, just the smirk of goodbye as he feels the topmost leaves of the treetops brushing past.

But no. Not because he wouldn't really do it, but because he really would, and still might, and yet the payoff would be too small, too slight. There would be no retrospect, no discovery, no chest to curl up in for later explorers to find you. Here comes another mental picture, another glancing snapshot, almost as if by mental telegraphy, and this one is simply a portrait of Stuart, posing sturdily in his role as devoted apprentice. A second picture shows him studying the newspapers that in former days he would burn. Picture three comes next, and it's a snapshot of himself, of Virge, in this case miles away, walking on the family path but in this case away, always away from the ocean. Life wins. Bones win. Virge turns away from the emergency exit.

But the feeling that he gets next, and would rather not get, now that the rest of his life is accounted for, is a sudden dejection, an urge to cry. This can't be right, these tears that come now, all from suddenly recalling, as he does now, the sordid business of San Grande, the miserable trip he may have to take there, in order to sit and stare awhile at old Mont. Damned Mont, would be one way of putting it. If the messages are real, and also if they're not, whether he's wearing the wig and also if he's not wearing it, the father has got to be somewhere, and all the contingencies to be considered are equally plain and bad. As for tears, he dries them, and leans out to take in the canyon once again, this time getting the smell of wet boulders, a glimpse of a reddish bird at the top of a tree, not a robin because much more of a songster than that, and what is the bird trying to tell him? To get going, nothing to see here, move it along, chum, no loitering allowed.

Here I am, cock robin, says Stuart, not far away at all, still going for a spooky effect with his voice, and the sentence echoes, as if spoken from a grand stage, striking and dying off the surfaces of the concrete tube.

Walk toward my voice, Patience, continues Stuart, needlessly hamming it up. No, do not walk toward the echoes of my voice, my voice, my voice.

Walk toward a voice, Virge whispers to himself, staggering forward, finding Stuart after a while, then reaching out a hand to touch his friend's shoulder, for stability, for sanity.

Meanwhile, says Stuart, ignoring him, speaking almost in a whisper, I'm keeping this shoe heel. Keeping it for luck. Maybe it's a Cat's Paw, and that's the one they say brings good luck. Better luck. Well, better bad luck anyway.

But Virge's mood, now nervous, can't be shaken by such considerations, and he really can't think about the heel, or say something typically dour, typically skeptical. He finds he can't be typical anymore.

You're the only heel I see here, he could retort, but instead mutely points out the aperture, and guides his companion over to that area to let him see the outside world for himself and maybe philosophize his own conclusions about destruction, either of the self or otherwise.

Let's get the hell out of this tunnel, says Stuart, briskly, uninterested in the window, having seen what he wants to see and striking out in the same direction that Virge had already been heading in.

But that's the way back home, says Virge.

No it's not. You got turned around. You were heading forward all the time.

And Virge shakes himself, thinking that Stuart's right, he's developing an instinct for moving forward, and it doesn't matter whether it's by car or on foot. Forward march. Follow your heart. Yet he has a little relapse. The tunnel turns abruptly cold, as if really and truly haunted. And he remembers then how Jansens had to dig a tunnel under the ice to get to some trapped men, to help them escape from something that had collapsed and buried. But finally, after heroic efforts, he got to the end of the slippery ice tunnel—but because it's a tunnel that had to angle upward, time after time he lost his grip on the ice and slid backwards, all the way back to the beginning. At last he finds, when at last he breaks through to the surface, that he's been digging the wrong way the whole time anyway, and has ended up further away from the spot he was trying to get to. But it's so hideously difficult to remember. Was it Jansens at all, or was it one of the other books, in which case he has combined two stories into one? Now there's a recurring pattern. Borrow the book, read the book, return the book, then spend years picking at the tangled knot. What is the name of that disease, symptoms of which include constant sharp recollection of things, but the same things? What is the name of that disease, symptoms of which include constant sharp recollection of things, but the same things? Har de har har syndrome, or something.

But now comes the surprise that again he's separated from Stuart, that he's turned counterclockwise somehow, and now stands alone, spine at a slight bend, palms to either side of his head, thumbs in his ear holes, a goon, suddenly, who won't hear things. When did he put fingers there? But there they are. Taking a cautious step back, that's it, it's all over, he straightens out. Stuart shows up and just guides him along tenderly through the darkness by the shoulders. They can march along in silence toward the pinhead exit of light now visible so far away, sticking close, single file, lockstep, chain gang of two.

But the silence and darkness are tolerable for only so long, and Virge ends up spilling his guts. He chooses this moment, above all other moments, to tell Stuart about the messages. About everything. Particularly, the wig transmissions from Mont. He wishes, after he's talked awhile, that he'd kept his mouth shut just a little longer, at least until they were back out in the sun, where such an account might not seem so preposterous and made-up as it suddenly feels to him here in the already eerie atmosphere of the tunnel. But Stuart is polite. He listens intently, head bent in a posture of honest thoughtfulness, as

Virge explains how first, soon after Mont's departure, the messages started coming in. How sometimes a sour ache was felt in the kidneys just before a message arrived, and when the transmission was over, the ache was gone. About the messages themselves, which Virge easily memorized and now repeats to Stuart verbatim. About the mirror. The expressionlessness. It's tempting to leave out the wig part, for reasons of sheer credibility. But the wig goes in. End of story.

Huh, says Stuart.

Huh?

Yeah. Huh.

That's your answer?

No, my answer is to ask you if you can't see the truth, if you can't see something you're missing here.

What? Which truth?

These messages that you say come from your dad, from Mont. What are they?

You tell me.

All right, and you won't like it. These messages aren't coming from the outside, but the inside. Transmissions from your head. You're like Flanig these days, always wondering where his hat is, and I'm always telling him, my dear fellow, it's on your head.

They stroll in silence for a while, straight toward the ever expanding circle of end-of-tunnel light. Virge keeps looking at his hands, noting more details. How the wrinkles around the knuckles look like parentheses within parentheses.

Do people always look this bad in tunnels? asks Stuart at one point, peering sidelong into his companion's face.

What do you mean?

Maybe it's just the light in here. But you look small. As if dwarfed by events.

I know. You said I looked bad because of my jazz about the wigs.

You look full-sized to me now, Virge. Handsome, even!

Look, I know that you're being paid, I mean paying me, to be my friend, but you don't have to remind me. You don't have to make it so obvious.

Okay, your face is, well, it's just that maybe you're a little sick. Sickly green. I'm paying you to be your doctor too. And I don't think you're in the best of health.

Oh, Doctor, I don't understand. Could you put that in layman's terms?

Well, says Stuart, shrugging, maybe a little sheepish, we've only a couple more steps, it looks like, and we'll get out of here. That's the one healthy thing we'll do today.

And they both hold out their hands instinctively toward the approaching sunshine.

But they stop. They hold it right there, and it's as if they are standing now just inside the door of a space rocket, looking out at the blindingly bright surface of another planet.

At the exact spot where Virge has stopped, he's right on the edge of this alien brightness, and he looks down to see the hems of his trousers in the shade, the toes of his shoes sticking out into the sun. They're the ones he left out in the rain, and they've shrunk some, which is good, they were his dad's before and too big. Stuart's shoes are lined up with his, and it's interesting to note how Virge's shoes are so bulbous at the front and old fashioned, while Stuart's shoes are thin, sharp-toed, brown and white, shoes of the future.

I don't want to go out in that heat any more than you do, says Stuart. But we've got to find a telephone.

Why?

To call a cab. To call Natalie Sandra for help of course. That's what we always do when the car breaks down.

I think that's a terrible idea.

So we'll go door to door, asking for a telephone.

I can't, says Virge, I can't see myself going right up to doors. Stranger doors to doors. I would *like* to learn how to do it. Just not in this heat.

Stuart pays no attention. He starts talking and can't stop, and turns out to have a lot to say, for the first time that Virge can recall, about this girlfriend of his, this Natalie Sandra, how she isn't from the area at all, like the rest of them, but in fact from El Damascus, at the bottom of the state, where actually it's pretty flat and hot, a pitiless desert, but friendly folks, a place where you can order eggs and cactus for breakfast, where the waitresses have equatorial suntans, and are all as pretty as Natalie Sandra, even more so, and how Virge ought to go down there and find a girl too, where they're sure to like him.

Oh knock it off, because I'm heading north not south, mumbles Virge, comfortable and uncomfortable with all the compliments. First San Grande, then further north.

All right, but don't expect to meet any Natalie Sandras on the way.

Do you plan to be married to her, asks Virge, vaguely interested. But the story seems to be over, and, as if they've agreed to this together, they step forward into the full power of the sun, left foot, right foot, and the heat of the day is a powerful entity, a bomb going off every second, and both of them stop again, shudder, breathe it all in, in ragged gasps, but then on they go, step by step, and Virge especially is wilted and defeated in spirit, sure that he won't make it before he falls and dies, but not sure what it is he's supposed to make it to.

Well that feels good, Virge leers. It's so hot I feel like I could reach out and shape it. Sculpt it. I'm more the artist than you, Stu. May I call you Stu?

Most of what he says goes unanswered.

The road angles up from there, gaining in altitude and, as they move forward, the walking and the heat grow that much worse. The landscape is remarkably alien, bright with a sulfurous, sunflower dustiness.

Climbing to hell! sputters Stuart.

But it's a slope like the slope of my progress chart, Virge reminds him, but Stuart seems to have forgotten all about that. They climb up steeply to a spot where the road bends even more drastically uphill, and they have to stop for a moment, to think about the potential killing power of the heat, and whether or not they can manage to climb at so miserable an angle in that fibrous air with nothing to drink.

Look, says Stuart, turning around, pointing at the great wet expanse of the Pacific behind them, and Virge, slow-witted, still wearing his horrible suit jacket, his viselike shirt and collar and tie, turns his head to see that by this point the ocean no longer looks blue and refreshing, but more silver in hue, more medicinal and corrosive.

But now look up there, replies Virge, pointing forward again, and though the air is rising in distorted sheets all around them he shows Stuart where to catch a glimpse, about fifty yards up, of a little spot where the road maybe flattens out, and where two figures, two people, stand to the side of the road, real human beings, two folks too far away to wave at, or be waved at by. Virge's first thought is that these could be not devils looking down on them, waiting, like buzzards, for them to die, but no, maybe they're angels who have found a shady spot, a travelers' oasis that isn't that far away after all.

I think they've got guns, says Virge. You think?

Trying to keep us off their property, maybe, croaks Stuart.

They're up to something, Virge concurs, but of course now there is absolutely no choice but to walk up the hill to see what their badness exactly consists of. It's a death march either way, so up they go, somewhat terrified, but after a time they can make out the fact that it's just a plain older man and a plain younger woman, no knives nor guns. Stuart grins at Virge and Virge grins back, as if to say, what idiots, it's just a couple of Okies or something, and a minute later it's clear that they're not even that, not farmers, but something lower on the human scale than that. No, not lower. Just apart.

What the two of them are both standing behind is a table covered by a bright white and red checked tablecloth. In front of the table is a big sheet of plywood, a sign that spells out

COLD CHERRY
ROOT POP

and a bit below that, in smaller letters, hastily painted in red, so that each letter has a little drip running down from it, like blood, like a Halloween party announcement:

try it why don't you HGP product
HGP = Health Giving Properties
all products 5¢ no loitering

Virge mouths all this under his breath, getting a sense of tremendous invitation, if not to the banquet of life, at least to the wellspring. Terminally thirsty, his tongue as large as a cow's tongue and pressing his teeth forward, his mind races ahead in time and pictures himself drinking, tongue shrinking, but it's more than that. Some other dimension of his life, he's certain, is on the verge of upheaval and change, perhaps as a result of staring at the old man, or the young woman, or simply the pale hand that one of them, it's not clear which, reaches down to open an ice chest that sits on top of the table. It's paranormal, a pair of Normas, a wild presentiment from beyond, and he keeps his head down and eyes fixed on the leaves and acorns and a penny or two that have drifted down around them and lay scattered in the springy, sponge-cake dirt.

Look inside that chest, will you, hisses Stuart, nudging Virge repeatedly as they stand side by side at the table.

Don't push me, Virge says out of the side of his mouth, uncomfortable with the fact that they're so far only talking to each other, but does at last allow himself the nearly unbearable luxury of looking carefully, and understanding carefully that there inside is one unfractured and weighty and solid block of ice, ice man's ice, with no milky center to it, clear all the way through, a block that has melted down to a softness, a roundness, but what's remarkable about it is that there are holes drilled or molded into it, four or five hollow tubes, each a few inches in diameter, and in each of these, like honey in a cell, there rests a skinny bottle, the contents of which must be delightfully cold. Cherry root pop. He's clear about it now. Root pop is not some kind of obscenity. A cherry root, or roots plus cherries? The delicious flavor, maybe, is what strikes the taste buds first. The young woman mechanically angles one arm, wordlessly extracts a bottle as if to offer it up. It's just now shedding its skin of thin ice, appearing even darker and rootier as she extends it forward, then just as quickly deposits it back in its cell.

Two of those please, speaks up Stuart, eyes starting out, eyes feeling the thirstiest.

Two of those please, echoes the girl in the quietest voice, so whispered that Virge strains to hear, though he can tell without looking closely that she's tall and sagging and has a large but tightly bound hairdo, though wisps do fall down around her face, shining red, and he reasons from that that she by all rights ought to have a deeper voice, a mother nature voice.

Our car broke down, rasps Stuart, acting required to speak.

Our car is dead on us there in the tunnel, he elaborates, Virgil shooting him looks of impatience.

Stuart's sunburnt cheeks make him look like his dad got up as a fake Indian.

First tell me your health problems, the girl instructs, not sounding sympathetic to any response.

His arms and hands are paralyzed, answers Stuart, kicking Virge in the ankle bone as a sign to play along.

Poor kid, says the girl, and Virge finally glances up and finds her smiling but not exactly looking at him anymore, eyes drifting off, which is a relief, but her hand at the same time angles again, this time out for a tentative pat on his shoulder. Despite her look of nervous shyness, she seems an important personage. Her cleverness is evidenced by the language of the advertisement, if it's her and not the old man who composed it.

To Virge she looks, first, trustworthy, and then her face clarifies, and becomes familiar.

There's a slight blurriness to her, that gives the impression that she's often trembling, and he remembers that about her more than anything else.

Soon up walks the other figure, coming up from the background.

Look, this one says, unknotting a bandanna from around his neck, rubbing it lightly on the block of ice, draping around his neck again, all as if it's a trick he's slyly encouraging them to copy.

So how about those pops, says Stuart, addressing the old man in an irreverent way.

Where's your two nickels, or where's your dime? says the girl, switching off her smile. While Stuart fishes for and finally comes up with a dime, and presses it into her outstretched palm, Virge studies her for the first time, trying to understand what it is he should learn there. Her face, he sees now, is long and square in the chin, and to block the heat she wears something like a baseball cap, but more cubical, with a flat bill that sticks out extra inches, keeping her eyes in shadow. But none of this is exactly what Virge sees directly—it's more that he wants to aim for the whole impression, to let his eyes wander all over her, and he feels that his eyes are as good as the eyes of a bird, perhaps a crow, gauging, wandering, a bird that is not wise nor is it foolish, just scientific, preparing a report for the others.

And then, with a surge of new knowledge, he recognizes this girl, since, not surprisingly, given the scant population of the region, it's somebody he went to school with, and maybe she'll recognize him too, though it's been many years since that time, since the days of grammar school and recess, but here she is with the same chin and same general outline as before, just more inflated and knotted now, like a balloon tied into the shape of a girl. And of course he recalls that her name is Alice, the polio girl, the classmate he knew and even talked to, the only one he ever talked to, then lost track of because she had to quit school and stay home, and had to be treated to the iron lung, and stay home from school forever after. So she could not reasonably remember him, since even if she had gone back to school, then he was the one who started missing quite a lot as well, because they were, the two of them, Alice and Virge, though neither knew it, the famously sickly kids, spoken of and scorned by all who were more on the incessantly healthy side.

As for Alice in the here and now, she shows no reciprocal recognition of Virge, and says nothing, just looks at him, but it's nice that, once she pockets the payment, the young lady gets friendly again, and launches into the story of how they make the pop themselves, she and her companion, whom she refers to only as Abuelito, introducing herself as Alicia, though Virge knows that this name is equivalent to the name Alice. Next she grabs an ice pick and brandishes it menacingly for a second, almost as if she were going to come around the table and go after the customers. But then she laughs and flips it expertly in the air, catches it by the handle, and only uses it then to enlarge the holes in the ice a little, and the whole process is torture for someone with a mouth as dry as ashes, or maybe potash.

Two cherry pops coming up, she mutters through clenched teeth, concentrating. At last, anticlimactically, she extracts first one, then two, of the sodas, neither quite the same as the first one she displayed. The pop in these two bottles looks thinner, weaker, but her customers don't say anything, because after all the bottle is the same, horizontally ribbed, again dripping beautiful skins of ice while she swings them out, like bowling pins, toward Virge. But Virge, recalling Stuart's nudge, though not sure what exactly is the point of lying about his paralysis, just shrugs, and Stuart, grinning approvingly at his friend, grabs the proffered bottles.

Two helpings of pop, she continues. Two flavor explosions for two handsome gentleman today.

You got some way to open these? asks Stuart.

Over there, says Alice, pointing with a shoulder at the trunk of the massive oak, where, a few inches off the ground, somebody has hung a church key opener on a string, and that is where the two of them retreat. Finally, there in the deep shade of the oak, ten degrees cooler than elsewhere, the ground carpeted for them with bristly leaves, Stuart and Virge sit cross-legged, and Stuart opens and takes a swig and then, continuing the fictional paralysis, opens the other bottle and holds it up cautiously to Virge's lips, like he's giving the baby his bottle.

Virge's turn to drink, and when the cherry fluid finally does touch his tongue and throat—too slowly, because Stuart is so cautious not to spill—the carbonation burns him, the liquid twirls down his gullet with the sensation of a snake spiraling down a hole, and when the liquid hits the bottom of his gut, it feels, even down there, almost too cold and sparkly to bear. Bitter to the abdomen, and so freezing, but healing enough to take another swig right away. Yes, please. But still, at the back of his mind, he's thinking, what kind of cherry pop is this? It comes to him, on the second sip, that it's not really so good, tastes nothing like he's ever had, full of something puckering and tangy, with an effect half way between a sigh of sweetness and an instinctive sticking out of the tongue.

Stuart tips the bottle away from Virge's lips, and looks at him, eyes screwed up to say that Stuart too has noticed some peculiarity.

Don't bolt it, cautions Stuart, but then himself goes on guzzling, draining his own bottle quickly, managing to spill the last drops of it down the front of his undershirt, staining it dark, staining it the color of tree-bark, but not offering any more of the other bottle to his friend.

Don't pick it up, Stuart says. You're still paralyzed.

I know, but why?

To make you more likable.

How do you mean?

To make you into some kind of a gimp, says Stuart. You have to be more interesting. You can always recover later, as if her soda is, let's say, a kind of miracle cure.

I have to be more interesting to Alice?

She said you were handsome, grins Stuart.

She said that in the way of a general observation. About you, too. She meant you.

You don't want a pair of Normas? A pair of Alices? A pair of Beas?

There was only one Bea, says Virge, smirking at the mistake. Anyway, I wanted to meet that woman with the clenched hands. Your Miss Elmwood. It seemed to me like I had the outside track with her.

Inside track.

Right. Inside, because we had both seen trouble in our hands.

But she was much too civilized for you! laughs Stuart, sinking to a new low, though tilting the remainder of the pop onto Virge's babyish lips.

The bottle empty, Virge shrugs in gratitude, and peers over at the table to re-examine Alice, complimentary Alice, who has resumed her roadside pop stand demeanor, stonily watching the road for the next customer. It's clear to Virge that he'll have to figure her out on his own, in his own time. The Stuart way of looking at things, with all its spotting and singling out, its judging and teasing out of weaknesses, is one way to go about things, whereas the Virge approach, invented now, is to think of people as belonging to certain categories, like sections in a cemetery, not that they're dead but that they're not readily accessible, and all the struggle and pain of getting to know somebody comes from finding that they don't belong exactly in the same section as the others. As oneself. This is how he will have to renew his acquaintance with Alice, even though no one will ever pay her to be his companion, nor can she pay him to be hers. It's comforting, from this perspective, to contemplate her convex plainness, just as it is to contemplate Miss Elmwood's elegance. It's the contrast that counts.

Stuart, meanwhile, is putting up his dukes, punching at the air, at the heat, like it's his opponent, and looking, in his undershirt, like a prize fighter.

Virge, it isn't so hot. I mean it isn't so hard. Don't worry about it.

Worry about what?

About jumping straight down, you know, into the thick of things. What's stopping you?

But they don't move for a long time, as the heat is just too much, and Virge starts to think that he can hear a gong being struck, somewhere far away. At length they plop down in the leaves again, bodies absorbent and heavy as hardened lava. Neither of them can move an inch. From a distance they can hear Alice's block of ice melting, dripping into the leaves on the ground, and the bottles sometimes slipping further down into the ice.

No cars drive by at all. The old man, Abuelito, finally makes a move, and wanders around, crunching leaves, finally sitting down with them where they are, smiling at nobody in particular, showing off the largest teeth Virge has ever seen, chewing thoughtfully on some twig he's brought along, cleaning his tall teeth with it, spitting out small morsels of something near their shoes.

Dear Alice. How to start a letter to her? Virge's brain draws a blank on that, and what if there is something wrong with his brain? It's true he's the quiet and shy type. Speaks correctly when necessary, though he finds he has nothing at all to say to this old man who has sidled up right next to him, so close that they are almost touching. Again, already, Virge is murderously thirsty. This feeling passes, he wills it away for a whole minute, and then again he is desperately parched, more even than before, when climbing the road. There is still after all his own dime, one he keeps in a tiny vest pocket, the dime pocket, as it's called. It's tragic to him now to think how that dime has occupied that position for years.

Well, let's at least get another bottle, says Virge, backs of both hands suddenly burning in a shaft of sun now.

You just said the magic word, replies Stuart, getting on his knees and crawling, maybe to mimic a dying man. Then he scrambles erect, returns to Virge, lifts him to his feet by grabbing him under the armpits, and shoves him in the direction of the soda table.

I'll wait here, says Stuart.

All this time Virge is having trouble with his eyes, at least so he believes, because when he approaches Alice she seems less distorted to him now, less blurry around the edges, but now seems as if she is too close to him, as if magnified by prescription glasses. A wasp arrives to circle over the smell of sweetness, and to his exaggerating eyes it keeps diving right toward him and her, nearly the weight and size of a hummingbird.

You know that there are no wasps or bees or any kind of animal like that north of a given latitude, he explains, ducking his head, avoiding the insect as best he can.

Then, supremely confident, a show off, he supposes he can snatch the wasp out of the air, and forgetting entirely about the pretend paralysis, he steps forward, throws out one hand like a frog's tongue, and easily gets it. Afraid of the sting, he crushes the insect immediately, so when he peeks inside his fist, it's full of yellow and green jelly, disgusting but cold, like a healing ointment. Not a bad therapy for the heat, and perhaps he's on the track of a new invention. Cool yourself lotion. Little jars of processed guts.

But then he remembers the paralysis, and this is where Virge learns that people sometimes don't pay close attention to you, because Alice doesn't show the slightest surprise or displeasure at his movements, and the only conclusion one can come to is that she takes all this in without really looking at him, without thinking what it means, or remembering much about him after all. He sneaks a glance back at Stuart, who holds his head in his hands, as if it has increased in weight.

I know the wasp can be thought of as a stinging insect, continues Virge, with an apparent calm, rubbing his hands together and then letting them hang down limply again, but staring into the palms as if they contain not cooling wasp balm but the script of his remarks.

Then what do the Eskimos use for paper? asks Alice. Don't wasps make paper?

I never thought about writing on it.

There is something in her voice, an enunciation, a sarcasm, that reinforces Virge's memory of her in the old days. She was quite the item then, as now, a lively girl who was funny to listen to, given to bossiness, anxious to speak in class, prone to sing songs out loud, share surprising facts, make fun of him. Might she, at this very moment, recognize his face, or some part of his body that she used to mercilessly tickle?

Wait, I *have* written on that kind of paper, lies Virge. I wrote a whole book on waspy paper.

You did?

I did, but I don't have it anymore, because it got splashed, or stained I should say, and I had to throw it away, and I don't remember now what it was about. Wait. It was about my life.

Well, you writers, says Alice, placidly, but she has walked away a few steps to see where Abuelito has gone off to, and when she turns back and looks at him from a distance Virge can see her entirety, and observe for the first time that, besides being interested, and interesting, she's wary, that a cautiousness is there too, and abruptly he feels terrible for himself, in case he's the one inspiring this fear in her, and likewise sad for her, that she sells pop by the side of the road. However, like him, she can talk comfortably about wasps and who knows what else, but really is more advanced, further along with things, because he, after all, mostly stays in his room, one tiny room out of all the rooms in the world, and here she is inhabiting one room too, but it's the largest room there is, the great outdoors.

But wasps aren't animals, she points out. They're bugs.

Why does this soda taste so bad? he asks, looking at her straight, learning from her some more.

Wait a second, says Alice, digging a scrap of paper out of a pocket, along with a pencil, producing these items with gestures suggesting practice and poise. She quickly writes something, folds the paper many times, reducing it to the size of a penny stamp, reaches out and tucks the message into Virge's vest pocket.

Don't read that now, but later, she frowns. It's not written on waspy paper, but it's for you to unfold and take a look at, if and when you make it home. I mean when.

I know a joke, says Stuart, approaching them, his appearance somewhat enchanted, as his clothes are covered in brown leaves.

Okay, says Alice, interested.

It's dirty, says Stuart.

That's all right, she says, sobering.

I'm not sure about this, puts in Virge.

Who invented soda?

I don't know, says Virge, perking up.

Adam. Because he made Eve some cherry pop.

I don't get it.

Neither do I, says Alice.

I said it wrong, smirks Stuart, as if saying it wrong were the best part of the joke.

Back downhill to the tunnel, back all the way to the moribund automobile. At least they can better survive the heat in there, they guess, and maybe someone will come along who knows something about the way things break and the way things get fixed. After half an hour of idleness, of Stuart trying to sleep behind the wheel, Virge in the passenger seat, Stuart, on a hunch, says they ought to give the old Bellevue one last try, and goes around to the front of the car to poke around in the engine.

While he's gone, Virge takes advantage of the privacy to wander over near the window again, to get some reading light. He doesn't look out into the canyon this time, just extracts Alice's message from his pocket, and, though it takes forever to undo all her minute folds, finally he gets it flattened out.

I am truly sorry about the rough times behind you. Someday I know I can help those who are like who you are. Alice p.s. You and your friend do wear clothes well. However, tell him I'd prefer his if they were more laundered and white.

Back at the car, he watches Stuart hop back in the driver's seat and hold his finger down hard on the button. Nothing. Holds it down again, maybe from a slightly different angle, and the engine kicks right in. And stays on, purring like a million cats. It just needed to cool off, he shouts to Virge, who has already refolded the note exactly along its fold lines, then made it even smaller, the size of an aspirin, and put it in his pocket.

Everything has three dimensions: a body of flesh, a scaffolding of bones, a glow of fire or soul or spirit. Even words written on paper conform to this arrangement. There's a body of expression, a scaffolding of letters, a glow of love.

It's evening by the time the two of them get back to the farm, and by then the sun is almost down, red and oval and cool as a distant planet.

Flanig is outside waiting for them, pacing in the driveway, hands clasped behind his back, trouser bottoms fluttering up in the breeze to display a smart new pair of button shoes and button hosiery. When he brings his hands forward, what he's holding is the old dumbbell, the one Virge threw off the roof some days before.

What do you make of that, he asks, holding out the item for their inspection.

Virge and Stuart hesitate.

It was your father's, intones Flanig, keeping his eyes cast down, then lifting the weight to his chin, a show of remaining strength.

What about my dad?

God bless the saintly man, says the old man, majestically.

Thank you, says Virge, looking around, turning to the house and finding Almy inside, visible through a window, staring at him and frantically gesturing—waving her hands, shaking her head, wagging her finger—as if she wants to keep him somehow from listening to what the doctor says, or perhaps asking that Virge just bring the gentleman back inside.

But you never met him, did you? inquires Virge.

I hope to read a book about him, says Flanig, casting down his eyes, as if the reading were to begin any minute.

Which book? asks Virge, but there's no answer to that question.

When Virge looks back to the window, Almy has vanished, and when he looks back to Flanig, the doctor, eyes shifting back and forth, looks terrified.

What should we do with you? whispers Virge, dropping the dumbbell to the dirt, nudging it with his toe, feeling impatient, wanting to help the old man, just as Alice has promised to help him. It feels like an afternoon to devote to a lifting up of troubled spirits. However, the moment he takes the doctor by the hand, thinking to lead him back inside, Flanig snatches it away.

Not those hands! he bursts out.

But doesn't offer any others.

Virge retains, every day since his recovery, an appreciation of life without paralysis. How now he can write, create great art, perform on a musical instrument. None of these are within his reach, but look how well he does what he does do. Flicking away lint. Snatching wasps out of the air. Taking up a downcast fellow's hand and patting it in a reassuring way. Later he tries this with his mom, and though she doesn't snatch it away, neither does she ever reach out for his.

What else? Playing with buttons on his shirt front. Taking a shoe heel that is being offered for inspection, revolving it in such a way that the shoe heel can now be said to be resting on the heel of the palm. Har har. Opening pants to pee, wetting fingers slightly with the urine.

Striking forehead, in frustration, with the heel of the palm. Don't be so clumsy with the pee. Plucking a handkerchief from pocket to wipe his hands, then a ring of sweat around the neck. Opening Almy's Bible with the difficulty that comes not from weak hands but weak morals. Hefting a bone—in fact a real bone, one he's had for years, a vertebra found in the fields back when Mont used to plow and things would get turned up from time to time. Maybe there really was someone buried out there in olden days, and maybe the bone is homo sapiens, but more likely an animal, or maybe a new species, part human, part animal, since such things have been known to happen. And, as if to test such a theory, he breaks his promise to himself, puts on the wig again, wipes all emotions from his face, and stands in front of the bathroom mirror.

But before any of the transmission comes through, Virge rips the wig off his head and slams it down into the trash can, thinking, in all that time, I never said a word to him about myself.

They fight a half real, half bogus fight. While walking out toward the ocean to put on a picnic, Stuart, instead of welcoming Virge's brotherly hand in his, snatches it away, seizes Virge by the collar, yanks hard, and spins his companion down into the dirt with great animosity.

Or so it seems to Virge, who rolls around passively in Stuart's wrestler's embrace, and since after a few seconds this gets boring, he allows himself some flailing, merely for dramatic effect, but in fact nothing is any clearer now than before. He isn't sure whether Stuart is just horsing around or really intends some kind of pinning down. There's just a painful flurry of pine needles and the smell of wool and saliva and dirt, and Virge sees, not for the last time, that there is something about the ground that is welcoming, that tends to bring him down to it. That the dirt is becoming a hobby of his, in a way. Or the ants and the mites. The bad part is that Virge's banana yellow tie gets badly scratched, and then wrapped around his neck, with the attendant danger of strangulation, and then Stuart's shoes both fly off at the same time. When finally the two men separate, shoving each other away like strangers who've collided by mischance, the fun, if there was any, is over, there are new beads of blood on both sides, and they stagger to their feet and walk in opposite directions.

Now *you* can be my hired companion, sings Stuart, and when Virge looks back he sees that his adversary is not looking back in return, but keeping his eyes glued on a tree about his own height.

And I'll be the one, continues, Stuart, who has to have his friendships negotiated.

This last remark comes out in a definitely nonjoking way, and leaves a bitter curtain hanging between them. Virge blinks hard, turns around in a circle, doesn't know where to direct his stare. There comes to mind a time in school, years before, when he won a prize for most beautifully decorated Christmas card, but when he put it on his classmate's desk to show it off the boy knocked it on the floor and quietly pulverized it with his great dirty boot.

Then Almy and the doctor both come up, and Virge's mom says something, not unexpected, about how grown-ups hate to see boys fighting, and Stuart turns more civil then, even servile, and comes wheeling back to dust off Virge's clothes with the flats of his hands, but it's a much-too-thorough dusting that quickly turns into a funny semi-slapping routine. It works, though, in that everyone laughs, even Virge, and the mood is clear again, until Virge starts reciprocating, dusting off Stuart in the same way, and this seems to bring back the curtain, and the discomfort.

Can we have the picnic here? asks Virge, breaking off, trying to change course.

Why not? cries Almy, looking giddy.

I think the ground here is soft enough, Virge whispers to Stuart, for the doctor to sit down.

What?

I meant his frailty. How he's a twig waiting to be snapped.

But Stuart only gives a blank look in reply, and gets the quilt out, choosing a spot not far off the path, where there's a little clearing thickly upholstered, to Virge's satisfaction, with pine needles. Next, they all pitch in to spread out and distribute the great feast and get a better idea of how much food is really involved. And Virge, with his lifelong fear of the beach, is pleased that they stop to eat where they do, and though the afternoon shadows are getting a little long, the picnic begins pretty well, with comments all around on the quantity and quality of the food arrayed before them. The young wrestlers need attention, before they eat, from the doctor, who, apparently working from sheer memory and habit, pulls out what looks like a fountain pen but turns out to cleverly contain within it a styptic pencil, and this he applies to the injuries sustained in the preceding fight: a cut on Stuart's lip and a scrape on Virge's left knuckles.

Almy says grace in her other language, nodding her head as she prays, like she's already sure of some approval. Mostly, they eat, though they do save the cake for a little later.

The salt air, claims Stuart, is good for digestion.

Salty, says Flanig, with some aplomb.

Virge, finished with his sandwich, liverwurst, keeps looking at his slightly scraped up knuckles, not thinking about the fight so much, but the styptic pencil, and how he wishes he'd invented that instrument, and how it's the only care he's received in recent weeks that can unequivocally be termed a success.

Thank you for the food, Almy more growls than says, then laughing, her mouth full, taking in the last buttery bites of her sandwich, speaking in such an uncouth uncharacteristic way that both Virge and Stuart look up in sharp surprise, and laugh.

Why did you do that, asks the doctor, turning and speaking to the trees.

You mean laugh? asks Stuart

Why did you boys fall down?

Oh, well. Okay. You know what? I'm a little embarrassed to say.

Boys are forever falling, Virge pipes up. We tend to fall.

Silence rules after that, and they go on, individually, watching sun and shade patterns creep slowly across their arms. Then the doctor removes his suit coat and makes a tidy folded pillow out of it for Almy, and she bends toward the ground a little stiffly, complaining about mussing her hair, not really wanting to lie down, but perhaps not wanting to seem rude. But at last she's down and then almost instantly asleep.

And though the others don't have any way of making a pillow, they all end up lying down too, staring up into the treetops, breathing audibly for the longest time, each perhaps weaving some kind of connection with nature in the way that suits each one best. The pine trees moving in the wind issue poetic susurrations. Almy meantime saws some delicate logs. For Virge, always between tenderness and crossness for Alice, his mother's raspings bring to mind the workings of the ocean, an entity that likewise snores, and signifies flow and escape. She'll be going soon, he knows, and he can't help but sympathetically match his breaths to hers and smirk, watching the color in her cheeks always change in his favor.

By and by there's another sound, a metallic crescendo, but Virge is the only one who seems at first to hear this and after a moment he identifies it as the rattle of the army train moving by slowly some distance behind them, as they aren't far from the tracks, only a hundred yards or so, and the grinding and pumping is pretty loud. But everyone else just lies there as if sound asleep, and Virge is left alone to contemplate that he is the only one, certainly, who is thinking about both Alice and Mont at that moment, and he can't help picturing Mont emerging from the trees at any moment. Maybe Alice too.

It's all right Dad, he would say, if that were the case. We're all okay, so get back on the train, we'll be just fine. But Alice, please stay and join us, won't you?

Did you hear the train go by? he whispers over to Stuart. My dad was on it.

Your dad, your dad. Maybe your dad is dead. Now close your eyes and forget about it.

I like to keep an open mind, says Virge, eyes wide and in this way taking in thousands of acceptable possibilities. The conversation has all been in whispers, lending a funereal atmosphere, and Virge has to admit that there is such a thing as death, and that to talk about it at all is to talk, between the lines, about your own death, a death that makes everybody else's seem a little less shocking.

Anyway, adds Stuart, let's go take a walk or something, but don't wake up the old folks.

So they end up tiptoeing away, and continuing down the same path, which Virge in his life has taken this far only a few times before, and it's not long before the trail emerges out of the trees and comes up right to the edge of the cliffs, which are not terribly high, but Virge quakes, subtly, tips of his shoes at the edge of things again, except that here he stands at a kind of summit, a vantage point, and here he can look down, quaking but also slightly spiritual, on the whole panorama of ocean, and, at the horizon, the dreamlike smudges of distant islands, or are they battleships heading to the northern wars?

Closer, down near the breakers, they are surprised to see a female figure walking among the rocks, threading between them or leaping across them with concentration, and Virge realizes that they are staring at more or less that part of the beach where the bonfire was built, and the young people danced, and how Stuart has of course been down here before, probably taken this exact path recently and then scrambled down the cliffs somewhere, and could this lone figure on the beach be one of bonfire kids, returning to the scene of the crime, or perhaps it's someone who never left. He knows that some people, like Alice, live outside most of their lives, or like certain others, live only in tents, or, he imagines, shacks laced together from driftwood, elegantly roofed with kelp.

Virge recognizes the girl a minute later as Natalie Sandra, but how blasé she looks as she approaches, catching sight of them in her turn and leaning suddenly to direct her steps toward the base of the cliff, where she peers right up at them, holding her hand over her eye, squinting, ears red in the wind, wearing her taxi uniform, everything sharp and beautiful. Her hair, probably just windswept from the ocean breeze, seems too large for her head, or is it, Virge thinks, that her head has reduced in size? But Stuart says nothing, doesn't even go so far as to acknowledge her. Even when Virge pokes him in the ribs a little, and looks back and forth a dozen times between the two of them, Stuart and Natalie, wondering what's going on between the two of them, Stuart pointedly keeps his gaze fixed on the horizon, and when Virge looks down again once more to try to read her emotions, she's already walked away, already out of earshot, and all this while Stuart rocks back and forth on his heels, whistling, and Virge understands that whatever romance there may have been there at one time is over, at least on Stuart's part, but it is Virge's heart, for some reason, that sinks.

What a day for outcomes this has been, says Virge, mostly to himself, and feels a welling of tears.

Time for lunch? asks the doctor, wide awake and fidgety when they get back.

He means, says Stuart, time for dessert.

Yes, Doctor, shouts Virge, not sure why he's shouting. Time for lunch.

Almy is awake too, and has removed the cake from its baby blanket, and now it sits atop a kind of china pedestal, and there's writing on top, along with some fleurs de lis, and voila, it turns out that Stuart made the cake himself, in secret, late at night, and maybe that is the secret of the picnic. The words are, Congratulations You Two, as if someone has accomplished something, but it doesn't indicate who.

Now it's time for a special announcement, says Stuart.

Let's just eat the damned thing, says the doctor, showing an unusual and unappealing anger, rummaging through the basket for a knife.

Is that the announcement? asks Virge, feeling an anger of his own.

But the topic has to go on hold for a while, and they all take time, a little uncertainly, to eat a few slices of the dessert, cutting through the farewell message on top without waiting for the explanation.

All right, says Stuart, wiping his mouth in such a way that makes his lips look rubbery and moronic. Also he's got a smear of chocolate frosting on one lens of his glasses, and no longer seems at all like he ought to be in charge of the proceedings.

Wait a minute, says Almy.

No, no. There's something that has to be announced to Virge. It's about the old folks. They got engaged.

To whom? inquires Virge, nonplused.

Meet the future Dr. and Mrs. Flanig, says Stuart, holding himself in a regal way, aware of the weight of the announcement, his spine as straight as that of a leader declaring war.

So that was the surprise, says Virge out loud, finally turning to look at his mother, who he knows has been grinning at him for a long time, and when he sees that she too, like Stuart, even like Flanig, has a rubbery and slightly kissy quality to her smile, as if it's been held that way too long, and also how she also has bits and streaks of chocolate on her face, a soft coldness begins to collect and pool all around him.

My dear, dear boy, says the doctor, reaching out for Stuart's hand, picking it up like a handkerchief, and there is a touch of spooky laughter under his words. It appears that he has mixed up the two young people.

Still, Virge notices that Stuart doesn't yank away his hand.

Dr. Flanig? puts in Virge, not wanting to be left out of the ceremony, even though, in a way, he abhors it. It's tempting to tell them about the ethereal letters that Mont sends via wig radio, proving that he's still alive. But it's more tempting to keep his mouth shut about that.

God made us in his image, says Flanig, turning to Virge, briefly lucid. Therefore, when we study anatomy, we study God.

He closes his mouth up tight. It looks like he has a thousand other aphorisms shut up in it, but there's the feeling that that's pretty much the last thing that Flanig is ever going to say. What he does then is extend and swivel his head, turtle-like, as if to show off the unattractive rawness that the old-fashioned celluloid collar impresses, as always, into the skin.

But Virge has gone back to staring at his mother, aware that she's not smiling anymore, and later he'll remember that particular expression as the worst part of the whole day, because, as far as he can tell, it's one of dark self-absorption.

She sees him looking at her, and swallows, and seems to search for something to say.

Oh, what a delicious cake, is all she can utter in the end.

The coldness continues to enlarge, and it's not the ocean breeze, it's the warmth of the air right around Virge simply seeping away. It's the chill of dirt, so familiar to him. It's his natural element in a way, but now it feels like the dirt, always dominant, is taking over the world in such a way that soon there will be little else, and dirt is soon all there will be to eat and drink and breathe.

The next day Virge mostly spends in the bath, naked but for boxers and undershirt, and no water, only a warm tub of contained air far removed from the hubbub of the packing and moving process. That's the other announcement, the one that was forgotten during the picnic and mentioned in passing later, that everyone will be moving to a new apartment in San Grande. The doctor's old place will be sold, Miss Elmwood will receive her settlement, Stuart will take over the practice, not as a doctor of course but as a practiced companion. Virge is more than welcome to live with them in whatever new place they take up residence, that's understood, but, given that he's an adult, free to do whatever he pleases, he can stay here in the country if he likes, and his mother, Mrs. Flanig, will send funds at intervals. Et cetera.

In the tub he finds, while examining himself, a pair of purple veins in his legs he's never seen there before, and he thinks, oh look, how intricate and beautiful. Veins like this have not been seen in the world before, veins that anatomically wrap and curl around his shins like delicate tendrils. Not river deltas, like on the backs of his hands, but baroque embellishments, arabesques. Like God's veins? At any rate take a razor and slice one open a little, and that would be one way to proceed into the future. Not to harm oneself, not like that, but only to bleed and judge the quality of the blood, examining it and tasting it and smelling it as it trickles, luminously, on the porcelain.

Of course it's similar to what happens in Jansens, the time when all of his men have got rickets and he, Captain Jansens, not only leader but doctor of the expedition, bleeds them all for it, and this only forty years ago or so, but still it sounds so old-fashioned, as nobody gets bled anymore today, not in the twentieth century. How would it be done? Do we bleed ourselves at the ankles, he wonders, or at the wrists? Or elsewhere? No idea, but it seems to Virge like he's come up with another invention, that is, a tub, not a bathtub, but a foot basin, that would be used when pricking these lovely veins that branch around the ankle bones, in such a way as to calm the blood when it is too hot, too overtly sexual, too abandoned, in order to siphon off the badness. People should stay away from each other most of the time, but when that's not possible, lie in the tub, where you have the drain right there ready for it, and spill a little something out. A teaspoon's worth. He hesitates to use the term, but wouldn't you have to call it a masturbation of blood?

He goes back to bed, and Almy a moment later brings in lunch on a tray.

Clearly, she's been crying.

Did they leave yet? asks Virge, for Stuart and the doctor, are to go to the city first to arrange things, then to return for the two of them, or one of them, given that Virge will do what he likes, though everyone already knows he will decide to stay.

No of course not, she says, and she's snappish. Do you think they would leave without coming in to say goodbye to you? They're not savages, not like your Jansens' Eskimos.

He didn't visit the Eskimos. Besides, Eskimos are the politest people on earth

Oh.

Now that's cleared up.

There are a few things I could say, she snaps, but I won't say them.

There are a few things *I* could say, he says, but I won't say them.

All right, let's leave it at that.

But he knows what she wants to say. Now that you're all better, she might or could say, go out and get a job. Not for the money, but for the undefinable value of such adventures.

If you need to leave the farm, why don't you go search for your husband, he might or could say in return. And he does at least arch an eyebrow, as if in provocation.

But she looks back at him dully, her eyes flat in her head, as if painted on, lipstick smeared sideways by a kiss or by a handkerchief. She's in a state of disarray. If she is moving toward the same mental condition as Flanig, he wonders, will it be easier to pity her?

And then they both hear the Bellevue rolling up the driveway, and realize that their guests are gone without coming in to say goodbye.

He wishes there were time to hang a banner in his room and letter it to some gay effect, for example, to say, I am happy for you. And whoever reads it could apply it to anyone who happens to be in the room.

Almy moans, rolls her eyes at him, doesn't really look at him, but does reach out to brush a thread off his shirt and then stamps her foot on the ground and laughs.

Oh you, she says. Dios mio.

And then Stuart and Flanig do come roaring back down the driveway, having forgotten something, and there is the sound of doors slamming, and then someone can be heard rummaging in the living room, and then they are off again, still without further ado.

There are those who would be curious to know: If tulips die back, but the bulbs stay in the ground, and the green stalks with their tips of tulip flowers come back the following year, can human corpses, planted in the ground, achieve the same? Bad mood follows bad mood. If a hand is filled with growing bone, can the bone cells reproduce faster than flesh and blood, and in some cases overtake everything else and turn the hand into a clenched fist? The bravest question is, is it all quackery? Are the soft tissues the center of life? Are bones only passive receivers, with no internal importance, beautiful antennae for incoming messages?

After a week spent for the most part in the empty bathtub, a good dry cleaning, Virge can and must transform. Sleepers awake! More so than ever, and more so than the mass of men.

One day, done with bathing, he teaches himself to ride the 3-speed, the one that Stuart pedaled, with Virge a passenger on the handlebars. He considers asking Almy to help him out, to run along behind him with her hand under the leather seat until he strikes a balance, and a momentum, and then letting go. He's certain that's how it's sometimes done, though often the office of fathers. Ultimately he goes on his own, and naturally falters and falls off, and falters and falls off again, repeating this procedure several times, a sorry sight, with his face tilted and forlorn, his hands greasy, his tie popped out of his vest, his stocking marked with the link-to-link pattern of the greasy chain.

All men, he reminds himself, fall, there's no disgrace to it, and he sticks to a bare outline of a plan, and with time he gets a little better at it, up to sliding back and forth in the driveway, using his feet on the ground instead of the pedals, until in time he finds that his legs can pick up the balance trick, and then a moment later, can pick up the pedaling trick, the purposeful revolution of the gears, which seem out of his control or concern now, like the whir of an electrical appliance. Soon enough he learns how to coax the pedals backwards for braking, and learns how to let his hands know how, without specifically teaching them, to juggle and tip the handlebars until he can ride in tight circles, leaning at just that angle that doesn't let him go straight nor fall to the ground, and he feels, really, like he could stay in this tight pattern forever, and never leave this particular circle of dust.

But then he's off like a rocket, without needing to think about it anymore, just determined that this is the day that he'll execute the plan, and the plan is to retrace the route of the eventful automobile trip of the month before. Up the hill he rides, up Highway Number One, without delay, and the riding, before long, turns much harder than before, something you don't notice when you're driving a car, and in fact he's almost instantly exhausted and miserable. Also there's a little confusion in the beginning, as he grinds through the three gears, about which one works best for hills, though he does get to it, but in such a way that he falls off the bike again.

No harm done.

But then how hot. He had forgotten how hot. He's thirstier than he's ever been, thirstier than during his first visit up the road, and he's only ridden twenty minutes, and the slope is always increasing, and almost, at this point, is vertical, and therefore a miracle that he doesn't just start rolling backwards. After another minute of this he's had it, and has to stop and take off his jacket, and tie it to the frame, then push the heavy vehicle by hand, guiding it up the hill, sweat fingering its way in a dozen places down his face and neck. He's lazy too, morally unfit for the task, like a non-worshiper who has to push a holy statue in a parade. He made the wrong decision, he knows that now. Or having made the right decision, which is more likely, it would have been wise to bring a bottle of water. But what's left to do: turn around and try riding down the slope, or just keep moving toward the summit of the volcano, if that's perhaps what it is, which would explain the heat. There are those who, discounting the heat and the slope, would be curious to know: Is the young bicyclist's father dead? If so, can the dead send mental telegrams? Can they draw, if carefully prayed to, a curtain of beautiful cool cloud across the sun?

Hours later there comes some relief, though not in the form of shade. It's just that the road flattens out, progress is imaginable again, the pedaling takes minimal strength, but Virge does proceed slowly, slowly, as in a trance, until, without seeing where he is, he ends up back in the tunnel.

Then his brain returns to him to a degree. The tunnel is more marvelous than before because he has ridden a bicycle there himself, by virtue of his own virtue, and once inside he falters a little, and almost crashes, but rights himself, not stopping, swallowing in the ice box air and dark calm that is the virtue and gift of the cement, but doesn't hesitate now or slow his pedaling, so much is on his mind, doesn't slow down in the middle, doesn't stop to get off his bike, to lean his body out the window over the canyon, as before, in the Stuart era.

Because naturally it's Alice he has in mind, as well as her simple note that is too silly sounding to memorize, but nevertheless he has it memorized, and when he gets to the far end of the tunnel, there where the sunlight comes straight down at noon just outside, he does stop, and gets off the bike, and steps into that exact same spot where his shoes are in the sun and his trousers in the shade.

And, half surprisingly, half unsurprisingly, there they are. The two familiar soda pop figures have relocated themselves, setting up their table much closer to the tunnel than before, and this comes first as an unwelcome shock, and then a welcome one, when he recalls the slope he had to climb before. He steps back into the shadow of the tunnel, but it's all right, they haven't seen him. Dealing with a couple of customers, they are distracted, and so he gets back on the bike and rides back and forth in the tunnel for a while, still in love with the sensation of riding where it's cool, and he practices the tight turns, the braking, becoming expert at these while watching for the time when the customers have left and the girl and the old man are there alone, and in time, that's how things work out, and there they are, just so, holding a position behind the table, arms behind their backs, like soldiers at ease, silent with each other, as if rules forbid them to talk.

Virge has time to form his own rules of friendly interaction. Don't mention wasps. Don't feign paralysis. Don't show off dance moves. Don't give anyone any sort of a leverage point. Be interesting by being interested. Cultivate a verbal ease that distinguishes those who are known for their inhuman minds from those known for their inhuman strength. Debonairly, desperately then, Virge adjusts his tie, a tactic which has sometimes helped him to find his voice, and finally, without leaving the shadows, without getting off the bike, he calls out to them, staying back where they can't see him but can hear his voice, amplified as it is by the acoustics behind him.

Do you know who I am? he singsongs, jiggling his throat to try increasing the volume, sure that he will sound to them like an apparition, no matter what words he happens to use.

No evidence of that, though—it's that they can't or won't respond.

So he lets go of the handlebars and inches forward, and waves his arms this time, shouting the same sentence, but they don't even move their eyes in his direction. Still, he knows they have heard him, because their bodies, especially hers, he's sure, slightly stiffen. Without twitching a muscle, only bones maybe, she becomes taller, and stares straight ahead, as if prepared for attack.

This is the voice of someone you know, he says, loud enough for them to hear him.

We know who you are, states the girl emphatically, looking right at him and brightening. Or he believes it is a kind of brightening.

No you don't.

Sure we do, don't we, Grampa.

How do you know? yells Virge, a little nervously, starting to wonder.

We know it, you and your brother came by last week.

I was?

It makes it sound like he doesn't catch on but he knows in his mind he's all right. Just don't put on an act. Say, Oh yeah, Alice, you're right about that one.

Come on over and agree with me, she shouts in a breezy and noncommittal way.

You're partly right, about the latter but not about the former, Virge responds. That guy wasn't my brother, he was a companion hired for me, that's all.

Success. His words come out with exactly the accent he intends them to have.

Do you still need a companion? she inquires.

Seems like a loaded question. But sick of all the shouting, Virge emerges from his ogre's cave and rides the bike over to them, riding a straight cautious line to the table. There he squeezes the brakes, halts, and with masculine force slaps down a nickel for the bottle of cherry root pop, in just the way he has been rehearsing at home. The nickel makes the same reassuring noise it did on the night stand in his room.

I used to be paralyzed, he explains, shaking his wrists. I was a victim of paralysis. Please excuse the joke about your name. But that was only in my extremities.

Extremities of what?

I mean, I had a paralysis in my arms.

And then it's her who goes on to tell the Alices joke.

I found a pair of socks, she recites, but is it a pair of yours or a paralysis?

But Virge spends that time looking her over, still needing to study her height, her dutchboy bangs, the ponytail she swings behind like a lariat. She's still wearing the baseball cap with the extra long bill. She still has a square nose the color of acorns.

My hired man would like to hear that joke if he were still around, says Virge, stroking his chin, not looking at her now, looking off, a trait that seems distinguished to him sometimes.

Was he a doctor too? asks Alice, because it looks to me like somebody did a good job curing you. Still he can't make out her exact words because he's too busy watching her hands again, studying as she begins the exact ritual that he has often dreamed of witnessing again, in which she plucks a heavy glass bottle out of the ice-block honeycomb, and this time, foregoing the church key, gets off the bottle cap by grabbing it with two strong fingers and pulling it straight off with a pop, like drawing a cork straight out of a wine bottle.

You wanted to know last time, she continues, watching him guzzle, leaning toward him as if to share a secret, why it tastes a little bad. It's because it's not made from cherries like cherry pop is made, or roots, like root beer is made. It's made from the bark of cherry trees. Well, sometimes there's one cherry per bottle. Or one root.

Virge, heedless of this, pays for a second one, thrilled with the coldness and even the taste of the stuff, thrilled to learn that Alice can pull the caps off barehanded. So guzzle on, letting the sting and bitterness of it reach every cell. A possible ad for the side of a barn, with him as the sultan, could read, in the speech bubble: *It doesn't take all that long to get used to the flavor.*

Using both hands on this second bottle, just to show her how electric and unparalyzed he is, he gets pointedly cavalier, and bolts the last of it so fast that some spills down his vest and shirt, and Alice, ready for it to happen, whips out a wet rag and dabs at his clothes with it, hurriedly gets the color of the pop out, with an expression not so much of apology but of interest, as if applying some test to him. She puts the rag away and pokes a finger against the fabric of his vest.

I like the merchandise, like I told you in the note, she observes ambivalently, letting out something like a hiccup, taking up a bottom corner of the fabric in two fingers and rubbing it in a professional if kindly fashion.

Virge is wary, excited, thinks he now understands what sex is, what the sexes are, though particular details remain a mystery. First there is the fingering of the fabric. He keeps one eye on her and the other on the old man, and both of them come off as uncomplicated and friendly to him, and this is what puts him off his guard somewhat, makes him hesitate, and he casts his eyes down and digs the toe of his shoe in the hard black dirt, and stops talking for so long that it's awkward when they all stand there, nothing to say. She doesn't lean back, but stays tilted toward him. He leans toward her, and it puts him further off guard to stand that close, but partly because the sense of progress is always there. He understands perfectly that all this is central to the next step, to the next phase of his life. That this is exactly how to get there, no matter how dumbfounding it all can seem.

I figured you'd come back up here after what I wrote to you in the note, explains Alice, jovially, throwing at the same time such a wicked look at Abuelito that he retreats to take a distant seat on a wooden pallet.

I knew you'd be back to find out whether or not I meant when I wrote. And when I wrote what I wrote, I meant I could help you in some ways.

It doesn't take all that long to get used to the flavor, he suggests.

It's just that it's a bark beer.

Okay, says Virge, losing interest. Is there a—a place. Do you know what I'm talking about? I mean when I say that?

No.

Neither do I. But is there something big around here? Virge is hopping up and down slightly on the balls of his feet, getting upset. Is there something like a big ranch around here?

What do you mean by ranch?

A big ranch. I think it's called Mystery Ranch. Or maybe that's what I call it because I don't remember the name of it. Haven't you heard of it? What do you mean when you say what do you mean by ranch?

I mean what kind of ranch is it?

I didn't know there were different kinds.

Why sure. There's cow ranch, sheep ranch, chicken ranch, fruit ranch.

Oh, then, I don't know. Probably cow. El rancho of the cows.

Come here a minute. Abuelo, you watch the store. And she reaches out across the table, takes hold again of a corner of Virge's vest, and starts to lead him gently across the dirt lot, in a way that he can't not follow, and a minute later they are in the woods, walking single file, Alice leading the way, no longer holding him, on a thin dirt path that winds back through some oaks and then goes down, always down, through some mustard plants that are so high that at times Alice turns a corner and for a moment is lost to view among the yellows and lacy greens and bees.

The heat goes down a few degrees, to something less horrible and more green, a heat full of shade and sounds, the humming foliage and the thumping red dirts and clays.

Alice keeps up a strange dry chatter while they forge forward, hard to follow, but speaking enough for the two of them, enough to keep him thinking and verging on responses, and anyway by listening to her verbiage it's easier to follow her when she goes out of sight sometimes in the labyrinth.

Then suddenly she is walking behind him.

If you're looking for a ranch, she says, where you can find some work to do, there's not much in that way around here. You ought to try making something in your kitchen, if you got a kitchen, the way I make the cherry soda, and sell it on the side of the road. We don't make out too bad that way, you know. Well we just don't know any other way to go, is all.

To Virge this is starting to feel like the hundredth time she's told him this story, and he starts to wonder how many hundred more times there will be. Nevertheless he has to admit that he mostly focuses on the sound of her voice, the movement of her shoulders as she walks, the way the muscles work under the overalls, the way her ponytail bounces like the cord of the venetian blinds.

Now we are on the ranch? Virge asks, winded by all the swift marching. The idea that comes to him is just to give up and lie down and curl up in some feather bed he can put together out of green mustard stalks and yellow mustard flowers. Lately he has a problem. There's something permanently inside that makes him want to lie down at intervals, relax the whole body, get horizontal, achieve breadth in lieu of depth, but in this case he just has to shut up and press on, always trailing behind several steps, curving away from her path, then self-correcting, wondering how a tall and ponderously figured girl like her outwalks a soul so easily. True, he's dressed in vest and tie, a costume that would be hot in the big city and hot here, though Alice doesn't break a visible sweat, stays fresh as you please, a movie star too in her own way. Maybe all women turn into movie stars. But how? How is that done? Finally the slope flattens out and they arrive at the edge of a clearing, a place from where they can see a wide green bowl of country spreading out all around and above them.

I like ranches and I like this ranch, he states, turning to hurry back the way they came, not sure why, but Alice grabs a hold of his hand, not for the last time, and spins and adjusts him slightly so that he's looking out over this landscape, and points out to him what he hadn't noticed at first glance, as if explaining to a simpleton, that it's a cattle ranch, that this little valley, this bowl, is inhabited by cows, so look at the cows, any moron can see the cows, and here, no more than fifty feet away, are two brown and white Holsteins that are also slightly green in the green light, giving off their own stinky heat, chomping listlessly at the grass, so unblinking and so unaware of the world that Virge, fascinated, gets sleepy again, and yearns again for a short nap, maybe in hayloft, in a barn.

Here's your ranch, indicates Alice. Cattle ranch, just like I said. Mystery ranch? Maybe. The mystery is that everything to be seen from here belongs to one owner and I'll tell you one thing, and that's that I am not that owner. Whoever he is, and maybe his name is Mr. Mystery, if you want to think so, has got money to burn, never mind the rest of the country. Is that what you're looking for? I brought you here to ask you that question, you know. What are you looking for?

You do help me. I mean to say that you help me a lot.

Well, that's nice. Sweet as honey. So is that the ranch you want, Honey?

I don't know yet. Yes, yes, it is. And I guess I will take a job on that ranch, if they have jobs on ranches. Thank you. I'll head over there in a minute.

She stares sideways at him, and he in turn eyes her occasionally from one eye or the other and can't help but focus in at intervals on the plain facts on the surface: her big blue overalls, her lips cracked but red and round as tulips. Or radishes, because her teeth are as white as the inside of a radish. Everyone he has known and met in his life up to this point seems to him now not properly completed, not quite human, because of something lacking and unnamable, whereas she, this Alice, is all there, even more than human. Does that make her insatiable? If so, for what? In any event, she hasn't buttoned the sides of her overalls all the way up and it's easy, furtively, to catch glimpses of skin. The skin, though, seems red from chafing, and this is not good. This is like Flanig's collar that scratches crimson rings around his neck. You don't want him to take off the collar, and you don't want Alice to take off her overalls.

So what should we do now? she says at last.

I need to be more horizontal, says Virge, meaning only that he wishes he knew a wide range of people. But she takes it a different way, and leads him back a short way to a little vale of oaks that feels like an orchard, as the trees are spaced almost in rows, and they clear a space in the mustard plants, like dogs who walk a little circle before lying down, and they stretch out in the fragrant mass of greenery as if following some plan. There and then they find themselves lying side by side, almost touching, mutely watching the clouds, and when later there are no clouds, the sky, each with various stalks of grass to chew, and both of them staying quiet but listening to the thousands of bees around that sound so heavy and dopey in the chewy heat.

Eventually their hands drift together and take hold, though without any particular electricity, and indeed it's as if someone has just laid their two hands atop one another to save space. Also there is the vibrating of the hovering bees and Virge himself slowly begins to buzz, though ever so slightly, like an elongated insect, and in this condition he moves toward the brink of sleep, without ever quite arriving there.

It would be better to be wasps instead of bees, he says, so sleepily.

Why?

Because then we would not only make paper, but write little books about our lives as wasps.

But what kind of moment is this, he wonders a moment later, to arrive at in one's short life, where one lies, as in a bed, but vibrates all over, and frankly comes close to being in love with someone, but not quite, not quite. I'll be in love with her a little later. And yet they are holding hands, and that is another item to add to the list of important and majestic uses of the hands.

And then Virge sleeps.

When he wakes up, it's much cooler, Alice is gone, and he gets up in a dither and runs back toward the soda stand, first thinking that he has lost his way, but then finds the exact place, yet everything is deserted—no table, no pop, no people, only his bicycle leaning against a tree, as if the whole sequence were a dopey dream. So back he runs to the woods and finds there, to his relief, that everything is real, or was real, and knows this by the fact that there is still a cool large area of flattened foliage, an oval, where she had lain down next to him.

Not in embrace, perhaps, but at least in contiguity.

The bicycle ride home is divine—once he's out of the tunnel it's all downhill, and though at first he lets himself creep down toward the ocean quite slowly, squeezing the brake levers with all his might, using the power of what feels for the first time like a pair of ridiculously strong hands, his suit coat catching the wind like a sail to slow him further, at last he untightens himself, gains courage, and shoots down the last bit of slope as in a racing motorcycle, head kept down near the handlebars for cutting through the wind, keeping his eyes on the asphalt, using not just legs and hands but eyes, the all-important eyes that can pick out potholes in the road ahead and send messages to the nerve centers that send messages to the hands to guide the front wheel just around the perimeter of each cavity with pinpoint accuracy.

—

Back home, putting the bike away, he thinks about what he would like to say to his mother, something he never thought of saying before, in so many words. Take away certain beliefs, he'll say to her, certain destructive beliefs, certain phrases rolled over in the mind, and rolled over and over and over, and observe the change, see weakness change to strength, see invalid become valid. And perhaps she'll note the differences. You're not in such bad shape after all, she might observe. Look how handsome you got, she might muse, as if seeing him for the first time. Pretty soon, she might say, pretty soon you'll be running this farm yourself, and I don't see any problem.

But when he walks in the door the first thing he feels is the spooky, shabby emptiness of the place. Nobody home. A note on the breakfast table comes into view:

Stuart came to get me, but you weren't home. We waited a while. Then since we guessed you would not be coming with us, and we all thought we should get a move on, well, off we go. I'll be back to see you, and you catch the bus and come up to see us really soon.

5

Virge wakes up this time saying something out loud. He's in the tub first thing in the morning, while it's still mostly dark out, and stays there in a state of sculpted but awkwardly bent nudity, wondering if there is some possibility that this is the last time he will ever wake up in his own house, and clings to the possibility that it is. Still, in the bathtub, especially without water, there is a feeling of being miraculously cleansed, vaguely spiritualized. These are the positive effects on the human body of sleeping in a tub or, as he likes to think of it, a chest, one made of glazed cast iron, and it's clear to him that all men should experience, at least once, the regimen of the cracker chest, or the ice chest, or the bathtub.

Morning is slow to arrive. Outside the sun must be arousing slowly from its own bath of fog. It's the beginning of autumn and suddenly no longer hot; some spongy marine air has crept up over the cliffs overnight, and it's so gloomy everywhere that outside the bathroom window there is no good distinction between night and day.

He lies motionless, poised for action, heart beating too fast for one who might just prefer to go back to sleep. There comes the sound of something heard once already, the crunch of footsteps in the outer gloom. But after minutes and minutes of alternating between eyes open, eyes closed, eyes open, he still can't quite prepare himself to meet Alice. Oh, because it's her, no question, who has been moving around out there in the fog for a while now, shuffling and crunching her shoes in the driveway, it's her that's making his heart beat fast, and when in time the face of the girl he almost loves does suddenly loom up at the window, wraithlike and almost beautiful, even, perhaps because of his spiritual mood, almost saintly, he just keeps alternating eyes open, eyes closed.

This girl, thinks Virge, when at last he snaps upright in the tub, tired of playing games, this Alice is a little too everywhere, isn't she, too everywhere for him to occasionally and fondly treasure like the rarest of jewels. And how anyway did she find out where he lives? Does she remember from the olden times, when they were in school together? Did she come here once when they were kids? In the window, she looks a fright, her hair enlarged with dark ribbons, or it could be seaweed, because she has emerged from the ocean, swimming to him down the coast? Clammy hair, clammy eyes. When, because perhaps she can't quite see him, she mashes her nose up flat against the glass, this is more alarming, more marine, with her face turning flat and pale, her lips glossy on the glass like the feet of snails.

What are you want? he shouts, misspeaking, blurting ungrammatically, but enunciating in such a way for her maybe to read his lips from out there, but what is there to read but his tragic English, and she just keeps pressing her nose and lips flat, grimacing, waving her hands, wriggling her fingers like claws, like someone pretending to be funny and scary. Finally, since he shows no signs of getting out of the tub, she taps the glass lightly. Come on, come on, come on out here, she gestures, seems to gesture. And he nods a big yes because though it's so cold he can't bear to stay bare and self-paralyzed in the tub a moment longer, not knowing what her mystery is, and because he can't after all refuse to change his life, can't not respond to her gestures, which likely have some chance of initiating a desired effect.

Every journey begins with a single step. Getting to his feet now could be the beginning of a trip to Greenland, or green land. So Virge bursts upright like a launched rocket, grabbing a towel as he does so to cover his preposterous white nakedness. At least she didn't see my white penis, he thinks to himself, but can't really be sure she didn't. Then, barefoot on the ice cold tiles, unable to locate his shoes, he gives up and glides out silently through dark corridors all the way to the kitchen screen door, as if floating, as if slightly airborne along a lamplit path, a path of perfect destiny, though at one juncture on this path, at the juncture of the screen door, he stops, and throws on the porch light. And there, upon sticking his head out the door an inch or two, and not seeing Alice right away, just staring into the circle of light cast like honey over the darkness, he feels, like never before in his life, the sense of being home and never wanting to leave.

But why? Well, because I am leaving home, and the thing is, I am leaving home, he says to himself. Because this is more home than anywhere. Where to find another one? And the sudden attachment is so physical and striking that it makes him weepy on the spot, though tears don't come, since at the same time he has to think about vast horizontal spaces that fill the mind and flatten it.

Come on, Virge, he has to say to himself then, whispering it, feeling the need to speak. Crawl on your knees if you've got to. Crawl on your belly. Jump on Alice's back for a ride.

But then here comes Alice, stepping into the light, one leg angled in front of another, just a big and somewhat boyish angel taking one step at a time.

What is it? he asks, spitting these words across space toward her without sticking his head another inch out the kitchen door to see her, protruding his lips only a little ways out the narrow space between door and door jamb, while holding tight to the knob, which seems to prop him up. There she is, there she constantly is. He could take a mental snapshot, then imagine an alternative future, but too late, she's advancing right toward him through the fog, casting a shadow behind her that becomes gargantuan, twenty feet high at least and he poses the question again.

What is it, Alice or should I say Alicia? He says it even more hissy and spastic this time, and all the while there is no question in his mind that he's coming across as a boor. But she's fine with it, he finds, just keeps smiling, and it's the case that he can hardly think about her right now, so utterly numb is he that he can only blurt out information, too much of it, in this case about how in Greenland there is a ring of mountain peaks and how Jansens and his men figured out that if they stood on one peak in the fog that gathered every evening, each man's shadow would appear in outsized scale on the peak opposite, and that he and his men grew fond of strolling to the heights of these peaks every evening to observe this and that they ultimately reached the point after a while of putting on gargantuan and comic performances, all silent pantomime.

I'm just trying to bring you the milk of human kindness, that's all, she pants, ignoring, as usual, everything he says, and coming to a stop a few feet away.

You're the very first person I knew, he confesses, sharply aware of their scholastic past, embarrassed by his endless Jansens stories, and he flings the door wide and emerges out onto the porch into full view, thin but approximately good looking in his towel, feet bare on the floor and freezing. The fog has never been this close to a state of pure liquidness, he supposes, and this fluid quality gives Alice's face the look of a plastic do-it-yourself masterpiece, an oval soft as cake and nearly close enough for him to reach out and sink his hungry fingers into.

But you have to hurry, she says, because they're out on the road waiting for us.

They?

I mean the workers. Me and the transport workers. They're waiting for me, for us, so hurry hurry.

But the word transport only makes him think of raptures, and great waves of emotion, and then he thinks about the words *waiting for me,* questioning whether she is or has become a in-commonist too.

I have always shown you the greatest respect and kindness, he says out loud, looking down at the crescent patterns in his toenails, his feet at the edge of the porch cement, the old standing-on-some-threshold posture.

Thank you, she says, and he thinks she blushes.

Oh, he goes on, it's just a turn of phrase. And he grins up at the moon, still not ready to keep both eyes on her all the time.

Hurry back in and get dressed, Hon, she urges, stepping up close and giving him a shocking but pleasant poke in the ribs. Remember the transport, she says, and remember the workers, and remember that that's us.

Okay Pumpkin, or Melon, he feels he ought to reply to her, in kind, but doesn't. There is always a catch, a hesitation. What that means, he thinks, is that he sees nothing significantly right or wrong with her. And so to conclude, she is not his wife, just contiguous to him. She is not there to embrace him, as he had guessed for a moment, but to provide a means of transport. So he will be transported.

The truck's waiting out front, she emphasizes next, stamping her foot when he hesitates.

Where?

On the shoulder, Brother. Willing workers waiting to work.

He looks at her blankly.

Okay, she sighs. Try to think, try to do this for me. I know it's early. I do remember you. I do.

Should I meet you out front?

Yeah, except I'll be in the back of the truck.

Okay, okay, I'll be right there, I mean. Me in the back of the truck too.

And Virge wheels himself around with a snort and heads back in the house without any special hurry, though directing himself as best he can to successive actions, still numb from the tub. What he lacks is any clear idea of what it is they are going off to do so early and so cold in the morning, but she said to expect something from her and probably this is it. Maybe the only thing he has to do is jump in the back of a truck on a foggy morning. Maybe it's enough that each new moment creates thousands of branching off moments, and each one of those, thousands more.

What Virge will discover later is that he's now one of those called not a hired companion, but a hired hand. Someone like him, with parents who did try to farm things once, though they couldn't succeed at it, might not guess that in truth there is farm work just down the road, farm work all around, though he has wondered about it, and suspected it, though not at this particular moment. So Virge, stumbling around in his bedroom, lights out, throwing on his shoes, fumbling with the laces forever, has no idea that he's to become a drone of sorts, starting today. How do the wasps make paper? Very slowly, very intently, without at all knowing that that's what they're doing.

At length, deciding that he's most probably on his way to some public gathering, like a picnic or a church service, he tiptoes right out into the soup of fog and then, almost getting lost, making a louder sound with each step, to remind himself where he is as he makes his way up to the road.

What he finds there is somewhat familiar, in that it's an army truck, painted like the army train, green in all its parts, with a canvas stretched loose over the back ribs, reminiscent of the army train, and Virge, nonchalantly, fully inflated now with cold morning air, leaps up onto the high tailgate and peeks inside into the mystery space under the tarp, wondering if his dad might be inside.

Exhilaration! he says out loud, pronouncing it more like acceleration.

But, as his eyes get used to the dark, revealing a pool of upturned faces below him, souls in some transportational purgatory, he wishes he hadn't said it, that he hadn't started things off with an uninvited lecture.

There are many faces visible to him in the darkness, none of them Mont-like, and he sees that the mood within is one of solemnity and neutral contemplation, as if he's stumbled into a sacred place, a zone of concentrated thoughtfulness, where there is some muttering going on, but not conversation. He can see who and what they are—that everyone is awake in the dark with two open eyes, that they are the kind of people to be farm workers or something, that he is one of them now, that they sit glumly pickled together within this dark rectangle, cigarettes glowing here and there, and after a second someone hands him one and lights it up for him with a flame as large and brilliant as an orange. Hip to hip, rib to rib, these travelers have arranged themselves modestly, without complaint, legs tucked up and in like folding chairs, tail bones settled down hard on the oak plank bed of the truck, and he perceives, as the stares directed toward him grow harder and squintier, that he will do likewise in some little spot that, despite his best efforts, he just can't find.

Look, he says out loud, sort of to himself, and to them, since they are his audience, and because no one is moving at all to let him in.

Look, he repeats, moving forward awkwardly, planting a foot between somebody's feet.

Look, there's Alice over there.

Then, blushing at his own words, he looks for a way to maneuver his bony body so that he can sit next to her, next to his Alice, and really he can't figure out how it works, where he goes, and after watching his various scrapings and bendings Alice herself just snatches him roughly by the hand and yanks him down hard to occupy a space that she makes next to her, while the truck suddenly burps and lurches forward, moving but in a roughshod way as if there's a broken engine or axle somewhere deep inside. But it's not, everything's all right, the truck is just gearing up for the journey, and soon it's all smooth sailing, possibly with the arctic north as a destination, and before long Virge can sense under the tires some endless steepness, the truck grinding so slow up a long hill, back to its piteous noises, a primitive machine that nevertheless can manage a jagged progress.

You see, Alice whispers in his ear, still gripping tightly the hand she grabbed him with. You see the deal?

See what?

Here's the deal. We're all headed right up to the ranch.

Somehow this time she's more than what she's been, she's more intimate now, right next to him, her breath complicated and romantic in his ear.

Can you believe that for luck, she adds, and in the silence that follows, she whistles a short tune, sticking out her lips till they look like a bird's beak.

Do you remember who I am? he asks, after a while, stubbing out his smoke on the floor.

Sure I do. You're Virgil. Virgil Boner, they called you back then.

When?

When I knew you in grammar school. Your arms are just about as bony as they were then.

You haven't seen my arms.

What? Yes I did. When you had just your towel on a minute ago. Good thing you have nice clothes to cover up your bony old arms.

It takes him forever in that crowd to find a way to uncoil his famous arms, but at last, in acknowledgement of all her kindnesses, present and past, Virge puts one arm around her shoulders, though from this position she recoils, then makes up for the recoil, possibly, by putting her own arm around his shoulder—which feels unnatural to him, like the embrace of someone who has nowhere else to place the arm. So after a minute he squirms out from under her heavy limb, but holds on to it in front of him, like a package that has to be delivered.

Where is your iron lung? he asks, changing the subject, taking a calm thrill in the fact that his face is not only inches from hers, but inches from everybody else s.

What?

Your iron lung. Are you wearing it now?

Let me ask you a question. You think people could have a thing made of iron inside them? And besides they're not made of iron they're made of steel. Only talk to me about steel lungs.

So you don't need one anymore?

Never did need one, she answers, taking her arm back.

So why did you leave school?

Because I was sick. But it wasn't steel lung disease.

But you were sick.

I was sick, you were sick. At that school, we were the sicklies.

They bounce along for a while.

Alice?

Yes?

Where are we going?

I told you. We're going to your mystery ranch to work the gourds. Remember the cows?

Yes, but didn't you just say gourds?

Do you know how that works?

No.

She thinks for a moment how to go on. They're vegetables. But you don't eat them. They're just gourds.

I'm much obliged to you for the thorough explanation, he replies.

It's for you, Virgil Boner. This is what I told you we'd do. To get you into something new. Something where you're less obliged to that companion of yours.

Virge lifts up both arms over his head, mulls over everything in this posture reminiscent of a dancer, or a yogi. And, like a yogi, he knows all, sees all, in the growing light. There are vaguely comic and vaguely tragic people all around him now, people from probably near by and probably far away, Mexicans and Okies, hobos and old cowboys, a handful of kids. All the folded up people look to him like they're peering at him and thinking the same thought, and he's suddenly so self-conscious of his vest, his tie, the splash of toilet water he threw on his neck in the bathroom, while Alice waited, over-splashing to the extent that now he smells like something that better belongs in the garbage can.

It's all a case of bad timing, and a sour feeling rises in him, like vomit rising in the gorge, but in this case it's only a mental sensation. Who the hell are these people? His father, and here's the truth of the matter, would hate such folk, and hate Virge for becoming one among the common herd, the riffraff, et cetera, as Mont was of course a gentleman farmer with emphasis on the gentleman. Such considerations take Virge back to the episodes of the wig and the transmissions, and sense of shame to reflect on what drivel that was, but he finds himself doing something he swore he would never do. He finds himself making one up.

Dear Son, Waking up on a park bench this morning, and thought I'd send you a line or to. Lying here thinking that you are made of the same material as me, that you and me are like two hats cut from the same cloth. If I feel something you feel it. If an earthquake comes it rumbles through the both of us. What does it mean to be independent? In the best dressed families it's not always right to light out after the new scheme of things by yourself. An only child isn't always permitted to leave his family, and the only ones that do that are the ones who are somewhat wayward from the start.

What about the cherry root pop, he asks, prodding Alice, who appears to have nodded off. She snaps awake.

What about the pop? he repeats, turning to her, trying to change his mood from inside to outside. What about your old grampa?

Oh, she replies with a sniff. That business only works out well in the hot weather.

Okay.

And as for Abuelito, she shrugs, open your eyes and take a good look. Don't you see him over there?

And sure enough when Virge squints in the direction she's indicating with her thumb, when he stares into the mass of faces, he catches sight of the old man; nodding and smiling, to himself or maybe to Virge, as if to convey to the world how much he looks forward to doing whatever it is one does to gourds. Virge's staring seems to make Abuelito smile more broadly, then click his teeth, then use his hands to pantomime the drinking of pop from a bottle. But the act isn't over, as he goes on to pantomime tossing the bottle away, then pantomime, oddly, if Virge interprets it right, two people smooching, then slapping one another.

All this time Alice can't keep her hands off Virge, or at least keeps lightly moving her hand over the surface of Virge's clothes. What she likes to do is keep at him with her fingers, like she did at the soda stand, but now going further and lingering there, picking lint off his wool vest, pinching up the pleats in his trousers, at times inadvertently pinching his skin, reaching up to wiggle the knot of his tie, perhaps hoping to see if she can make him come out a little snappier, a little more sharply etched.

If I had a girl like you, she sings out in the middle of all this, a popular song, and some of the workers around them laugh.

Here's the whole ball of wax, she confides, later. I think they're going to want to make you a foreman.

She makes this pronouncement too boisterously, loud enough for all to hear, and several people turn to examine him more closely.

What do you mean, Virge whispers, shrinking from the close attention.

I mean you might have to stick with us for a while but I bet when the boss notices you he'll say something like, Say now, bring that boy over here, that boy's sharp, that one's got the mark of quality to him.

Well I don't suppose it's any of my business what he says, replies Virge, nervously.

The fellow closest to them leans in even closer.

So you're the new foreman? he asks, sharpening his gaze.

Sorry? says Virge.

Oh, don't apologize, continues the man, nodding, head loose, like a puppet. I like you, Boss, I'm devoted to you.

If I'm qualified for anything, says Virge, blinking a little, taking the man's words as a compliment, I'm only qualified for special and undefinable activities.

He could go on in this vein, but Alice tugs at his sleeve.

Don't bother with him, she whispers. Don't talk to any of them.

But Virge keeps blinking pleasantly at the man, trying to get him to say something else.

What's your name? the guy demands, obligingly, after a moment.

It's Virge, he answers, and holds out his hand halfway for a shake, despite Alice tugging further at the sleeve.

Not a-gonna tell you my name, says the man, shaking hands nevertheless.

Virge guesses that he's not a lot older than himself, but like himself, is perhaps aged beyond his years. Another convalescent. That's one possibility.

His name's Lank, Alice whispers, and all you need to know about him is that he's not so nice.

To Virge, this Lank fellow looks all right, seems sort of old-fashioned in his droopy hat, though what's striking is that he's all bruised up under his eyes, so that it looks like he's got heavy purple makeup, or blood that's trickled down both cheeks.

Are the gourds for drinking from? Virge asks, comfortable in conversation mode, more so than with Alice, truth be told, but it's at this point that the truck pulls noisily off the road and stops, and they all have to rise to unload themselves and he's separated from Lank before he can get the answer to his question.

Outside the truck it's still foggy, but Virge can tell they've gone inland, because here there's no more homey smell of kelp and ocean, just the sour mash smell of cow manure and mustard grass and freshly sawed pine.

It strikes him now, as they all mill around the area, stiff as the walking dead, that something remarkable and somehow rather unappealing is about to get underway. His new theory is that it's a kind of incarceration, or forced labor. He wonders if Alice meant, when she spoke in the truck, that it's his destiny to become a prison foreman or a chief guard, and the others, including Alice, will be his prisoners, and he will be in charge of bringing the drinking gourd around to every cell, dipping it repeatedly into the bucket, dispensing generously, and so rising to the highest levels of popularity. But he keeps his mouth shut as everybody, standing and waiting in the fog, subconsciously sidles in a little closer to each other, looking for a little warmth in the semi-arctic hills.

But there's nobody to greet them or instruct them, no explanation of what is to happen to them or why. Virge looks this way and that, hoping to find someone who will take over, someone to escort him toward where he is meant to be, because Alice just stands there with a blank look, not much help anymore.

Where's your gourd, Brother? he asks the man named Lank, who has reappeared nearby. Are we supposed to get one yet?

Oh you'll have plenty of gourds soon enough, shouts the fellow, taking on a crazy, arms out posture. His eyes look worse and more stained now, but he seems friendlier than before. And Virge is about to ask more questions about everything, but then there appears, out of nowhere, a figure towering over them a few yards away. Though at first this seems like a freakishly tall person, Virge realizes it's really just someone standing elevated on a couple of overturned crates, a heavily bearded man wearing a strikingly yellow and black flannel shirt, plus a baseball cap with a long bill, who says nothing, just puffs on a cigar, all the while scowling and blowing out dense spheres of smoke, little planets that seem to orbit him for a while. Then, as if by signal, he goes into a frenzy of action and starts throwing things at them, hurling little black objects out toward the workers, and they appear to be items of value, because others near Virge dive to the ground to grab one. When one of these appears next to Virge's shoe, he snatches it up and finds that it's a heel detached from its shoe, one nail sticking out of it still, maybe even the mate to the one from the tunnel, except that this one has the number thirty-four painted on.

Then there's Alice again up close against him, grabbing the heel away from him to read the number.

You got a good one, explains Alice, excited, wheeling her arms and prancing around him, dancing, making fake jabs at him like a prize fighter.

Because, she goes on, still dancing, it means you get an extra 34 cent bonus on every twentieth box you bring in, and see, that's ten cents more than me, my number's only 24. Say, would you split the difference, since I'm the one who got you the job?

Alice stops moving, and the next moment she seems awfully exhausted.

What's not so good, she goes on, is that it turns out we're doing gourds all day, without any of the Indian corn. Corn is easier, you just have to shuck it, but I'm glad we're together on the gourds because that way I can give you help. Not that you need help. But, you know what? I can give you hints about how best to do it. Stick close to me is all I'm saying.

Then there is a wave of general movement, chattering, shoving, and Virge finds himself trotting ahead of almost all the others, running in synch with Alice, relieved to be with someone who understands systems so well, since so far this workaday world makes little or no sense to him. Holding hands to keep each other steady in the rocky soil, they manage to be the first to get to the picking area, and there they are, standing in a large flat piece of farmland, something growing there in rows, fog at all corners but slowly burning off, taking with it a reek of old vegetable matter that hurts the nose, and there again is the bearded man who threw out the numbered heels, and now you can see that he's standing on a pair of crates again, as if he always carries such platforms everywhere he goes. He's a tall man but it seems, with those crates underneath, like he has managed to be the tallest man for miles.

That's Boss Wasp, says Alice. They call him that on account of his yellow and black shirt. He's the one who's going to notice you, so we'll see if we can't work some rows near him, near where he's bossing today. But we've got to start picking now, Hon, if you're planning to make that dollar today.

What dollar?

What dollar? Why, the dollar you'll go home with if you work hard today, that's what dollar. Nearly guaranteed. Your 34 cents on your way to it already.

But turning her face away from him then, scowling, as if she suddenly dislikes him somewhat, for reasons that he can't understand, she grabs some wooden crates from a pile, hands a couple to Virge, and demonstrates how to bend at the waist without straining, like a ballerina, gently stretching the hamstrings, she says, because the upper part of the body, the part with the arms and hands, all that has to get low enough down to pick the gourds out of the mess of vines and leaves that stretch all around them in somewhat dumbfounding rows. The main thing, as she explains, is that you have to work quick as a wink, that you have to fill two wooden boxes before you carry them on up toward where Boss Wasp is, so you can show them to him and he'll make a mark in a book, next to your heel number, for every box you show him and go on to empty in the back of the wagon that's parked there.

The more you pick the more you make, she keeps repeating under her breath, apparently thrilled to be present at such an event, thrilled with the raw simplicity of it, the ease with which physical movement turns magically, if slowly, into cash money.

So they begin, and Virge, still working on getting his posture right, on stretching his legs, is shocked to hear Boss Wasp, in dripping tones, already calling out the number of a worker who has brought in two boxes worth.

What are these things, asks Virge, after Alice has been to the wagon twice, and he's filled up only one box and his hands are pink and stinging from something.

Oh, they're gourds of course. Gordo gourds, they call them. Fatties. They're just a kind of squash after all. You eat squashes don't you?

Do we eat these too? he asks, straightening up, tapping on one, finding it hard as a rock. Already Virge is winded, awkward, angry enough to start strangling himself, or someone nearby.

Oh no, not for eating, only for decoration. And other stuff. See what pretty colors they come in? They get all shellacked later on and used for Halloween, Thanksgiving. For making egg cups. Parts of dolls. You name it. But here I am talking to you and you're losing a nickel every time you open your mouth.

So he goes back to work, chastened, burning up. After tossing a few more gourds in his box Virge chooses to resign from this line of work.

I could have done this job if I'd had a pair of gloves, he announces, and holds up his hands to reveal to Alice how his palms are as red as cinnamon candy and dotted, festively, with a dozen little snow-white blisters.

Oh no, you don't want gloves. Gloves'll slow you down to a crawl. Your hands have to toughen up. But come on. Finish filling your box and I'll finish mine, and we'll go up together and maybe Boss Wasp will notice you, like I keep telling. You shouldn't be picking at all. Someone dressed like you should be inspecting.

He bends down as if to pick some more, as if to finish the box, but just stays there, motionless, concentrating his mind toward willing the poor stinging hands to stop stinging, as though it's a problem he'll be able to solve with one minute more of mental power. It's not just his hands that bother him, but also he can't help but think there is something in Alice's voice, something unheard before, low and menacing and dusty dry in every word she says to him now. Virge glances sideways at her whenever he can and sees how somewhere along the line she's tied up her hair in a red handkerchief and that her hands too, to be honest, are kind of red and awful, but that to look at her, he realizes she's a champion at this, snatching up and twisting dry gourds off the withering vines, shooting them into the nearby box like she's entered some manic contest, kicking the box ahead of her as she works, never pausing, apparently pretty good in the world of production and money, good at sheer accumulation, a talent he wouldn't have dreamed of her having. Look at her, he marvels, she's ready to go over to the wagon again, but as for himself, forget it, his attitude is that the gourds don't need him and he doesn't need the gourds, he can just go home after all, and get back in bed, or, even better, the tub.

But, after a long pause, a pause more hellacious than the actual picking, he goes at it again. It's a courtesy to Alice, the way he sees it, and there are pictures he can look at in his mind, snapshots, anything that distracts, whatever moves the mind from one level of torture to somewhat lighter one, and he keeps one eye on his shadow, which has become visible as the sun burns harder, and says to himself, lectures to himself, that it's really just the shadow feeling the torture, not his body, and such fictions do help for a time, for maybe a minute. Meanwhile he sticks one hand behind his back, with one finger curled in an awkward gesture of affection toward Alice, which he half hopes she'll see and, maybe when she does see it, she'll come up to him for just a second to curl her finger into his.

But she doesn't, and so all his cleverness and then all his cultivated attitudes and tricks and refinements fail. He stops, because he can't go on doing what he's doing, any more than he could grow new skin, or swallow the ocean, so there's no chance of filling that second box, his hands being incapable of that and, as he now understands, a whole long list of other tasks.

The air itself is unbreathable, as if it too has a rash, but it's only most of his body that has turned red, because, though no one mentioned this earlier, the vines that the gourds grow from are covered in tiny sticky hairs that come off when you grab the gourds, and the hairs get on your hands and then your wrists and somehow, like ants, or mites, these hairs crawl up your arms until your whole body under your clothes is consumed, and nothing will put an end to the burning until you can maybe plunge into a lake or brimming bathtub at the end of the day. Which is what all the others are good at, more than they are good at picking—they are good at patiently waiting for a reward at the end of the day. As for him, all he can think to do is rip his jacket off and throw it down on the ground and sit on it, and turn in-commonist, if ripping their jackets off is in fact what in-commonists do. Rip off their jackets and go on strike!

Bad bad bad, he thinks, simply, staring into his palms. I hereby wish for them to be paralyzed again.

No you don't no you don't, someone is saying and he looks up and it's Lank, the guy from the truck, who has in fact become their foreman for the day, beating Virge out for the job, and given a badge to wear on his droopy hat to signify authority over any lazybones in the crew, though nobody has ever mentioned a word of warning to Virge about this or bothered to tell him to look sharp in case the foreman comes by.

Is it time for the drinking gourds yet, asks Virge, going for the charm again, the humor, smiling in the fresh and innocent manner of someone who has been an invalid most of his life and a shut-in, and not used to dealing with elements of structure in the world or for that matter frankly intolerable working conditions. He even holds his hand out to droopy Lank as if to say, pull me up my friend and, yes, let's get that gulp of water now please.

So Virge is surprised when Lank does not take his hand, but reaches down and pinches him by the shoulder, as if his collar bone is the handle of a suitcase, and in this way he lifts Virge to his feet with an easy, unlooked for strength, but stops just short of actually lifting him off the ground.

It's all up with you, he announces for all to hear, speaking without any measurable degree of human kindness. Looks to me like they made me foreman today, not you, and here's what the foreman says: you no picky, you no get ticky. And besides, I kicky your ass as well.

Laughter erupts somewhere. Is it that they are laughing at the man's bad English? And though Virge takes him to mean something else, Lank is true to his word, and after revolving Virge to face the other way he then does kick him square in the pants seat, as if to launch him all the way home, but Virge doesn't fly far, just comes to earth square among the thickest part of the planted rows, so that now the skin of his face too gets a good strong exposure to the stinging hairs that, so far, he's managed to keep away from that one last portion of his anatomy.

Go away and come back later, he hears someone shout out, and then realizes it's Alice's voice, that she's speaking to him, and through a veil of tears—his tears or her tears?—he sees her gesturing at him to get lost, to do as he's told.

Also, through a pair of bleary filthy eyes, he can't help but see that Lank is quite the gentleman in that he's pouring the gourds out of Virge's crate into Alice's, and handing her, with a deep bow, Virge's numbered shoe heel.

I'm obliged to you for your support, says Virge, speaking to the dirt, crawling away, looking for slightly different dirt to lie in.

People fall, and he has fallen. Nothing special there. Meanwhile, every inch of him is under the dread power of inflammation, and then the most wonderful thing that can happen, happens—he puts a cheek down cautiously on the ground, and is carried to the land and dirt of sleep.

It's later in the day, and not quite as hot, when Virge regains anything like an understanding of where he is, and where he is, he sees, is naturally flat on his face on the ground, but away from the gourds, discarded to the side, offstage. He awakens to the sensation of skin still burning, but sees he's ended up on a stretch of ground where there are no gourds, no dust, just a knot of young flame-shaped cedars and a carpet of green weeds that feel like someone's matted hair underneath him and also, when he twists his head, there's water nearby, a brook that gurgles so close to him that all he has to do is what he does: crawl one more foot forward and then protrude his lips out right to the surface and drink, and it's so cool and good as it flushes the filth out of his teeth, then fills his throat with arctic purity, that he ends up more or less deciding to live there from then on, fitting his whole fiery body into the water an inch at a time, though the stream is only as wide as he is and he has to stretch and wriggle quite a lot in order to get every square inch of his conflagrational skin in there to where it can be doused by the mud and water and the cold green strings of algae that he ends up draping across his neck, a scarf of scum.

Thus Virge presents himself to the world, as a mud man now, a crawdad, a folk tale, but he has found his salve, or salvation, finds that soon the discomfort and dissolution gradually just disappears. Maybe he could try a job again tomorrow, not this one of course, but every day presents a new opportunity, a chance for one more inch of headway. Now he must and will just relax, loll into motionlessness, let go of his idiotic formality, because now he's a primitive, a part of the general trickle, flat on his back, elongated, and now, if an observer were to come along, that person would hardly see any traces of the young man there, just a length of something in the stream bed, even perhaps step on him to cross the stream, he's that much a part of things.

Life in the outside world, the great breadth of things, is simple then: a question of agreement, immobility. Seep and spread. Know a lot of things well, rather than one thing excessively well. There's shade, water, songs of birds somewhere. But, admittedly, there's a snag. There's a sensation underneath his joy that nothing of significance has changed—that the creek and the ocean and the mystery ranch and his mother's farm and his little bedroom are physically adjacent, or nearly so. That to be sure he hasn't arrived anywhere, that he is by now, effectively nowhere.

Later he has a new thought, and it's to beware of the man nearby. Beware of anyone, someone, who might be watching him all this while. No, it's not Lank, but it could be someone waiting to pick him up and give him another kick like the last one. There's a kind of chair-shaped rock upstream, a natural throne, and some particular fellow is sitting on it, motionless and oddly familiar. Not moving. Well, he does move from time to time, but it's only to scrape his behind on the rock seat, like a cow rubbing its haunch against a gate, and Virge's good eye takes this in after a long while and finally recognizes that, all right, it's the overseer, it's Boss Wasp, the man who earlier was cutting a figure here and there on his portable podium, and he's lost the podium but found a throne, so he's still elevated, still wearing the black and yellow shirt and baseball cap, still smoking a cigar, coolly taking in the various spectacles of nature that surround him, including that of the young man in the brook who might pass for a log, or a pile of manure, or a cow carcass, or a fired farm worker.

A quiet stretch of time passes, and Virge begins to feel self-conscious. Why be on display when he can never really be at his best in front of others? Why meet new people when he has a gift for meeting new people under prostrate circumstances? If a pariah, down on the ground again, abject, the salt of the earth, why should he feel superior to the drunk in the gutter, the boxer on the canvas, the peasant in the ditch, the father on the park bench? Still, he does feel superior, and it must be because of his views, which are broader than any of the foregoing. When you are what you have become, what by rights your character destined you for, then you don't care how others achieve the same, and there, in a nutshell, is your superiority.

Still he'd like to get up, but can't. Paralyzed again? Not in your life. Everywhere he attempts the experiment, his body responds. Toes wriggle, fingers flex. Eyelids go up and down, and his lashes flick away little gobs of mud. With eyes stuck open in the end, he can twist to allow for self inspection, learning that the pain in his knees comes from pebbles embedded in the skin and that a dull black crayfish has a claw clamped, clothes-pin style, to a shirt tail. More to the point is that when he looks at himself he realizes that right now he's proportioned himself, forever, from everyone he knows. Alice is not far away, he can and does see her far off, where she's half hiding behind a tree, watching him, and Virge guesses she's there to watch for the moment, if this might be the moment, not to be missed, when Wasp sees degradation as eligibility for health and success. After all, time is marching on, autumn is in the air. Already a few copper and yellow leaves are spinning down, beginning to blanket Virge, hiding him from view, ending every courtship.

Go to sleep, my darlings, and all will vanish, like a fairy dream. Those who have the gall to sit and stare will get tired of it and go away. When you wake up you won't remember a thing.

And Virge does move toward sleep. And then does close his eyes, but there's no drifting off this time.

You aren't afraid of me? asks someone.

Virge opens his eyes to find that Wasp is talking to him, but from a peculiar angle. Everything has changed. He looks up, and though the yellow and black shirt blinds a little, he sees he's inches away from the bottom of the bushy beard. It may be that the boss wants Virge to go to sleep, because he holds and rocks him.

I'm not one bit afraid, says Virge, speaking at a childhood pitch, because it's so much like being carried by your dad.

Holding firm, a soothing quality in his voice, Wasp strides up the path, a bear of a man. The only shame for Virge is for his cold muddy body to be held right up against Wasp's chest, so that the bold striped shirt gets foul and muddy too.

Not afraid of me? Because I mean no harm.

Well, says Virge, trying to capture the tone used in striking up instant friendships, one who knows the art of drawing others out.

They told me, Virge goes on, that I should stick close to you.

That may be.

I need new clothes.

Oh, you'll get 'em. You'll get new clothes, grumbles Wasp, in a warm but also threatening tone.

They proceed in silence, and Virge takes the time to look more carefully at where the boss's fingers curl up around his ribs. Notable fingers, because they're puffy, white-pink, the fingers of the ones who don't pick gourds. Otherwise, staring straight into the man's bosom, there's a scrap of scarlet union suit visible where one button has come undone.

The walk is far enough for Virge to start squirming, or letting his hands dangle in the dirt, but he notices how those are no longer reflexes. At last the two men emerge into a clearing, a little shelf of broken shale, and when Virge looks out he sees a funny brown structure, a kind of hut, except that it's all built what look like staves and ribs. While similar to a cabin in size, it's really a fishing boat turned upside down, or more probably built to look like that, with a chimney poking up from the stern, a door and a four-paned window with tulips in the window box.

Here we go, breathes Wasp, lunging down to deposit Virge on his feet.

Watering can! Shouts Wasp shoving one into Virge's hands.

But it's so slopping full of water and heavy when he takes it on, and his first thought is that he's being told to water something, the window box maybe. But together they hold the can above Virge's head and let the water down, let it clear Virge's hair and ears and nostrils, flushing out invertebrates, bringing color back to his shirt, in time to all the rest of him. Then suddenly there's a big bed sheet that gets wrapped and cinched around his shoulders, and he gets steered inside the ship and set on a bench in front of an iron stove, where there is already a fire igniting and cracking inside. Wasp, nearby, furiously moving in a rocking chair, scoots closer.

You're the kind who'll dry up pretty quick, he frowns.

So I've HEARD, shouts Virge, inappropriately, but always assuming deafness.

Wasp goes on unperturbed to tell the stories of others he's rescued from that stream, because hobos end up there once in a while.

And believe it or not, he concludes, drily, I once saw someone drowned in that creek, when there was no more water than there was for you.

A worker?

A worker's child.

Less about the child, thinks Virge, and more about the man. Some idea is pointing at him like a stick.

Not much of a farm hand, I guess, smiles Wasp, his eyes moral-looking, but not widening as if he expects an answer.

Virge has the feeling that a particular buzz he keeps hearing is coming from the scrappy little stove, not from inside Wasp's head. It's the expansion of metal, the movement of joints. Wishing Alice would just walk in, because she must have followed all the way and be just outside. So it's not surprising that when he turns his head toward the little window, he catches glimpses of tiny movements outside, and of course these are the movements of his Alice, familiar to him now, this crazy Alice of his, right out there in the yard, because naturally she's followed them, and now she just appears and disappears from view, with movements that can be described as flitting. Though a different word for it would be flirting.

That, says Virge, renewing a vow, is my girlfriend.

I don't see a girl.

Yes. Not now. She's gone. Sorry. She likes to make a pestilence of herself.

Well don't mention her anymore, says the Boss, working his rocking chair. Or do you want me to ask her in?

No, no. Better not.

All right. Now tell me about it—no, wait a minute, don't tell me yet.

But Virge can't help blurting out some words from the tip of his tongue.

I was lying in the creek because I'm sickly, he explains. Too sick to pick. I'm used to working with ice.

Sounds right, because we need all the ice we can get.

It starts to get a little dark outside, and the Boss at long last produces, on a plywood tray, two deep china bowls of heated up soup with cigar-shaped biscuits to use as stirrers.

Alice remains out of doors. The soup, with garlic in it, tastes rich and health-giving. The atmosphere feels more rarefied. The crickets have a lighter song. The hut is so narrow that it feels that people don't really belong inside it, and Virge pictures someone, a giant little girl, probably, opening the door and wiggling a finger inside.

Peering inside the stove, trading fire for fire, Virge listens for the signature footsteps.

Then there does come a more definite noise from just outside, a substantial crash and thud, and Virge wonders why Alice stays out there spying, instead of coming in, though he supposes she must be fearful of the boss.

Nothing to be afraid of, Virge says, raising his voice so that perhaps she'll hear him.

I heard that too, says Wasp. Likely it's the owner coming up the path to see me.

Shouldn't you put on a light? asks Virge, unhappy with the deepening darkness.

Usually I don't do that, says the Boss darkly. But because it's you, I'll do what you say. I'll light the lantern.

It's too dark to see one another anymore, so Virge only hears a series of movements, then a long sigh, a rustling and scratching, and eventually the room fills up with yellow kerosene light and the hiss of a moth soon burning up in the flame.

What kind of people live in the arctic circle? asks Wasp, visible now behind the lantern, his round shadow swelling on the wooden boxes just behind.

You don't live there, you just visit.

The Boss looks surprised at this news, but at the same time there is at last a more deliberate shuffle just outside, followed by a tentative knock on the door.

Come on and open it, says Wasp, warmly, and Virge is not at all surprised to see Alice, and smug to see that her hands are still puffy and red from the gourds.

I'm here to see my friend, she says, in a small voice, the voice Virge heard out of her mouth the very first time he met her at the soda stand, and made him mistake her for a reluctant soul.

Well here he is, announces Wasp, ushering her in, and after a few seconds of confused repositioning, they all manage to sit down, Alice next to Virge on the bench, and the boss back in his rocking chair throwing a big pulsing shadow, when he rocks, just behind him.

My name's Alice, she says, after a while.

Well, says Boss Wasp, Virge you already know, I believe, and I'm Virge's dad.

And the story rings true. As in a fairy dream, it all is accurate, and instantly established. Clairvoyance shows us our real lives, our real families. Virge sees that rocking there before him is his father, old man Mont, just a little different in appearance now, transformed into a foreman, with sporty beard, extra pounds, an outdoors beauty to the face and hands. But it's Mont in the flesh and Mont, missing for so long, from top to bottom. No wig, but the man is more Indian than ever in his skin color, and serenity. Virge, wound in the pale sheet, is his son.

Those burning fruits, says Alice, are going to be the death of me.

On the other hand, she hardly looks to Virge much worse for wear, so he ought to tell his own gourd story in contrast, inspire laughter, though he ends up just focusing all of his attention on languid Alice on his right, contemplating her commanding presence and wit. Those burning fruits! Virge stays silent, not ready to think all things through yet. He's not God, nor can he use clairvoyance to see everything, or, as of now, anything.

Are you sorry to see me, Virge? asks Mont. Do you have any questions for me?

What time is the owner coming? is all Virge can think to inquire at this juncture.

The owner of the ranch? asks Alice.

That's right, says Mont. He stops by every Monday night to go over accounts.

I'd like us to meet him, says Alice, and she gives Virge another one of her pokes in the ribs.

Well I'm sure he'd like to meet you too, scowls Mont, stroking his beard.

To think I'm going to meet both of them on the same day, laughs Alice.

Both who?

The boss and the owner. You and Mr. Mystery, or whatever his name is.

Oh, there's nothing so important about meeting me, says Mont, blinking, showing a genuine modesty, and he goes on to tell his story, about how barely qualified he is for an overseer position. He'd been looking for a job for such a long time, had gone to San Grande and beat around the bush there for months without luck, just soup lines and bread lines and sleeping on park benches there, guys getting grabbed off park benches and beat up. And then the morning coffee line, and by the time you got to the head of the line they moved the coffee so that now you were at the end of the line.

So you applied at the ranch, says Alice, drawing him out.

Yes, and then next you see comes the lightning stroke of luck. Promoted fast. So in a wink of the eye I'm a foreman, one they put away at night inside a wooden boat.

Wooden treasure chest, you mean, says Alice, leaning back and closing her eyes.

So you see, he goes on, angling the rocking chair more toward his son. Making decent money meant bringing home some soon. On the verge of a big wad of cash. A pillowcase full, to pay for the best doctors. You're better now, as I'm glad to see, but I'll give you the pillowcase anyway.

I've never seen a wad of cash, puts in Alice, fiercely.

If you wonder why I didn't write, continues Mont, it was because I was always of two minds. I could never choose between two anything.

Did you ever wear the wig while you were gone?

Wig? Mont's expression twists. What wig?

Never mind.

Two minds, or two anything.

I think I may have her address, answers Virge, his voice echoing as if it drifted up from the bottom of some well.

The echo effect rouses Alice and Mont to laughter, as if some joke were included. There's a cynical cast to the mouth, both of them moving their lips silently as if thinking hundreds of dismissals at once.

You're the one who's the slice of pie, declares Alice after a while, as if someone called *her* that, and she reaches over to grab one of Virge's arms, pull it out of the sheet and lean backward with it, away from him, holding on to it like a fishing pole.

The silence holds for a while.

Because, she concludes, letting the arm go slack, we've all got a job to go to in the morning.

All three? wonders Virge.

All three.

Then Alice gets up and goes into action, beginning to clean the place up a bit, and when Mont protests that she doesn't have to do that, she says no no, it's no bother, but it becomes clear after a while that what she's really doing is not so much cleaning as it is searching through all the boxes for something in particular.

Find me some cigarettes, Alice, says Virge, smooth as glass.

Oh, you're a smoker now? asks Mont. Well good for you, Son, and I've got a little present for you then.

And he pulls a pack of Sultans out of his pocket and tosses it into his grown son's lap.

It's the first full pack, never opened, that Virge can call his own, and he tears it apart and lights up a smoke immediately, then settles back in his chair to watch Alice move like a hired companion among all the boxes. In the end she has to step over Virge any number of times, sometimes planting a hand on his chest in order to steady herself as she peers into each plywood crate, until at last she mutters something he can't make out and, with a reach and a flourish, displays to all a bottle with a label that reads, in simple stenciling, Best Whiskey.

Virge feels like wrestling somebody, getting somebody down on the ground and pinning them there, humiliating them, but then reflects that that's probably something you only want to do once in a lifetime. No point in repeating, unless in the case of a rematch with one's original opponent. However, if no wrestling, then no conversation, either.

A minute later, when the two others are preoccupied, scrounging deeper in the boxes for something else, and it seems like they're not paying attention to him, Virge slips out the door.

Where to go? He's at least made it outside, and now, ten or twelve feet away, he peers back in through the window at Alice leaning toward Mont, formalizing the party, pouring up three little shot glasses of the Best, which looks sweet and smokily delicious to Virge, though he's never tried the stuff. Alice, without looking up from her careful decanting, calls out to him, yelling at him to hurry up and come back in because there's the toast to be made, a toast, she cries out, to family reunions. And the two of them, Alice and Mont, go on sitting there politely, not touching their drinks, comfortably waiting, it appears, for him, the third member of their party, to make his way back inside.

Virge turns away, choking a little. Coughing. He can't quite figure the two of them out. There may be something wrong with old Mont, and with Alice the farm girl. There may be something wrong with everyone.

The further he walks from the overturned boat the colder it gets, and he's grateful to still have the sheet to tighten around him. Then he turns back to see, exactly as he described it to Wasp earlier, that, yes, there is something extraordinary about a friendly cabin in the midst of a dark wood, with a lamp that has been set to flicker in the window and welcome in any tired stranger.

As he stands watching, another personage, almost a stick figure, approaches the boat from out of nowhere, and this, he imagines, has to be the previously mentioned owner of the ranch. And would it be so great a surprise to recognize this gentleman from a distance? Why not find out now, for example, that the owner of the ranch is really Dr. Flanig? Or Stuart? Or Lank the foreman? It seems like anyone you meet around here can be someone you already know. And, isn't it a fact that anyone can be your father? There's no way of knowing. Sure, you know who your mother is, she's there from the start. But it doesn't really matter in the end who your father is.

In any event, the man disappears inside the boat, and presumably, within seconds, sits down to enjoy that third glass of whiskey.

There is no room for anyone to judge, says Virge out loud, raising a hand, discoursing in his sheet like a Roman in a toga, though the cigarette spoils the effect. There's no way to know whether poison has an effect on the mind or not. People get poisoned everyday, then lead pretty normal lives. It doesn't matter who you are. It's normal, for example, to not want to go back inside that house. It's normal, it's paranormal, to wrap oneself tighter in a sheet, finish a smoke, grind the butt into the ground, head deeper down into the velvet darkness.

But it's the case that it's not that dark, because look, a full moon has risen, and he finds to his surprise that he's standing at the top of a slope that leads all the way down a few miles to the ocean, and that the moon is reflected back a thousand times on the surface of the distant saltwater, like thousands of broken bones.

There's no way of knowing how I would have turned out anyway, and maybe it would be just the same, he thinks. Childhood incidents, from here, feel small, drops in an ocean, a few crumbs in the banquet of life, and he starts walking down the slope toward where he sees another light, a flame flickering in the heart of a little grove of eucalyptus.

It must be a hobo camp, he supposes, and then wonders if these are men who have gotten off the train, though one thing's sure, his dad won't be among them, and it's a good bet that they will share their dinner with him, because he can smell something cooking, and feels a hunger pang, and he wonders if they know how dangerous it is to light a fire next to the eucalyptus.

But when at last he reaches the light he's drawn toward, it turns out it's no hobo campfire, and not located among the trees, but just a number of steps further downhill.

It's a part of the slope that lies under some electric lines. A large crow, maybe a monster among crows, has fallen to earth here, dead, flat on its back, its wings spread out wide, like human arms in resignation. Presumably it got crossed up in the electrical lines, this birdbrain, because now its feathers and skin are slowly burning, licked by playful flames, a nasty and moralizing scene to gaze upon, but good smelling, as in crow pie.

It's warm enough here by the fire that Virge lets drop the sheet, and finds that his clothes, underneath, while tattered and caked, are completely dry. How good to remember that he has a whole pack of equally dry smokes, and that he can take one out, drop a knee, and light it in the crow's soft fire.

Everything's normal and all right, he thinks, remaining crouched. No matter what else had happened in his life, he would have ended up here, smoking, kneeling over the poor bird. No matter what or who, he's savvy enough to pick up a pile of dirt with his hands and drop it on the burning crow, then mold it all over to make a burial mound in the approximate shape of the deceased.

ACKNOWLEDGMENTS

The author would like to gratefully acknowledge the help of all those who provided motivation and inspiration during the writing of this novel, including Katharine Haake, Mona Houghton, Annette Leddy, Terry Myers, and Hilary Roberts. Also, thanks are due to the Millay Colony, the Ragdale Foundation, and the MacDowell Colony for their gifts of time, community, and space. Lastly, thanks go to Mary Bellino, for her help in the editing process.

This volume is the ninth recipient of the Juniper Prize for Fiction, established in 2004 by the University of Massachusetts Press in collaboration with the UMass Amherst